Chocolate Fondue

by Martha Reynolds

DEDICATION

For Ray

CONTENTS

Acknowledgments   i

Chapter One   1

Chapter Two   10

Chapter Three   17

Chapter Four   24

Chapter Five   30

Chapter Six   44

Chapter Seven   49

Chapter Eight   60

Chapter Nine   71

Chapter Ten   79

Chapter Eleven   87

Chapter Twelve   94

Chapter Thirteen   101

Chapter Fourteen   113

Chapter Fifteen   124

CHOCOLATE FONDUE

Chapter Sixteen	129
Chapter Seventeen	137
Chapter Eighteen	151
Chapter Nineteen	161
Chapter Twenty	175
Chapter Twenty-One	189
Chapter Twenty-Two	197
Chapter Twenty-Three	210
Chapter Twenty-Four	220
Chapter Twenty-Five	226
Chapter Twenty-Six	233
Chapter Twenty-Seven	245
Chapter Twenty-Eight	252
Chapter Twenty-Nine	259
Chapter Thirty	265
Chapter Thirty-One	275

ACKNOWLEDGMENTS

As always, I have many people to thank for helping to make this the best story I could tell.
Libby Mercer, Sharon Arthur Moore, Susi M. Nonnenmacher, and Lynne Radiches read and reviewed the manuscript and provided valuable feedback. Thank you. My friend Peter inspired me to write this sequel. My writer friends in the CLG Group are a constant source of encouragement and support. And, of course, to Jim, who read and praised and made suggestions.

CHAPTER ONE

Nani Karas blew into the Hotel de la Rose like a Mediterranean sirocco. From the rear of the lobby, Jean-Michel Eicher raised his head and watched the petite figure breeze across the lobby. As usual, Nani was dressed all in black. He checked his watch and finished up some paperwork at the reception desk as she approached.

"*Salut*, Michel!" She stood on her toes and kissed him on each cheek. He felt her lips press against his face. She pulled back and tipped her face up to his. Her lipstick was bright red against olive skin and nearly black eyes.

"Nani, hi," he replied. She'd been his colleague for three months now, and still he was disarmed by her. Nani had attended the same hotel school, where she'd perfected her English, as Michel had done three years earlier. French and German were still a challenge for her, so they always spoke English when they worked together. Michel didn't mind; he spoke English at home with his wife, also. He pictured Lucia, waiting for him to come home.

"You're on time," he remarked as he logged off the computer. He slipped his phone from his pocket and laid it on the counter, a reminder to call Lucia before he left the hotel.

"I am on time? Oh, perhaps I should go outside and return in ten minutes?" She made a fist and soft-punched his upper arm. Standing next to Michel, Nani barely reached his shoulder. She pulled her long black hair from her face and secured it with a yellow plastic hairclip. Michel wondered if she had ever cut her hair. Lucia's hair was light brown and soft, and curled around her neck.

"I see you chose some color today," Michel teased. He usually wore tan or gray slacks, a light-colored shirt, and a dark jacket, clothes befitting the day manager of a traditional hotel. His one concession to the conservative attire was a whimsical necktie, and today it displayed brown and white cows on a green background. Very Swiss. The tourists seemed to like it.

"I like to wear black," Nani retorted with a laugh. "I never have to worry what I will wear today, because always, it is something black. But wait! I do have something colorful," she said, sticking one tiny hand into her big black shoulder bag. She pulled out a pair of bright red designer eyeglasses and put them on. Nani grinned at him and Michel noticed her teeth were very white and straight. And that red lipstick... Michel looked away, and stared at his phone.

Nani dropped her bag to the floor and crouched down to fiddle with her boot. Michel stole a glance at the expanse of skin showing between her short top and low-rise pants. Nani had a tattoo on the small of her back, something in Greek. It was a word, and he didn't know what it meant, but he wouldn't ask her. He pulled his eyes away.

"Well, I have to leave," he said, ducking his head and feeling the warmth on his face. I need to get home to my wife, he thought. "Lucia is waiting," he added, more to himself than to her.

Nani removed her cropped jacket and hung it on a hook just out of sight behind the reception area. "When does the baby arrive? Soon?"

"The baby comes at the end of December. It will be our Christmas present." He smiled at the thought.

"*It?* Don't you know if *it* is a boy or girl?" She hopped up onto the stool he'd just vacated. Michel could smell her, and her scent reminded him of candy. Sweet and forbidden.

"We want to be surprised," he said. He picked up his dark brown messenger bag and strapped it across his body so it hung in the back. "So, have a good night, Nani. See you." Jean-Michel hurried across the lobby to the front entrance. As soon as he was outside the hotel, he remembered his phone on the desk and had to go back in. Nani held the phone in her upturned palm, grinning at him. He felt himself blush again and took the phone from her hand. Once again outside, he took a deep breath and exhaled. His heart was pounding. Michel pictured Lucia in their apartment, preparing dinner. But he kept seeing Nani's red lipstick, like a siren.

Michel walked up the hill to the station, where his bus waited. He would never cheat on his wife; he knew that better than anything. Lucia meant the world to him, and soon they would have a baby to complete their family. For the past three months, he'd made an effort to help Nani learn everything about the hotel. When she arrived in early August, they'd worked side by side every day, so he could mentor her. She was so shy and quiet then, he mused. Perhaps it was his friendliness that encouraged her? He kept walking, and with each step he resolved to be more professional with Nani. He would not give the girl reason to think he was interested in her.

His parents would join them for dinner tonight. Michel ran the rest of the distance to the train station, and boarded the bus that would take him to the outskirts of town. At the end of the line in Givisiez, he stepped off the bus and walked down the narrow road to his house, thinking "Lucia, Lucia" with each stride.

Michel and his wife lived in the same house where he was raised. The large, three-story building was constructed to look like an old farmhouse, but was intended for two families to live side by side. Two thick oak doors stood next to each other. Flower boxes, now emptied of the red geraniums that had bloomed for months, cupped each window. Michel glanced to the left side as he reached the door on the right.

When he was a boy, Michel and his parents occupied the left side, where his parents still lived, and a family of five inhabited the other side. The three children were all older than he, but everyone got along in the quiet, respectful way of the Swiss. When the children all had married and moved out, the house was too big for the Wecks, so they sold their half to the Eichers. Bruno purchased it as a gift for his son, a place for him to raise a family when the time came.

Michel knew he was adopted. When he was about seven years old, one of his classmates asked him about his orange hair. Emmanuelle was the prettiest girl in school, with blonde braids that fell in two straight lines down her back.

"Where did it come from," she asked, her brown eyes large and round, like chestnuts. "Your parents have dark hair. Are you adopted?" She scrunched up her face, as if the word smelled bad, and still she looked so pretty, Michel recalled.

"No," Michel said in a loud voice and stamped his foot. He wasn't sure at the time what adopted meant, but it didn't sound good. He had spent the entire day at school in a dark mood, was disruptive in class, got into a scuffle outside with one of the boys, and when he arrived home that afternoon, he headed directly to the kitchen, where his mother was grating potatoes for supper.

"Mama, what is adopted?"

Klara Eicher spun around and nearly grated her finger. "What is this talk, Michel? Who said something about adoption to you?" She handed him a slice of raw potato with a trembling hand.

"Emmanuelle asked me about my hair," he said as he crunched into the potato. He raised his eyes to his mother, waiting for an answer. "Is adopted bad?"

Klara straightened her shoulders and said, "Your hair is a special color, my son. It was a gift from God; I've told you that before. There is no need for any more questions." She looked at the bowl full of grated potatoes and onions and directed her attention back to young Jean-Michel. "Now it's time for your schoolwork before Papa comes home," she said, pointing to the stairs. As Michel climbed the stairs, he heard his mother let out a long breath.

Michel's mind returned to the present and he placed his hand on the door handle. It wasn't until four or five years later that his parents told him the truth: that he was indeed adopted. They'd explained that seven was too young for him to understand, and he knew they were right. He'd asked once about his birth parents, and was told they were both dead. He never asked about them again. It didn't matter. Michel opened the front door and was enveloped by warmth and a delicious aroma.

He entered the kitchen to see his wife standing at the counter, tossing greens in a large bowl. She wore a loose-fitting top over what he knew were her favorite stretch pants. His mother bent to remove a large, rectangular pan from the oven. With thick oven mitts on her hands, she maneuvered around Lucia, whose expanding belly kept her inches back from the counter. A small kitchen made smaller by a pregnant woman, he thought happily.

"*Salut*, Lulu," he crooned as he tilted his head to kiss his wife on the neck. She turned her face to his and gave him a weak smile. Michel could see how tired she was. Her eyes were puffy and her skin lacked its usual glow. Lucia had not had an easy time with this pregnancy, he knew.

"Michel, go sit with your father, please. We bring the food to the table." His mother gestured with her eyes toward the dining room, where Bruno Eicher sat by himself, a big man alone at the table, seemingly lost in thought.

Michel entered the dining room and kissed his father. "*Salut*, Papa," he said. As if on cue, his father pulled the cork from a bottle of red wine and poured Pinot Noir Grand Cru into three of the four glasses. Michel picked up a bottle of sparkling water and filled the fourth glass. Lucia waddled into the dining room, carrying the bowl of salad, and set it on the table. She sat heavily in her chair and watched as Klara brought the pan of lasagna to the table and positioned it over a red ceramic trivet. A long baguette rested on a wooden board at Michel's elbow, ready to be cut.

Michel and Lucia spoke English with each other because Michel's Italian was not very good, and Lucia's French was only marginally better. Klara and Bruno could both speak English, although Bruno often grew impatient when he couldn't remember a word.

Michel took his wife's hand before they began eating. "Thank you, my love, for this wonderful meal," he said. Lucia's tired eyes met his and she squeezed his hand.

6

"Your mother did all of the work. I sat down a lot," she added, with a sincere smile to Klara.

"So, we eat," Bruno declared, slicing into the bread as Klara cut squares of lasagna for everyone and Michel doled out salad. Plates were passed until everyone was ready to eat.

"How was your day today, my son?" Klara asked, grinding pepper onto her salad.

"Good, good," he replied as he blew on a forkful of lasagna before placing it in his mouth. He emitted a little groan of pleasure and saw his wife grin in return. "*Molto bene,*" he said to her.

"Were you busy today?" Lucia inquired. She always showed interest in hearing about his job, and what was going on at the hotel. Since the arrival of Nani three months ago, Michel thought she showed an increased interest. She had not yet met his colleague, and now that Nani worked nights, Michel tried not to talk about her. It felt like an intrusion into his home when her name was mentioned.

He nodded as he chewed. When he'd swallowed the food in his mouth, Michel said, "We had a few new guests today. A professor who will stay for two weeks. He is doing a special lecture at the university. A young couple checked in for only one night, stopping in Fribourg on their way to Italy. And two American women arrived today." He chuckled. "One of them cried the whole time at check-in this afternoon."

"Cried! Sad to be in Fribourg?" His mother shook her head and picked up her glass of wine. Bruno grunted a laugh and continued to eat. He would be ready for a second helping before anyone had finished their first. Michel glanced at his father and shrugged.

"No, I don't think she was sad to be here. She said she was in Fribourg as a student in the late 1970's and coming back was very emotional for her. Funny, she kept staring at me." He shrugged again and went back to eating. "Oh, and she called me Michel. Everyone calls me Jean-Michel before they get to know me. My name badge is Jean-Michel. It was strange," he added.

When he looked up at his mother, he saw the wine glass trembling in her unsteady hand. Klara was staring hard at Bruno. Michel watched his mother lower the glass to the table. She picked up her fork but it, too, trembled in her hand, so she set it down and clasped her hands in front of her. She cast her eyes down at her plate.

Lucia said, "Imagine that! So she was returning to Fribourg after many years."

Michel nodded. "Mama, you don't eat?" He turned his head to say something to his wife when Klara spoke.

"What is that, Michel? There, back by your ear. Is that blood?"

He stared at his mother as his father, to his left, leaned forward to peer at his ear.

Michel pulled his napkin from his lap and rubbed vigorously. He knew it was not blood.

There was silence at the dinner table. Michel focused on his empty wine glass.

When he raised his eyes and met his wife's stare, he could see she knew as well that it was not blood.

Michel cleared his throat and looked to his left. His father was glowering at him, his eyes dark and fiery.

"Would you mind terribly if I excused myself?" Lucia pushed back from the table and struggled to her feet. "I'm afraid I'm not feeling well at all." Michel stood to help her.

"Of course, Lulu, I'll help you to lie down." She waved a hand in the general direction of his face.

"I'll be fine. I would just like to rest." She turned to Klara and said, "I'm sorry, mama. Thank you for everything."

Klara stood too, as Lucia walked slowly down the hall to their bedroom. When she had shut the door behind her, Michel and Klara sat again.

Michel could no longer ignore the hard stare of his father. "Papa, it's nothing. The girl at work, she kissed me hello and left behind some red lipstick, that is all." He wiped a finger across his upper lip and tried to smile, but his father's glare was stony.

Bruno raised a hand and pointed a long finger at his son's face. "You don't do one thing to hurt that girl," he said in German. "She is the mother of your child. You treat her with respect."

Michel nodded. He stood and cleared the plates. Dinner was over.

CHAPTER TWO

Joan Weston surveyed room 345 at the Hotel de la Rose and nodded with a satisfied look on her face. "It's nice," she said.

"I know it's not the Hilton, Joan, but believe me, these Swiss rooms are the cleanest you'll ever find."

"It's perfect, Bernie," her aunt replied. Bernadette Maguire agreed. The room was quite spacious for a Swiss hotel, with a double window overlooking the blue-green Sarine River. There were two beds, each with a soft white featherbed atop a thick mattress, and a small table between them with a lamp for bedtime reading. A large painted armoire for their clothes stood against the far wall, and the bathroom had a deep tub for soaking. There were fluffy towels on the shelves above the tub, which had a shower attachment. An overstuffed chair and ottoman, in a blue patterned fabric, nestled into the far corner near the window.

Bernie sat on one of the beds. Tears came to her eyes again as she thought about Michel, her Michael. It had to be him. That was her son! She'd seen the carrot-colored hair the day she gave birth in 1979, just before the nurse took him away. She'd been back to Fribourg years ago hoping to find him, but she never did, instead spending most days sitting at sidewalk cafés, drinking too much wine, hoping for a miracle that never occurred. Her friend Hanna Schmidt knew where he was, but she'd made it clear that she couldn't tell Bernie. That was part of the arrangement Bernie had agreed to when Hanna, her obstetrician, had arranged for the adoption, and Bernie had stopped asking. Now, after her mother's funeral, after Bernie had made peace with her past, she walked into this hotel and came face to face with the boy she gave up twenty-three years ago. Perhaps it was her mother's spirit guiding this reunion, she thought. Either way, it was a miracle.

Joan sat on the bed next to her. "Quite a remarkable young man down there," she said, and put an arm around her niece's shoulder.

"Yes," Bernie said, wiping her cheeks. "I so wanted to reach out to him. I wanted to gather him in my arms. But I can't do that. He may not even know he was adopted. Perhaps he wasn't told anything about me. I can't just walk up to him and tell him I'm his birth mother. And it hurts, Joan. My heart hurts."

"I know, dear, and you're probably right," Joan replied. "He's an adult now, and even if he does know that he was adopted, if he had wanted to find his birth parents, I'm sure his parents would have told him."

Bernie jumped to her feet. "Come on, let's get out of here. We can unpack later. We're only here for a couple of days anyway. Um, unless you're exhausted, Joan. Are you?"

Joan stretched and stood up as well. "Let me just wash my face and change my shirt."

By the time the women stepped out of the elevator and into the hotel lobby, Michael was no longer at the front desk. Instead, Bernie saw a slight young woman with a dark ponytail and red eyeglasses. A pretty girl, she thought, and smiled at her.

"Hello." Bernie approached the front desk.

"Hello," the girl replied, looking directly at Bernie. "May I help you with something?"

Bernie glanced at the girl's name badge. Nani, it said. She was quite stunning, Bernie thought. A Mediterranean beauty.

"My aunt and I just arrived today, and although I lived in this town many years ago, I'm sure things have changed. We're looking for a restaurant in the *basse-ville*."

Nani frowned as she thought about it, her otherwise smooth forehead lined with concentration. "Let me see if I can find something for you," she said and began typing on her keyboard. She leaned toward the computer monitor.

"Do you know the Café des Epouses?" Bernie wondered if she dared to enter the place where there were so many memories. Could she handle it? She watched as Nani typed and peered at the monitor. That red lipstick really works on her, Bernie thought. I'm more suited to coppery colors.

Nani pushed the red glasses to the top of her head and looked up at Bernie. "I have never heard of this Café des Epouses," she said. Those red eyeglasses were adorable, Bernie thought. She wanted to compliment her, but held back. I don't need to make friends with everyone I meet, she reminded herself.

"You could try the Restaurant du Schild," she said. Nani reached behind her head and unfastened a bright yellow clip holding her ponytail in place. Bernie watched as dark hair spilled around the sides of her face and down her shoulders. In an instant, Nani had gathered it all back up again and refastened the clip.

"Yes? Is this restaurant a good place?"

"I don't know," Nani confessed. "I don't go out to restaurants very often." She blinked at Bernie and Joan. "You are Americans?"

Joan piped up, "Yes, we just arrived this afternoon. My niece here was a student in Fribourg, at the university, many years ago."

"Many!" Bernie chimed in, rolling her eyes in Joan's direction. "Well, thank you for your help."

"Have a nice evening," said Nani, turning back to her computer. The women waved as they headed out the door.

"Joan, let's just walk," said Bernie as they crossed the square and turned the corner. She knew the area well enough. "I want to see if my old café is still there."

And straight ahead was the old sign above the street, the couple in traditional Swiss garb, joined hand in hand, with the quotation in French, something about the fidelity of married couples. The sign was old and worn, in need of paint, not quite the way Bernie remembered it.

"How quaint!" Joan exclaimed, looking up at the sign. She fished her camera from her shoulder bag and snapped a picture of Bernie standing beneath it.

"This way," said Bernie as they walked underneath the hanging sign. She couldn't help but think of Karl Berset, the Swiss banker she'd been so attracted to, the married man who had seduced and fooled her, the father of her son Michael. Michael couldn't possibly know about Karl, unless Hanna had told his parents, and his parents had told him. But Hanna would never have breached that confidence, certainly not without alerting Bernie. Besides, Hanna Schmidt had been Karl's wife's obstetrician, too. Bernie recalled that cold day in February 1979, when she had stepped off the bus and was walking up the hill to the hospital for her appointment with Hanna. It was Valentine's Day, and she had frozen in her steps when she saw Karl Berset and his very pregnant wife exit the hospital and climb into a waiting taxi. She was sure Karl had seen her. That one time. She had never seen him again. She never wanted to. For the most part, Bernie had pushed Karl Berset out of her memory, but being back in Fribourg, here he was, front and center.

Bernie stopped. This wasn't the Café des Epouses, but she knew this was the right building. It was a jazz club, the Moonwalker. Bernie could hear the strains of saxophone and bass guitar from the outside. She shook her head.

"What, Bernie?" Joan stared at the door to the jazz club, then turned her face to Bernie.

"Let's keep walking." Bernie tucked her arm into her aunt's and led her in the opposite direction.

They ambled down the cobblestone street that led to the older section of town, the *basse-ville*, the original town of Fribourg. There were no supermarkets, no banks. Everything looked as it might have a hundred years ago, with the exception of a neon sign here and there and cars parked on the street.

"Bernie, look," Joan said, pointing. Straight ahead was the sign for the Restaurant du Schild.

Bernie laughed. "Well, what do you know? We might as well try it then," she said, and pushed hard against the heavy door.

The interior of the restaurant was dim, with small pools of golden light from wall sconces and short, fat candles in glass holders on the tables. A young man walked up to greet them, and seated them along the far wall. The wall was stone and plaster and cold to the touch, but the restaurant itself, like a cave, was warm and comforting. Their table was heavy dark wood, smooth in places and nicked in others. Someone had etched their initials in one corner of the table; Bernie showed Joan where "CP 91" was carved. The restaurant was about half full, and there was a pleasant ambience that comes from the sound of laughter mixed with the clinking of glasses and silver against china.

They ordered red wine and the restaurant's specialty, as described by their waiter: roasted venison with lentils. Joan was a wonderful traveling companion, game to try anything new. Toward the end of their meal, a duet assembled on the other side of the room. A young man played guitar, accompanied by a woman with an earthy, soulful voice who sang bluesy ballads in French. Bernie relaxed and swayed to the music. She was so comfortable here, she thought.

"So Bernie, tomorrow we take a walking tour of Fribourg? We're only here until Thursday. I want you to show me where you lived." Joan used a piece of bread to sop up the rest of the sauce on her plate. Bernie poured more wine for both of them.

"Yes, it's our one day to see as much of the town as we can." She thought again of Michael, and wondered if he'd be working tomorrow. She could ask that young woman at the front desk. Bernie needed to see him again. Joan was right; they weren't in Fribourg for long. When she had planned the vacation, Bernie had no idea she'd find her son. Now the thought of traveling away from him bothered her.

"Are you thinking about him?" Joan's eyes were glassy from drinking half a bottle of wine. Bernie felt her own cheeks flush, probably from the wine. Probably.

"It's weird. I don't want to do anything to disrupt his life, I really don't. At the same time, how can I leave Fribourg without talking to him? It's as if I was given a sign, Joan. Maybe this was all meant to happen." She laughed at herself; maybe she really was drunk.

"Let's see what tomorrow brings," Joan said. She picked up the empty wine bottle and tilted it, then made a sad face. "What's for dessert?"

CHAPTER THREE

Hanna Schmidt's telephone rang and broke the stillness of the evening. She checked her watch. Nine o'clock was late for a phone call, she thought, but that would be the case for anyone else. As an obstetrician, she was accustomed to late-night calls all the time. Hanna was prepared to leave her house within three minutes of a phone call, and she lived close to the hospital. She marked her place in the book she was reading and answered the telephone.

"Hanna, it's Klara Eicher. I am sorry to bother you so late."

Hanna laughed. "Klara, it's not late and you're not bothering me. Oh! Is it Lucia?" She was treating Klara's daughter-in-law and knew it was early for labor. Lucia had another two months to go, Hanna recalled.

"No, Lucia is okay. Well, she is very tired, but otherwise she is fine. This is something else, Hanna, something difficult."

"What is it, Klara?"

"Tonight, Michel came home and we all ate our supper together, Bruno and me and Michel and Lucia. And I ask him about his day, you know, 'how was your day' and so on. He is telling us all about the guests in the hotel, always funny stories from my Michel. He says there are two American women who check in today. One of them is crying and looking at him all the time. And she says she is a student in Fribourg many years ago. This is what he tells me, and Hanna, I don't know, but I have a feeling inside about this. It worries me."

Hanna leaned forward in her chair. She hadn't heard from Bernadette in months. Bernadette would have let her know about a trip to Switzerland, Hanna was sure of it.

"Klara, I'm sure it's nothing to be concerned about. I keep in touch with Bernadette, and I know she would have contacted me if she were coming to Fribourg. She hasn't been here in many years."

"Yes, yes, I know, Hanna. And I am being a silly old woman. I just had an uneasy feeling when Michel was speaking, you know?"

"Okay, I understand, Klara. Listen, I'll find out for sure. Don't worry about anything."

Klara let out a long breath on the other end. "Thank you, Hanna. It's just that, you know, I was wrong. We should not have lied to Michel about his parents being dead. But so much time now, and how can I tell the truth? He would never forgive me for lying to him."

Hanna paused. She knew that Klara and Bruno had told Michel that he was adopted, and that his birth parents were both dead. That was their choice, and although she didn't agree with it, she couldn't do anything about it. When Bernadette returned to Fribourg years ago, hell bent on finding her son, Hanna had been quite forceful with her, and it seemed as though Bernadette had let it go. But the connection between a mother and her child was stronger than anything, and Hanna felt a prickle of queasiness in her stomach.

"Klara, get some sleep. Everything will be fine."

She hung up the phone and sipped tea that was no longer hot. Would Bernadette return to Fribourg without letting her know? They still exchanged emails a few times a year. Klara had mentioned two American women. Perhaps her sister? Hanna knew that Bernadette's mother was ill, yet she could be here with her sister. Well, only one way to find out, she thought.

Hanna dialed the number for the Hotel de la Rose. She waited and heard a female voice at the other end.

"Yes, good evening. Would you connect me with one of your guest rooms, please? I'm looking for Ms. Bernadette Maguire." Hanna waited and felt her heart thump inside her chest. She heard typing on the other end and then the woman's voice returned.

"One moment, please, let me look. Yes, room 345. One moment, I will connect you."

Hanna gasped. Bernadette is here! And she has seen Michel! Hanna steeled her nerves and waited to hear Bernadette on the other end. She listened to the phone ring and then suddenly she was reconnected with the front desk.

"I'm sorry, Ms. Maguire is not in her room. May I leave a message for her?"

"No, that's not necessary," Hanna snapped and slammed down the receiver.

She stood and paced back and forth across the antique Persian rug in her living room. Klara was right. Had Bernadette returned to claim Michel as her son? Surely this would cause havoc in the Eicher house. And Lucia – she is too close to term. Nothing should upset her now, and surely this situation would upset everyone. Hanna clenched her fists and made little punching gestures in the air.

"Bernadette, what are you doing?" Hanna glared at the wall, expecting it to answer.

I'll go there myself and speak to her, Hanna thought. She pulled her coat from a hook by the door and shrugged into it. Damn it, Bernie! Hanna grabbed her keys and locked the door behind her.

Nani was bored. Nothing happened in this hotel lobby after nine o'clock. Most of the guests were back in their rooms, except for the American women, who were out for the evening. Nani smirked to herself; they don't realize that everything closes at ten. She wondered who had called looking for them. That woman was very rude. Imagine, slamming down the phone just because her friend is not in the room! It wasn't my fault, Nani thought. She slipped off her stool and headed behind the reception desk. In the small kitchen, she brewed fresh coffee for the long, boring night ahead.

A woman entered the lobby and Nani looked up from the magazine she was reading. This woman was very pretty, for someone older. Short dark hair. Nani thought perhaps she should have her hair cut, but quickly dismissed the idea. She liked it long. Men preferred long hair. She loosened her ponytail a bit.

The woman unbuttoned her coat and pulled it off, then folded it and laid it on the sofa. She plopped down in one of the plush, overstuffed chairs. Nani could only see the top of her head now, as the woman sat facing the entrance doors, as if she was waiting for someone to walk through them. Nani slid off her stool and checked the pot of coffee in the back. With a full pot in her hand, she returned to the reception desk.

"Hello," she called out, "Would you like coffee? I just made a fresh pot."

The woman stood and turned to face Nani.

"Thank you," she said, nodding. "That's very kind."

Nani returned to the kitchen area and was preparing a tray when she heard voices in the lobby. She left the coffee preparation and hurried back out to see what was going on. The two American women had returned and the younger one with the red hair was hugging the woman from the chair. Ah! So the woman in the chair must be the rude one who had called earlier, looking for, what was her name. Nani checked the guest log. Yes, Bernadette Maguire. And the older woman stood there grinning. She looked drunk.

Nani stayed behind the desk and strained to listen to the conversation.

"But why didn't you let me know you were coming, Bernadette?!"

"Hanna, it was kind of last minute. After the funeral..."

"Funeral?"

"Oh Hanna, my mother died at the beginning of the month. I'm sorry I didn't write to let you know. We had the funeral and Joan and I decided to take a vacation. We really needed it. Oh, this is my mother's sister, Joan Weston."

"I'm so sorry." The woman named Hanna turned to the older woman, who embraced her. That older woman was definitely drunk, Nani thought, as she watched the little scene play out in her hotel lobby.

"We're traveling around the country. I wanted to show Joan the best of Switzerland, and we just arrived today." Bernie turned slightly and Nani could see her face. "Hanna! Michael is here, working here! I know it's him, isn't it?" Her face was alive with joy, and her eyes were shiny with tears. She grabbed Hanna's arms with both hands. "I know it's my Michael," she sobbed.

My Michael? Whose Michael? Michel? What? Nani frowned again, confused, and listened harder.

"Bernadette!" Hanna snapped, and Nani's eyes grew wide. "What did you say to him?"

"Nothing, I said nothing. Hanna, I don't want to cause trouble. He didn't recognize me, or ask anything. I knew him, but he didn't know me. He doesn't have any idea who I am. I didn't say anything, Hanna," she repeated. Nani watched, transfixed, as Bernadette sobbed and wiped at her eyes.

"Bernadette, you must not say a word about this, please. He has a wife, and she's pregnant. His parents..."

"His wife is pregnant?" Nani watched as this woman Bernadette cried even harder now. She stayed out of sight behind the desk, even crouching a bit so that just the top of her head would be visible, in case any of the women remembered she was there. This woman is Michel's mother? And who is this Hanna person, she wondered.

The older woman Joan spoke, practically shouting. "Bernie would never do anything to hurt anyone. She didn't come here looking for her son, but obviously she's found him. Does the young man not know that he was adopted?"

Hanna said, in a much quieter voice, "He knows he was adopted, yes. But he does not know that his birth parents are alive. He was told at a very young age that they were dead. It was easier to explain this to a young boy, and it was the parents' choice to do so. And he still believes it. To change all of that now could be very detrimental, to his relationship with his parents, to his wife. There is an unborn child to think about. You must consider all of this." Hanna gestured with her hands to the Americans.

22

Bernadette nodded, subdued. She turned toward the front desk and Nani pretended to be deeply engrossed in reading. She peeked up through her lashes and saw Bernadette turn back to Hanna. Her voice was low and Nani couldn't hear what she said.

"Come to dinner at my house tomorrow evening, please," said Hanna to the women. "Bernadette, you remember where I live?" She touched her on the shoulder.

Bernie said, "Of course I remember. I lived there, too, you know. Thank you, Hanna, we'll see you tomorrow. Good night." They all kissed good night and Hanna left the hotel.

Bernie and Joan walked to the elevator. Nani kept her head down, absorbed in her magazine and did not raise her head until the elevator doors had shut.

CHAPTER FOUR

Lucia couldn't sleep. She rolled to her side and swung her feet to the floor, leaving Michel sleeping soundly. She padded down the hall in bare feet and peered into the kitchen. Everything was clean and tidy; no doubt her mother-in-law had cleaned up before leaving. No Swiss woman would leave kitchen duties until the morning. When she used to visit her brother and his wife in Rome, Lucia would often find a sink full of dirty dishes in the morning. Bits of dried pasta and marinara on the plates, tiny pools of red wine in the glasses, bread crumbs dotting the tablecloth.

Lucia couldn't sleep because when she closed her eyes, all she could see was that red lipstick on her husband's neck and ear. She wondered if Michel had been unfaithful to her, and what constituted infidelity. A kiss? A long kiss? Groping in a closet? She was seven months pregnant, a big fat cow with bags under her eyes, tired all the time, often too tired to respond to Michel at night. And her big belly in the way. He suggested other, more comfortable positions, but she turned him away. As tears moistened her eyes, Lucia imagined him finding solace in the arms of another. A woman who wore bright red lipstick. Who was this woman, she wondered. His co-worker? He'd mentioned her a few months ago, when the hotel hired her and they worked together, but Lucia understood she worked nights now. One of the maids? A guest? Her husband was a handsome and charming man. She knew he loved her, he always told her so, but had she driven him to find love with someone else? Lucia was tortured by uncertainty and doubt.

She eased herself down onto the sofa and raised her feet. With her hand resting on her stomach, Lucia could feel the baby move. She thought back to when she and Michel first met, three years ago in the village of Morcote on Lake Lugano. Lucia was nineteen years old and on vacation with her parents from Milan. They had rented a house in the hills above the lake, and spent one sunny day after another walking the village square, hiking up in the hills, or taking one of the boats that traversed the lake, stopping at all the different grottoes for pan-fried lake fish with risotto, or gnocchi with butter and sage. Michel was working at the Hotel Walter on the lake, and on a rare day off, had taken the boat from Lugano to Morcote, where he intended to climb the steep hills to the Chiesa di Santa Maria del Sasso. He had stopped in the Ristorante della Posta for lunch, and sat directly in her line of vision. She noticed his burnt-orange hair and his soft brown eyes, and remembered nothing of the conversation with her parents, or the meal she'd eaten. He'd noticed her, too, and had asked the waiter to give her a small card for the Hotel Walter with his name written on the reverse side. She'd purchased a postcard of Morcote and mailed it to him at the hotel after she had returned to Milan. She included her email address, and they corresponded for nearly a year by email, always in English, because Michel's Italian was not very good, although he tried, she recalled with a smile.

The following summer, as their relationship had grown over correspondence, Lucia invited Michel to Milan, and at the end of a two-week stay at her parents' home, he approached her father, and in halting Italian, asked permission to marry his daughter. Lucia convinced her parents that her love for Michel was true, that he came from a good family, that he had excellent prospects in the hotel industry. And, she added, if they said no, she would marry him anyway. Lucia's father liked the young man. He found Michel to be intelligent, mannered, and clearly devoted to his daughter. Fulvio Pizzi relented, and Michel and Lucia were married in June of last year. She didn't expect to get pregnant so soon, but they welcomed the news with excitement.

Now, though, Lucia had doubts. Doubts about herself, doubts about her husband. She knew he was affable, and attractive, and it wouldn't surprise her to see women show interest, even after seeing his wedding ring. She saw evidence of this when they strolled the town on a Sunday afternoon; she saw the smiles and meaningful glances from the young women who passed them. She couldn't prove anything, and he certainly was attentive to her. As tears wet her cheeks, she prayed for strength in the coming months.

Around midnight, Nani began to nod off, even after three cups of strong coffee. As was customary, the hotel doors were locked, and Nani had retreated to the loveseat situated in back, next to the small kitchen, where employees could relax, or, in Nani's case, nap. The buzzer at the front entrance sounded and she opened her eyes. She hurried to the front and saw the large figure of a man against the double glass doors. He raised a hand and she bounded through the lobby to the door, pressed a button to the left of it and allowed the big man entry.

"*Salut*, Alain!" Nani turned her face up to the tall man in a dark policeman's uniform.

"*Salut*, Nani," Alain replied, bending low for the customary cheek kisses. He stopped her from turning away and planted a soft kiss on her open mouth.

Nani didn't bother to lock the door once he was inside; after all, Alain was not only a police officer but a six-foot, two-inch tall police officer. Armed and dangerous, she thought with a grin.

"How are you?" She slipped in back to get the pot of coffee. She returned to the reception desk carrying a tray and waited while he cleared a space. She set down the tray, which held two white mugs, a bowl of sugar cubes, a spoon, and a small plate of cookies. This was their routine on Tuesday night: Alain visited just around midnight and they spent the next half hour together, chatting comfortably.

Alain hadn't yet asked her out on a real date, and Nani wondered if he ever would get around to it. She liked him, and she knew he liked her a lot. He would return to the hotel at eight in the morning, when her long shift was finally over. Nani's apartment was a fifteen-minute walk from the hotel, and Alain always walked part of the way with her, until their directions diverged and they waved goodbye. Then she wouldn't see him again until Thursday night when she worked again. She thought it would be nice for them to spend a quiet Sunday afternoon together sometime. She wanted to make dinner for him, but she felt he should at least take her out to a restaurant first. Besides, her kitchen was so small.

They sipped coffee in easy silence. Nani thought about the big news she'd heard earlier in the evening from the three women in the lobby. Should she share it with Alain? No, she thought, Alain had only met Michel once or twice. Nani would hold onto this bit of information. It might help her to get closer to Michel, somehow.

She took a small bite of a cookie as Alain read the previous day's newspaper. *So Bernadette Maguire in room 345 is the birth mother of my Michel, and Michel does not know. And this woman Hanna thinks he should not know. What does Hanna have to do with all of this? And Bernadette's aunt, Joan, who appeared too drunk to comprehend much of what was going on earlier this evening, what part does she play in all this? And who, then, is Michel's birth father?*

"Don't you think so?" Alain's voice cut through her thoughts and snapped her back to the present.

She turned her head to smile at him, and fluttered her long lashes at him. "Whatever you think, Alain," she purred.

Bernie lay awake in her bed. Joan snored softly in the bed next to her, but Bernie could not sleep. Seeing Hanna again was unexpected, and Bernie recalled the anger she saw in Hanna's dark eyes. At least until she explained her reasons for being in Fribourg, and the fact that running into Michael was pure coincidence. Or fate.

She didn't even know if Michael would be working tomorrow, but what she did know for certain was that she would have to see him again before she and Joan left for Lucerne. *I want to know my son,* she told herself, confirming the thought that had been at the back of her mind since she first saw him earlier in the day. She held up her wrist and squinted at the watch face that glowed in the dark room. Two in the morning.

I want to meet his wife. I want to know the kind of woman he chose. And what about that dark-haired girl who was at the front desk tonight? How much did she hear of the conversation between Hanna and me? Bernie knew she'd spoken too loudly, but then the girl never raised her head again. Was she close to Michael?

We'll go to Hanna's house for dinner tomorrow night, Bernie thought. I'll show Joan where I lived right before Michael was born. Bernie turned to her side and Joan murmured in her sleep.

I don't want to leave Fribourg now. He is my son and I want to know him. She stared into nothing.

CHAPTER FIVE

Michel showed up for work early on Wednesday, relieving Nani of her long shift.

"*Salut*, Nani," he called as he strode from the hotel lobby to the reception desk. Nani appeared from the back room. She had loosened her ponytail and her long hair curled over her shoulders, almost to her tiny waist. She must have applied fresh lipstick as well, but Michel was careful not to kiss this morning. No more red marks on his face.

"*Bonjour*, Michel," she said as she slipped her eyeglasses into a case and placed it in her big shoulder bag.

"How was your long shift? Uneventful?" He busied himself with logging onto the computer, getting his paperwork in order.

"Yes, it was fine," she said. "I met the two American women." Michel continued to type as he felt Nani standing very close to him.

He nodded and stared at the monitor. "Yes, they stay until tomorrow. So, I will see you back here tomorrow at five?"

"Yes, Michel, I'll see you on Thursday. But you know how to reach me if there is something that comes up." She skirted the desk to stand directly in front of him, and he had to look at her. She had such thick, dark eyelashes. His wife's coloring was light, delicate. Nani was bold and striking.

"If something comes up? What would come up, Nani? I won't need to call you; you can enjoy your time off." He tilted his head at her and tried to give her a friendly smile that conveyed nothing but professionalism. Some pretty girls were dangerous.

"Nothing, nothing. I don't know why I said that. But you have my cell number anyway."

Michel twisted the gold band around his finger. When he realized what he was doing, he stopped, feeling the warm flush creeping up from his neck to his forehead and knowing she would see it.

"Um, how are your parents?" Nani rested an elbow on the desk, in no hurry to leave.

He narrowed his eyes at her. "My parents? They're fine, why do you ask?"

She gazed at something behind his head and ran a hand through her hair. "Just asking," she shrugged. "I think of my parents a lot."

Michel's tense muscles softened. Poor girl, away from home, so young. He remembered her first day at the hotel, and how nervous she was. She was probably the same age as Lucia, but Nani was different. She looked younger, due to her small size, but she was not naïve, he knew that. Lucia had been very sheltered growing up; he imagined quite the opposite of Nani Karas.

"Can you go home for a visit sometime?" His fingers drummed lightly on the desk.

Nani shook her head, and her black hair shimmered under the lights. Michel looked away.

"No, I work here now. It's better, not so much opportunity in Greece," she said. She crossed her arms over her chest. "But I miss my parents. We're a very close family," she added in a tight voice.

"Yes, I'm close to my parents, too," said Michel. "Well, have a good day, Nani, and I'll see you tomorrow at five." He gave her a brief smile and returned to his computer. Please leave, he implored silently.

"Okay, Michel, see you," she said and walked to the front entrance. He watched her leave. The glass doors parted when she stepped on the mat. She turned and waved, then stepped outside. A big man approached her and they kissed. Ah yes, Michel thought, the policeman he'd met once. Alain Bouchard.

I am weak, Michel told himself. A weak, pitiful man whose head is turned by a pretty face with red lips. I have a beautiful wife at home, who loves and cares for me, who is giving me a child. I must think of Nani only as my colleague. He smacked his forehead with the heel of his hand.

"*Pardon, monsieur?*" An elderly woman stood in front of him with a questioning look on her face. He hadn't heard her approach.

"May I help you?" he croaked. The old woman had a complaint about the shower in her room, and Michel was suddenly focused not on Nani's long dark hair and red lips, but on his job as hotel manager. He picked up the phone to call maintenance and smiled at the old woman.

Bernie and Joan descended in the elevator with a young couple who could not stop kissing. Bernie did not see Michael at the front desk and thought perhaps it was too early for him to be working. When they walked into the hotel restaurant for breakfast, Bernie was transported in time, back to Christmas Day in 1978, when she and her best friend Lisa enjoyed Christmas dinner in this very restaurant, thanks to the generosity of Lisa's landlady, Erika Stangl. Bernie could see the restaurant as it was then, with twinkling white lights, the scent of pine all around her, a charming waiter who looked like Paul

Newman, and a memorable meal, probably the best meal either she or Lisa had eaten the entire year. She closed her eyes for a minute to see it all just one more time.

They made their way to the breakfast buffet and surveyed the offerings: glass jugs of orange and apple juice; platters of croissants and dark, raisin-studded bread; white ceramic pots filled with jam, red and orange. A yellow bowl filled with cut fruit and another platter layered with slices of cheese, ham, and salami. And waitresses in starched white aprons serving hot coffee.

"It all looks so good!" Joan exclaimed. "I want coffee first," she added, patting her head and laughing. "I had a little too much wine last night."

Bernie chuckled. "Yes, let's have coffee first."

They found a small table and a waitress appeared immediately, holding a silver pot in each hand. Joan's quizzical expression turned to a grin when she saw the girl pour steaming dark coffee with her left hand and at the same time pour frothy hot milk with her right into the large cups on the table.

"*Café au lait*," Bernie explained. She sipped the hot coffee and sighed as the caffeine infiltrated her system. When they'd finished their first cup, the women returned to the buffet. Bernie chose a *pain au chocolat* and some fruit. Joan filled her plate with dark bread and cheese, a buttery croissant, and a smear of strawberry jam.

After breakfast, they walked back through the hotel lobby, and Bernie spotted Michael at the reception desk. Her chest tightened at the sight of him, but he was engaged in conversation with one of the guests, who seemed to be complaining about something, and Bernie didn't want to bother him. Besides, what was she going to say? Still, it was hard to tear her eyes away from the young man. She stood motionless, unable to move.

Joan touched her arm gently. "Do you want to speak to him, dear?"

Bernie shook her head. "No, not now, Joan. I don't know what I'd say. I can't just stand there and make idle conversation, and he's working. I think I need to fill our day to keep from thinking too much about him. Come on, there's a lot I want to show you." She linked her arm with her aunt's and they headed to the front door, but Bernie turned back to look at her son before they stepped out onto the cobblestone square. A sharp breeze met them, and both women were glad to have scarves to loop around their necks. They spent the entire day in and around Fribourg, from the university to the boulevard where Bernie had lived. She pointed up to show Joan the tiny window that once was hers. They did walk up to the building, but, as Bernie suspected, there was no name plate for the Zellers. They must be both dead by now, she imagined. A woman who looked to be about thirty years old appeared in the lobby and opened the door to them. She spoke only French, so Bernie attempted a conversation with the woman, explaining that she had been a student at the university many years ago, and had lived in the building. The woman told them the Zellers were both, indeed, dead: Monsieur Zeller passed away in 1981, and Madame Zeller died just two years ago.

"Bernie, ask her if that room is open. I'd love to see it," Joan said.

Bernie shook her head, and then told the woman, in halting French, that she had lived in one of the attic rooms and her aunt was very curious about it. The woman replied that each of the apartment owners had use of one of the rooms, but that no one lived in any of them anymore. She said that she would be happy to show them the one room she had, although it was used for storage now and nothing more.

"Okay," Bernie said, and felt her stomach muscles quiver with the thought of returning to the place where she'd spent most of her time as a student. Where she'd let Timmy Lyon into her room on New Year's Day, after spending the previous evening with him at his place. That New Year's Eve, when she already knew she was pregnant. And what led Timmy to believe the baby was his.

Bernie and Joan followed the woman, who introduced herself as Véronique, to the elevator. Bernie recalled the first day she'd arrived in Fribourg and had been dropped off at this building. She remembered the brusque Madame Zeller and the struggle to haul her suitcases into the tiny elevator.

Véronique pulled the wrought-iron gate shut and the elevator began to ascend, just as slowly as ever. Well, this hasn't changed, Bernie thought wryly. All the memories of her first day in Fribourg came back in a flood and she was quiet as the small lift inched its way to the fourth floor.

When the elevator stopped, Véronique pulled the gate open and the three women stepped out. Véronique led the way up the final flight of stairs to the dim hallway.

"Joan, that was my bathroom," Bernie said as she pointed to the closed door at the end of the corridor with a sign on it marked "WC." It could be the same sign, Bernie thought. Véronique stood before a door and fished a key from her pocket. The door was right next to the one that had been Bernie's room.

"There was an old woman who lived in this room," Bernie said in French to Véronique. "I never knew her name, but she was very sweet to me the first day I arrived. I only saw her once or twice after that."

"Yes, she was the widowed aunt of my mother," said Véronique. "Her name was Mathilde Piery, and after her husband died, she had very little money, so my parents, who owned the apartment I now live in, provided the room to her. She took her meals with us when she was able, although I recall, as a child, that she often preferred to stay in this room."

"Yes, she was very quiet," said Bernie softly, remembering the tiny woman with the warm, bony hands. Mathilde Piery. Now, finally, Bernie knew her name.

Véronique opened the door, revealing the same kind of room where Bernie had lived. This room, however, held a stack of plastic storage bins, a broom, a mop, and a bucket filled with an assortment of cleaning products.

"This was your room?" Joan exclaimed, her mouth open.

"Yes, just like it. Mine was right next door," Bernie replied, pointing to the wall.

"Wow, Bernie. I had no idea," Joan said. "How did you live in a room so small?" She swiveled her gaze around the tiny room, to Véronique and back to Bernie.

Bernie shrugged. "It was fine, Joan, really. I was a kid. I had some privacy," she added, remembering Timmy's visit. "It was fine." She wrapped her arms tightly around herself and turned to Véronique.

"Thank you for allowing me to relive some of my memories here as a student. My aunt was able to see where I spent much of my time many years ago." Bernie walked away from the suffocating space and stood in the hallway. That was all a long time ago, and unless she was able to have a conversation with

Michael, she'd be just as happy to say goodbye to Fribourg.

Bernie and Joan thanked Véronique again and descended in the slow elevator until they reached the ground floor. They walked a few blocks down the boulevard, and Bernie pointed out the small market, Migros, on the corner, the tea-room, the cinema, and the park where she would often sit alone and reflect on the course her life had taken.

"I lost my virginity to Karl Berset three weeks after arriving here," she said to her aunt as they sat on a bench in the park. The breeze had died down, and they were warmed by the October sun. "I was sure I was pregnant pretty early on," she added. "This was a spot where I could think and breathe." She looked out over the town, all the way across to the spire of the cathedral.

Joan patted Bernie's arm. "What a time you had, Bernie. You didn't feel that you could tell any of us, did you? You were so young and on your own. Did you ever consider not having the baby?"

Bernie stared again at the far-off cathedral spire, tall and alone amidst the red and orange rooftops. The trees had shed some of their leaves, and the few that still clung to the black limbs were brown and dry. A fountain in the middle of the park made a soft, splashy sound as water cascaded down a concrete rim. She remembered the day in November, on the train to Paris with Erika Stangl. Bernie was going to a doctor that Erika knew, one who would terminate her pregnancy. Karl Berset had disappeared, and she had convinced herself that termination was the most logical choice. Then something happened. She still couldn't explain it, not that she wanted to, but something had gripped her, hard, and she had changed her mind, right there on the train, minutes before they arrived in Paris. Erika had been so kind, so understanding. Bernie took a deep breath and turned her face to Joan.

"No, I never considered not having the baby. Come on, let's walk. I'm hungry."

The women stopped for lunch at the Bella Vista, a small bistro with views of the city from its enclosed rooftop café. Bernie led Joan on a walking tour of St. Nicholas, although the stairs to the roof were closed for repair. Too bad, thought Bernie, on a clear day the views from the top of the cathedral were stunning. They returned to the hotel in mid-afternoon, leaving time to rest and change clothes before taking the bus to Hanna's house.

Upon entering the hotel, Bernie looked again for Michael, but he was not at the reception desk. She felt her heart drop in her chest, too heavy to stay in its place. He's a busy man, she imagined, always dealing with a problem or a question. Still, the hope of seeing him had lifted her steps as she and Joan walked back from the cathedral.

They returned to their room and changed clothes for the trip to Hanna's house. On the bus ride uptown, Bernie tried to remember what she could about the neighboring town of Villars-sur-Glâne. She'd moved into Hanna's house after the unexpected death of her father, but before the earlier than expected birth of Michael.

At the end of the route, Bernie and Joan exited the bus and Bernie easily found Hanna's address. The big gray house looked the same, and Bernie felt her mouth go dry as she aimed her finger at the doorbell. Some of this traveling back in time was difficult, she thought. She swallowed hard and waited.

Hanna opened the door wide and grinned at the two of them.

"Welcome! *Bienvenue!*" she cried, extending her arms and motioning for them to enter. Joan handed Hanna a bouquet of flowers and Bernie held up the bottle of red wine she'd purchased on the way.

"Ah, flowers and wine! It could not be more perfect. But Bernadette, what about the chocolate?" Hanna's eyes sparkled.

"You'd better have some here," Bernie cautioned, then broke into laughter. Turning to Joan, she explained. "Hanna understands my addiction better than anyone, and she's kept me in supply all these years. Because we all know," she said with a wink to Hanna, "Swiss chocolate is far superior to anything we might find at home."

Hanna laughed. "But of course it is true," she said. "Our cows eat grass and flowers, only the best!"

Over a delicious meal of veal with mushrooms, prepared the Zurich way in cream sauce, with Swiss "*rosti*" potatoes and salad, the women caught up on all the news. Hanna again expressed her sympathy to Joan and Bernie at the death of Bernie's mother. She asked about Bernie's sister, Joanie, and shook her head in disbelief when Bernie told her that Joanie and Lou's twin daughters were now fourteen years old. Joan dug out her wallet and produced a photograph of the girls, who had the dark good looks of Lou. Well, of a younger, thinner Lou, thought Bernie.

"Lovely girls," Hanna murmured. "And will they too travel abroad like their aunt Bernadette?"

"Perhaps they will," Joan interjected. "But my niece keeps them pretty sheltered. I don't know."

"I was pretty sheltered, too, Joan," said Bernie. "Look where it got me."

Hanna cleared the dishes and brought out coffee and Calvados brandy. Bernie waited and counted silently to herself in French: *un, deux, trois, quatre, cinq*...there! Hanna opened a large cabinet and retrieved two unopened bars of Swiss chocolate: one in the bright red wrapper, Bernie's favorite, and another with slivered almonds in it. She met Hanna's eyes and grinned.

"Bernadette, you didn't think I would ever forget? Giandor, your favorite? But no," Hanna said.

As the women sipped coffee and brandy, the talk turned serious.

"Hanna, I know you were upset last evening when you first saw us," Bernie said. "You know, I didn't bring Joan here to Fribourg to look for Michael. It took me quite by surprise to see him at the hotel desk yesterday afternoon, and I still have a hard time believing it's him. In fact, I had no proof it was Michael, but I believed it. And that was enough. I don't want to disrupt his life at all, or hurt anyone, especially his parents. But seeing my son after all this time..." her voice broke and she felt tears fill her eyes. "Bernadette, I understand," Hanna replied. "Of course it was very emotional for you," she nodded to Joan, "to you both. And yes, that is Jean-Michel Eicher, the boy you gave birth to in 1979. His parents still live in Givisiez, where they always did, and he is married. His wife is expecting their first child sometime around Christmas, and I am her physician." She leaned forward and laid her hand over Bernie's. "Tell me what it is you want. What do you hope to achieve with this knowledge." Hanna's eyes were sincere and kind.

Bernie twisted her hair around her finger. "I guess I want him to know that I did what I thought was the best thing for him. That I didn't just give him away without regret. That I thought he had a better chance at life with two parents, not with a twenty-year-old American student. I need to know that he understands why I did it, and that I did it all for him. I don't want him to resent me for it." She swallowed the rest of the brandy and waited for the heat to fill her. "You said last night that he knows he was adopted, but did I hear you right? Did you actually tell me that he thinks his birth parents are dead?"

Hanna nodded. Her dark eyes held Bernie's. "Yes, his parents told him when he was about ten years old. There were questions, typical for a young boy, especially with the orange hair." Hanna smiled. "Once he understood what adoption was, he wanted to know about his other mother and father. Klara was at a loss. She was afraid that he would try and find you; you know, sometimes a child gets angry with his parents. Klara tells me she wishes she had never told him this, but he accepted it then and never asked any more questions, so she and Bruno let it stay that way. They thought, what is it you Americans say? No harm, no foul?"

"But Hanna, dead! He thinks I'm dead. And I am here. In his hotel." She stood up from the table and paced to the window and back. "She didn't have to tell him that I was *dead*." Bernie raked her hands through her hair, and it spiraled out from her head, down to her shoulders. She looked at Hanna, not expecting an answer. What answer was there? There was no explanation that would satisfy her.

Hanna sat back slightly in her chair. "I don't know why she told him that, Bernadette. She did what she thought was the right thing at the time. Klara has always been a worrier. Obviously, she would find it very hard to tell him now that she lied to him, that you are alive. And here in Fribourg. At his hotel. That's why she telephoned me yesterday evening. Michel came home from work and spoke of two women from America, one who could not stop crying and kept staring at him. She feared it was you and called me in a panic."

"Well, it *is* me! His dead mother has come back to life." Bernie tried to control her breathing. She inhaled deeply through her nose, held it, and exhaled through her open mouth. It didn't seem to help. Dead! He thinks I'm dead! How could she ever make contact with him now?

"Let me speak with Klara." Hanna rested her chin in her upturned palm and cut her eyes to Bernie, who was still standing, her hands in fists by her hips. "You leave Fribourg when?"

"We leave tomorrow, Hanna," Joan said quietly.

Bernie raised her chin and unclenched her fists. She rested a hand on Hanna's shoulder. "It's alright, my friend. Don't worry about it. I don't blame you; I don't even blame Klara for doing what she thought was right. I have seen my son. I know that he is well; he's grown into a fine young man. That should be enough, shouldn't it? My wish, my sole wish for Michael all these years was for him to have a happy and loving home." With those last words, her voice broke and she sat down heavily.

"He is well, Bernadette. All is well. I'm glad you had a chance to see him. And I hope that you both will have happy travels throughout Switzerland. Bernadette, had I known you were coming, you could have taken the chalet. There is snow already in the mountains," Hanna said.

Had she known I was coming, she would have tried to banish us to the chalet, Bernie thought grimly. Then her mood softened. This wasn't Hanna's fault. It wasn't anyone's fault. It was just the way things were.

"Thank you, Hanna. Joan, we really should go," Bernie said, checking her watch. "When is the next bus back to town?" She guided Joan toward the door. They put on their coats. Bernie kept a smile pasted on her face.

Hanna also checked her watch. "Five minutes." She hugged Joan first, then Bernie, and handed Bernie an unopened bar of Giandor chocolate in the bright red wrapper.

"Put this in your purse," she instructed. "I know you like chocolate for breakfast."

Bernie smiled back at Hanna, beautiful Hanna, the picture of calm. Time had treated her well; there were tiny crinkles around her eyes, but Hanna looked as youthful and pretty as she had in 1979, when she was Bernie's obstetrician. "Thank you for everything. Come visit me sometime in America, won't you?" They hugged again and the women walked out of Hanna's house into the crisp air and empty street.

On the bus ride back to Fribourg, Bernie was quiet. Joan tried to make conversation about Lucerne, asking questions, but gave up when Bernie's murmured answers discouraged chat. Bernie looked out the window at the dark streets, the closed-up shops, and the occasional pedestrian. They might be leaving for Lucerne tomorrow, but Bernie would be sure they returned to Fribourg before flying home. She just wouldn't tell Hanna, or even Joan, about it.

CHAPTER SIX

On Thursday morning, Bernie and Joan ate breakfast in the hotel restaurant, then returned to their room and gathered their packed bags. They descended in the elevator and Joan rolled the bags into the lobby, then settled into one of the big lobby chairs while Bernie returned their keys.

Michael was at the reception desk. Bernie tried to imagine the coming days, away from him, but her mind was unable to see past this moment. Everything inside her was heavy.

"*Bonjour*," she half-whispered. She didn't trust her voice, not now, not with him right there in front of her.

"*Bonjour, Madame!*" he replied, his face registering recognition. Bernie couldn't believe it was only two days ago that she'd walked into this hotel and seen him. "You leave Fribourg already?"

"*Oui*," she said. She fiddled with the silver chain around her neck. "We had a wonderful time. Many memories, all good ones. Look, no more crying." She dared to meet his eyes. Soft brown eyes, not unlike his father's. But how cunning Karl's eyes were. She knew in her heart that Michael was nothing like Karl. Do you not recognize me, my son? Her words were spoken only inside her head; she could not say them aloud. She couldn't do it, not today.

"We're going to Lucerne, then to Lugano. I know a lot of the sights are closed at this time of the year, but still, the weather may be a little warmer." She played with her necklace again, reluctant to let the moment end.

Michael grinned. "I know Lugano. Where do you stay?"

Bernie wrinkled her nose as she tried to remember. "Hotel Walter, I think?"

He lifted his eyebrows in surprise. "I did my first training at the Walter. You will enjoy. It's a good hotel," he said.

Bernie just stared at him. That couldn't be coincidence, she was sure of it. Another sign?

Michael added, "I met my wife Lucia in Lugano. It is a very special place for us."

Bernie leaned forward, willing him to keep talking, to tell her everything he could in the few minutes they had. "Ah, she is Swiss, too? From Ticino region?"

Michael flushed, and Bernie's heart lifted. He blushes as easily as I do, she thought. "No, she is from Milano," he said as he printed out a receipt. He slid it across the desk to her and his fingers brushed against hers. She accepted the receipt, folded it, and put it in her purse, then extended her right hand.

"Thank you for everything, Jean-Michel. We enjoyed our stay here very much." Bernie smiled hard at her son and blinked rapidly, forbidding the tears that threatened to fill her eyes. He took her hand and she squeezed it.

He nodded his head and replied, "I do hope you will come back to see us again."

Bernie said, "You can count on it." She withdrew her hand from his and their eyes met one last time. "Would you call a taxi for us, please, Michel?"

"Yes, certainly."

He picked up the telephone and Bernie turned away from him. Those tears had a will of their own.

She crossed the lobby to Joan and said, "Come on, auntie, let's go outside and wait for the taxi." She could leave him only because she knew she'd return.

Joan sprang to her feet and looked back at Michel, then quickly joined her niece outside.

By mid-morning, Bernie and Joan were on their way to Lucerne, where they spent four days touring the old city along the Reuss River. They walked over the covered wooden Chapel Bridge and viewed the magnificent Dying Lion of Lucerne sculpture, carved into the side of a cliff. They took a side trip to Engelberg, where there was already snow. The smell of roasting chestnuts made Bernie nostalgic as she remembered the street stands around Fribourg with hand-lettered signs advertising "*heissi marroni*."

From Lucerne, they traveled by train to Lugano, where the temperature was decidedly warmer. Joan was excited to see palm trees at the stop in Bellinzona. When they arrived at the Hotel Walter, Bernie pictured her Michael at the reception desk, handsome and charming, helpful and professional. She even asked the older woman behind the desk if she remembered Jean-Michel Eicher, but the woman shook her head no. She'd only been working there for a few months.

The Hotel Walter provided a small but comfortable room, generous breakfast, and views of the lake. The boat ran on its winter schedule, and on their second day, Bernie and Joan boarded the "Ceresio" for a tour of the lake, stopping off at Morcote, the picturesque village on the shore of Lake Lugano. Joan looked up at the steep, terraced hill.

"Look, Bernie! We could walk all the way up." Bernie could see that Joan had that look, and the shiny eyes of childlike anticipation. Bernie smiled and thought again how Joan had been a fine companion, so easy-going, so agreeable.

"Sure, let's do it, Joan. Then we'll have lunch before boarding the three o'clock boat."

They disembarked and followed the signs pointing up. In no time, Bernie was breathing hard. It was all uphill and steep. Still, she followed Joan, who didn't seem to be breaking a sweat. All that tennis, Bernie thought. I really should do more aerobic exercise.

Thirty minutes and a few rest stops later, they reached the church of Santa Maria del Sasso. Even on an overcast day, the view from the summit was spectacular, with the lake spread out before them like a freeform blanket of heathery gray, cuddled by the surrounding hills. The women rested on a bench and took in the beauty around them before venturing back down the four hundred steps to the village.

They dined at the Ristorante Battello, and enjoyed polenta with roasted rabbit. A bottle of local red wine complemented the meal, and with a little time to spare before the boat returned, they shared a delicate tiramisu, better than any Bernie had ever tasted. With full bellies, they waited for the return boat and Bernie dozed on the slow ride back to Lugano.

"Honey, wake up," Joan said softly as the boat pulled into dock. Bernie stirred and for a moment she didn't know where she was. In her dream, Bernie could see Michael with his wife, Lucia, and she was lovely.

"Joan, I think I'm ready to leave Lugano." Bernie stood and stretched as they made their way off the boat.

"We don't fly home until Tuesday the fifth, though," Joan said, frowning as she tried to remember what day it was. "You don't want to stay here?"

"Well, I booked us through to tomorrow. There isn't much more to do here. Everything is closed for the season." Bernie chewed her lip, considering her words. They passed a souvenir kiosk with a sign that read "*chiuso*" nailed to a padlocked door.

Joan stopped walking and turned to face her niece. "Do you want to go back and see him?"

Bernie nodded. Her throat was tight and tears wet the outer corners of her eyes. She bit her bottom lip hard to try and stop them.

Joan's voice was tender when she spoke. "It's okay, sweetie. I understand. He's your son, and if you need to see him again, we'll just go back."

"It hurts to be away from him." Bernie hugged Joan hard, and they returned to the hotel.

CHAPTER SEVEN

That evening, while Joan and Bernie dined at the pizzeria next to the Hotel Walter, Nani sat on a stool behind the reception desk at the Hotel de la Rose. She checked the clock on the computer. Almost midnight. Alain should be here soon, she thought. I wonder if he will ever ask me out, and if he doesn't ask tonight, maybe I should offer to make dinner for him. Enough of these visits during work. We both have the day off on Sunday.

She lowered her head and tried to concentrate on the magazine in front of her. These nights were so boring. It was either read the latest magazine that featured tall, leggy models in clothes and shoes she could never afford, or play mindless games like solitaire on the computer. The buzzer at the hotel entrance sounded and she jumped off the stool. Alain stood on the other side of the door, his giant frame obscuring anything behind him. Nani wiggled her hips seductively as she approached the door, and enjoyed seeing Alain's expression. She let him inside and waited for him to lean down to kiss her, but he surprised her by grasping her tiny waist with both hands. Suddenly she was lifted off her feet.

"Nani, I have something to ask you," he said, as her arms encircled his neck.

"Can you ask me while I'm standing on the floor?" She knew she was small, and Alain was so big, but he didn't need to pick her up as if she was a child. He set her down gently and held out his hand. They walked to the rear of the hotel lobby together and he sat on her stool. When he stood, she had to crane her neck to look into his face. With him seated, they were practically eye to eye. He had a strong chin, she noticed, and a fine, straight nose.

Nani removed her red eyeglasses and blinked a few times at Alain. She had applied extra eyeliner and mascara that afternoon, a dab more of perfume, but Michel hadn't seemed to notice. Funny how she felt so powerful with Alain, and so powerless with Michel. Alain would drop to his knees if she asked.

"So ask me, Alain," she said softly.

He pulled over an extra stool for her, and Nani climbed on. Their knees bumped together and he moved his aside. "Sunday we are both off from work," he began. "Would you like to go to Bern with me?" She saw his Adam's apple bob in his throat and liked that he was nervous to ask her.

"To Bern?" Nani licked her lips. She had never been to Bern, even though it was only twenty minutes away by train. This would be a good first date, she reasoned. Walk around the city, browse the shop windows, and enjoy a meal together.

Alain twisted his big hands. "We can take a train at noon, maybe see the bears, have something to eat. If you would like, Nani." His face was full of hope.

Nani wasn't accustomed to being pursued; back in her little village, none of the boys ever called to her house, to ask her parents if they could take her for a walk, or to a dance on a Saturday night. At eighteen, her only kiss was from the fat pig who washed dishes at the tavern, where she worked during the summer before she left for hotel school. He was ugly and smelly and he'd cornered her one night after closing, pressing his thick slimy lips onto hers, thrusting his fat stomach against her until she wriggled away and ran home. She often dreamed of how wonderful it would feel to have a real man kiss her, with soft lips and just a trace of scratchy stubble. Someone who would use his hands to caress, not to grab and squeeze.

"Nani?" Alain's voice was subdued. His eyes, dark blue like the sea in winter, probed hers.

"Okay," Nani replied and gave him her best smile. "I would like that, Alain. Thank you." Why not, she reasoned. He's a nice guy. She angled toward him. "Alain, do you know anyone who is adopted?"

"Adopted?" He frowned at the question. His dark eyebrows joined as one on his forehead. "I don't think so, Nani. Why do you ask?"

"I just wondered, you know, if someone was adopted and wanted to find out who their real parents were, I mean, the birth parents, that could be done, right?"

Alain laid his massive hand over her tiny one. "You are a sweet, sweet girl. I will help you find your parents," he said, looking deep into her eyes.

"Oh," she exclaimed. "No, it's not me. It's…I just read about it in a book and it made me wonder." Let it be, she told herself. Don't share this information with anyone, especially not a police officer. Knowledge is good to have, she reminded herself.

Friday morning arrived and Michel nuzzled against Lucia's shoulder.

"It's holiday today, Lulu," he murmured. "We could stay in bed all morning." He traced his hand down her neck to her breast, fuller and heavier now. She turned to him and he teased her through the thin cotton of her nightgown.

"Michel," she whispered as desire won out. She put the red lipstick out of her mind. It was silly; she had overreacted. This was her husband, and she had no reason to doubt him.

He turned her back to her side, facing away from him.

"Let me make it comfortable for you," he whispered back, lifting her nightgown.

Half an hour later, Michel stood under a strong spray of hot water and sang off-key. He knew he couldn't sing, but he didn't care, not this morning. He turned off the water, stepped from the shower and wrapped a thick towel around his waist. He breathed in to catch the smell of breakfast cooking and it made him smile. Dear God, he thought, I am not a religious person, but I must have done something good for you to give me this woman. All he wanted to do was make her happy. He rubbed a towel over his head to dry his close-cropped hair and returned to the bedroom to dress in casual khaki slacks and a long-sleeved blue shirt. He wondered if the baby would have orange hair.

Lucia was setting plates on the table when he walked in. "*Bonjour*, Lulu," he murmured into her neck. "You smell like ham," he added with a laugh as he laid his hands on her stomach.

"Come sit. We have a good breakfast together for once."

"This makes me a happy man. Today we can have a relaxing day. Would you like to go somewhere? Lausanne?" He scooped up ham and fried eggs with a piece of bread and beamed at his wife.

"Yes, okay. For a little trip." Michel watched her clean her plate and grinned. There's my girl, he thought. Lucia was even more beautiful pregnant, and he hoped she wouldn't try too hard to lose the weight after the baby came. He loved every curve of her body, every soft place.

"Lulu, I know it seems very early, but the management at the hotel has set the date for the annual Christmas party," he said, wiping his plate with the last bit of bread. She was still glowing from their lovemaking an hour ago. Her skin was luminous as the morning sun slanted through the window and reflected off her shiny hair. See, he told himself, good sex has many benefits.

Her shoulders sagged. "Christmas! Oh Michel, I won't be able to attend. It's too close to the due date," she said.

"It's the fourteenth of December, a Saturday. Two weeks before the due date. We'll see how everything is then, but I really want you to be there with me if you can." He made the sad puppy face that he knew would get to her. "I don't want to be there without you." He laid his elbows on the table and cupped his chin with both hands.

And, he added silently, I want Nani to see us together. I want her to know that she has no chance with me.

"Okay, *amore*, stop making the face. I will go with you if we don't have the baby already. I must try to find a tent to wear." She carried the plates to the kitchen and called back to him, "Where should we eat in Lausanne?"

Early in the afternoon on Friday, All Saints' Day, a train carrying Bernie and Joan arrived back in Fribourg, and within twenty minutes, the women stepped into the lobby at the Hotel de la Rose. Bernie was so excited to see her Michael again, she practically skipped to the reception desk behind the lobby, but he was not there. That little dark-haired girl was talking on the telephone when she and Joan approached with their luggage.

Nani looked up and her mouth gaped open. She ended the telephone conversation abruptly and snapped her phone shut. Bernie saw the girl's eyes darken and her mouth set in a tight line.

"*Bonjour,*" she said politely, but Bernie could see something black and threatening in those eyes. "So, you have returned to Fribourg." Her eyes darted from Bernie to Joan and back to Bernie, where they rested.

"Yes, we came back. We fly home on Tuesday, so we decided to spend the rest of our time here." Bernie broke away from Nani's piercing stare and glanced behind her, toward the back room. "Is, is Jean-Michel here?" She combed trembling fingers through her unruly hair.

Nani smiled at Bernie, but her eyes remained flinty, like the hard pieces of coal Bernie had once used for a snowman's eyes. "He has the day off, *Madame.* Holiday today. He will not be back until Monday."

Bernie eyed her, trying to assess the dark looks she was sending forth. "Well, I know we didn't make a reservation, but I'm hoping you have a room available for us. We stayed in room 345 – is that room available until Tuesday?"

"Oh, I don't know. I will have to check. Perhaps you and *Madame* would care to sit while I check?" Nani turned her attention to the computer screen and began typing furiously.

Bernie tilted her head at Nani, like a bird would when hearing a foreign sound. When Nani did not look up, Bernie turned on her heel and sat down hard in one of the chairs facing the reception desk. Joan sat across from her, looking at the entrance.

"Bernie, I can't imagine they're fully booked. It's early November, hardly high season."

Bernie leaned forward to whisper to her aunt. "They're not booked, Joan. There's nobody here. That girl is just taking her time. I bet you anything our old room is available. She'll probably give us a smaller room. I wish Michael were here." Bernie bounced her leg up and down and chewed on a fingernail.

It was another five minutes, that felt more like two hours, before Nani slid off her stool behind the front desk and called, "Ms. Maguire?" She mispronounced it, of course, saying "Ma-GEER" the same way Karl Berset used to do. Another reason not to like her, Bernie thought.

"Stay here," she said to Joan, as she stood and walked to the front desk, where Nani gave her a saccharine smile. "You have good luck. Room 345 is available for you both. You check out on Tuesday the fifth of November?" Her eyeglasses had slipped down her nose a little, and Nani's eyes, so dark and fringed with thick black lashes, blinked rapidly at Bernie.

Bernie steeled herself and breathed out through her nose. "Yes, that would be correct. Thank you ever so much," she said, and squinting at Nani's name badge, added, "Nanny." Knowing she had mispronounced the name, Bernie met Nani's glare with her own sweet smile.

Joan wheeled the bags to the elevator and they stepped in. Just before the elevator doors closed, Bernie saw Nani whip open her phone and manipulate the keys at lightning speed. Their eyes met for a brief hard look before the doors slid shut.

The train from Fribourg to Lausanne was a pleasant, fifty-minute ride through the tiny towns of

Neyruz, Romont, and Palezieux. Lucia rested her head against Michel's chest as he gazed out the window. Someday they might leave Fribourg to move closer to the lake, he thought. Maybe even all the way to Lugano. Lucia would be right at home in Ticino, and his Italian surely would improve. They would be closer to her parents, but the thought of moving away from Klara and Bruno made his heart hurt. For now, they would remain in Fribourg.

His cell phone vibrated in his shirt pocket and Lucia shifted against his chest. Michel withdrew the small phone from his pocket and flipped it open. A text message from Nani read: "Amer women here again. B Maguire asked for u." He scowled at the phone.

"What is it?" Lucia raised her head and stifled a yawn.

"It's my co-worker, bothering me on my day off, to tell me about guests. Totally unnecessary," he added as he snapped the phone shut and returned it to his pocket. She is a bother, he said to himself. Just because Nani had to work today shouldn't mean she could pester him with unneeded information. Very nice that the American women had returned, he thought, but it has nothing to do with me. I have three days away from the hotel and I plan to spend it with my wife, not taking messages from an annoying colleague.

The train slowed and squealed as it arrived in Lausanne. Michel turned to Lucia and took her chin in his hand. "Today is just for us, Lulu," he said. "It's too bad the boat does not run now, but we should go to the lake anyway, don't you think?" He wrapped her scarf around her neck twice. "You will be warm enough?"

Lucia nodded, her light blue eyes like crystal against light brown lashes and brows. Those blue eyes mesmerized him the first time he saw her.

"Come, we're here," he said, as he stood and held out his hand to her. Together they descended the train and strolled hand in hand down the platform to the exit. They crossed the strcct and boarded the metro that descended the steep hill from the train station to Ouchy, on the shore of Lake Geneva.

It was breezy at the lake and there were more than a few tourists around. As it was a holiday, Michel and Lucia were not alone. Little children chased after pigeons, flapping their arms as they whirled through the park. An elderly couple sat quietly on a bench, their heads bent close together. A fat man in a cowboy hat snapped photographs of the lake and mountains.

"Come, let's sit," Michel guided Lucia to an empty bench, and they settled themselves, their thighs pressed close together. Michel stared out at the bluest lake, with the mountains of Evian, France, on the opposite side. Patches of white covered the highest peaks.

"Are you thinking about the baby?" Lucia broke into his thoughts, and he smiled at the intrusion.

"We still have to decide on a name, you know," he reminded her. He lowered his arm from her shoulder to her waist, and pulled her closer.

"But we must choose two, one for a boy and one for a girl," she replied, resting her gloved hands on her stomach. The coat she wore last winter would not button now, so Lucia wore a heavy sweater and wrapped a woolen shawl around her shoulders.

"You said you like Raphaela for a girl." Michel watched as a young woman pushed a baby stroller past them.

"I do like it, unless you think it's too Italian. What about for a boy? You choose, Michel. Do you want a little Jean-Michel in the house?" She winked at him.

Michel shook his head no. "Raphaela is fine. It honors your family. What about Nico?"

Lucia drew back in surprise, "Really? You like that?"

He shrugged. "We can just call it *bebe* for a while," he said and they both laughed.

The couple grew quiet again, and stared at the whitecaps on the lake.

Lucia turned to face her husband. "Michel, do you ever think about your birth parents? Wonder who they were?"

"Of course. I try not to think too much, because sometimes it makes me sad that they are dead, that I never knew them. I love my parents so much. They really are my parents, because they raised me, but yes, sometimes I wish I knew. Just something about them. Their names, where they were from, what they looked like." He touched the top of his head. "Someone had this hair, no?" He grinned, showing his straight, white teeth. Then the smile disappeared. "If I ask mama, it would make her sad. So I don't ask. Papa, too. But yes, I wonder about it."

Lucia stretched out her feet and made small circles. She looked up at Michel. "Maybe it would be good to try and find out. If you were born at the hospital in Fribourg, there would be a record perhaps. Or Dr. Schmidt. Now you're an adult, she would understand, I think. I mean, that you don't want to upset your parents, but still, you want to know. Maybe you start with her and you don't need to bother mama."

"I never thought to look at the hospital records," he said in a faraway voice. He snapped his head up and said, "Come, let's find a warm place for tea." He helped his wife to her feet. "Can you walk?"

"Of course I can walk!" Lucia cried. "I'm only at seven months, still two months to go. Want to race?" She threw back her head and laughed, and Michel caught her in his arms and whirled her around.

"I am crazy in love with you, Lulu," he said as his lips met hers.

She tried to reply, but he covered her mouth with his, and her words were lost.

CHAPTER EIGHT

Saturday dawned bright and cold, with a clear blue sky and a brisk wind from the east. Michel and Bruno planned to pick up the baby furniture today: a crib, changing table, dresser, all white. Lucia wanted primary colors for accents; she said they would work with either a boy or a girl.

The men left early for the drive to Lyssach. Bruno had borrowed a truck from one of the men in the village, who was all too happy to help the young couple. Lucia dressed and telephoned Klara.

"Good morning, mama," she said when Klara picked up. "Will you come over for coffee?"

Klara agreed, and thirty minutes later, the women were seated at the table, enjoying a second cup of coffee and a slice of the butter cake that Klara brought with her.

"So, you had a nice day in Lausanne, Lucia?" Klara sat straight in her chair and lifted the china cup to her lips. Her dark hair was veined with gray and pulled back from her face in a loose knot at the back of her head. Lucia thought that if Klara covered the gray, she would look younger than her fifty-eight years, but she knew it was inappropriate to suggest such a thing. Klara was not one for makeup or jewelry. She wore a plain gold band on her left hand and a simple watch. No polish on her fingernails. Lucia's mother was the exact opposite of Klara. At their wedding, it couldn't have been more obvious. Klara in a simple linen dress, light green, high neck, modest length, low heels. Lucia's mother Franca ablaze in shades of red and orange, black hair piled high, drawing attention to herself, just as she'd intended. Just as she always had done, thought Lucia.

"It was lovely, mama," Lucia replied, using the familiar term Klara had insisted on when Michel first brought her home. "It was chilly by the lake, but with such pretty views. And we found a small restaurant by the lake that had a spicy fish soup." She licked her lips just thinking about the memorable meal.

"And good for Michel to have a day away from work. He works hard, my boy," Klara said. She cut another sliver of cake for herself and pushed the plate toward Lucia. Lucia picked up the knife and cut a far more generous slice for her own plate. I eat for two, she rationalized.

"He certainly does work hard. Oh! Remember last week when he spoke of the two American women who arrived at the hotel? The one who cried? Well, they returned! Michel received a message on his phone yesterday, telling him they have returned to Fribourg. Isn't that so nice?" Lucia took a bite of the buttery cake and closed her eyes as it melted on her tongue.

Klara's cup clanked onto her saucer and Lucia flinched. Her mother-in-law looked pale and her lips were set in a thin line. Lucia watched Klara's neck muscles tighten and twitch.

"Mama? Are you okay?" Lucia reached for Klara's arm.

Klara looked down at her cup and saucer, at the remnants of cake on her plate. Her lower lip quivered.

"Mama, what is it? Please. Let me help." Lucia scraped her chair closer to Klara's, and put an arm around her shoulder. "Are you ill?"

Klara wiped at her eyes and pulled a white cotton handkerchief from her pocket. She dabbed at her nose and turned her eyes to Lucia.

"You know I love you like a daughter. You know that, my dear, don't you?"

Lucia nodded and tensed for what was to come.

"And you know that when Bruno and I adopted Michel, he was just a newborn baby." She looked up to the ceiling. "We were unable to have a baby of our own, and we were getting older. Dr. Schmidt found a baby for us, from a young girl who could not keep it. The girl was unmarried and chose to give up the baby for adoption. She was a patient of Dr. Schmidt. Hanna took care of the adoption, with the help of a lawyer. She arranged for us to adopt the girl's baby." Klara's breathing was labored as she struggled to finish. "Everything was legal."

Lucia kept her hand on Klara's arm, almost as if she feared the woman would flee at any moment. "Yes, mama, I know all of this from Michel. His birth parents are dead. An automobile crash, yes?"

Klara shook her head and wiped her eyes again. Her hands were shaking and she laid them flat on the table. "No, they did not die." She met Lucia's shocked expression and Lucia saw such sadness in Klara's eyes that she, too, filled with tears. "We told that to Michel when he was a boy because he asked a lot of questions. And I was afraid he would try to find his mother. That he would leave me. Boys sometimes get mad at their mothers or their fathers. I didn't want him to leave." She choked out the words.

"Mama. What are you saying?" Lucia's leaned forward, until her face was just inches from Klara's.

Klara blew her nose but would not look at Lucia. "Michel's birth mother is the American woman. And I'm afraid that the truth will come out and Michel will be so angry with me..." Her shoulders curled over her chest as she sobbed loudly.

Lucia gasped and put an arm around Klara. When she finally spoke, her voice was higher than she expected it to be. "Mama, Michel is a grown man, and married. He will understand when he hears the whole story. We are not leaving. We won't leave you, I promise that." She kissed Klara's wet cheek. "We will never leave you. But mama! This woman is Michel's *mother*?"

Klara nodded. Her voice was barely a whisper. "He will hate me for lying to him. She will tell him that she is his mother. I'm sure that's why she returned." She took a deep breath and let out a ragged sigh. "When Michel told the story last week about the American women at the hotel, I had a bad feeling. An American woman who had lived in Fribourg many years ago, who was crying, who kept staring at him. I called Hanna after that dinner. Hanna knew Bernadette – that is her name, Bernadette – she has stayed in contact with her through the years. But she was very surprised that Bernadette was here in Switzerland. Bernadette didn't tell Hanna because her motives are not good, Lucia." Klara sat straighter in her chair and pulled her shoulders back. She drummed nervous fingers on the table.

"And who is the woman with her?"

"It is her aunt. According to Hanna, Bernadette's mother died last month and the women came here for a restful vacation, at least that's what Bernadette told Hanna. Hanna told me that Bernadette didn't come to look for Michel, but when she saw him..." her voice trailed off. "I guess a mother always knows her child." Klara's eyes were still red and puffy. Lucia pushed away from the table to get her a glass of water.

"Mama, I can assure you that Michel considers only you and Papa his true parents. We just talked of this yesterday, in Lausanne. You are his parents. But I think you must tell him the truth, especially with these women back in town. Wouldn't it be better for Michel to hear the truth from you than from this woman who doesn't even know him?" She rested her hand on her mother-in-law's back and set a glass of water on the table in front of her.

Klara took a sip and turned her face up to Lucia. "You are right, dear. Yes. I will talk to Bruno tonight and we will tell Michel tomorrow. We will all be together tomorrow, yes?"

"Yes, mama," said Lucia, wondering how Michel would react to the news.

Bernie and Joan spent Saturday in Neuchâtel and took a guided walking tour of the old town. With Michel not working in the hotel all weekend, Bernie found it better for her mental health to plan things to do outside of Fribourg. After all, Fribourg was very picturesque, but she and her aunt had walked extensively around the town the previous week, and Bernie thought it better to explore other areas within a day's train ride.

On the ride back to Fribourg, Joan dozed with her head against the window and Bernie's rambling stream of consciousness eventually landed on Karl Berset. Her first love, who really wasn't a love, who seduced her for a weekend, one weekend, and then he was finished with her. The married Swiss banker who abandoned her after that weekend. Before she knew she was pregnant. Bernie recalled those first days when she had no idea what to do, the feeling of utter aloneness. She wondered if Karl was living in the area.

Back at the hotel, Joan headed upstairs for a nap and Bernie approached the reception desk. She was glad to see an older man there, not that little dark-haired girl with the red eyeglasses. There was something about that girl that Bernie didn't trust. She didn't want to have to ask the girl for anything.

"May I help you, miss?" Miss! Bernie liked him already. This man reminded her a little of Norm, the bartender at the Drop-Off back home. Those days seemed like ages ago now, when she'd spent nearly every evening in the bar, hooking up occasionally. Norm was like a great dad who didn't judge her. Bernie would have to pick up some chocolate for him, even though she'd already vowed to spend less time at the bar. She turned her attention back to the clerk behind the reception desk and spied his name badge: Robert. Yes, he looked like a Robert. Probably about her age, with thinning hair, gray at the temples. A large, bulbous nose. Small, close-set eyes the color of a Fribourg sky in November. Pock-marked skin, poor guy.

"I'm not sure," she began. "I don't have a computer with me, but perhaps you could help me. I'm looking for someone I knew many years ago, and I believe he lived around here, possibly as far away as Lausanne, but it's been a long time." She rested her elbows on the desk and smiled at him. His face colored and he ran his hand over his scalp. Bernie noticed white flakes on the shoulder of his dark jacket.

"Maybe I can help you, unless he has a very common name," he said. "By the way, my name is Robert." He patted the name badge pinned to his navy blue jacket. His face had the look of someone who had seen his share of sadness and heartache. His cheeks sagged and the corners of his mouth just naturally pointed down. But in his eyes, Bernie saw a flicker, a light, and she looked away, afraid that her kindness might be mistaken for something else. She saw him staring at her left hand. No ring. She stood up and took a step back from the desk.

"His name is Karl Berset. Here, let me write it down." Robert opened a drawer and took out a sheet of plain white paper. He slid it across the desk to Bernie. She felt his eyes on her, and concentrated on writing the name in large letters. She turned the paper around so it was facing him and glanced up.

Robert began typing into his computer. "We have an online directory for each canton," he said. "First I'll check in Fribourg, then I'll look in the others." Bernie could smell stale cigarette smoke; it was attached to his clothes and would stay with him, she knew.

She fixed her gaze on the elevator, waiting while Robert typed. Perhaps he won't be able to find him. Karl may be dead, or long moved away. It's okay either way, she told herself. It doesn't matter. She fidgeted on the opposite side of the desk while Robert peered at the monitor.

"Here he is," Robert announced, and Bernie drew her attention back to him. He was grinning at her with uneven teeth. Bernie looked away as he wrote an address on the paper and slid it back to her.

Bernie looked down at the paper. 23 Rue du Midi in Lausanne. She committed it to memory and looked up at Robert.

"Are you familiar with Lausanne, Robert?"

He shook his head and began typing again. "One moment, please, I'm pulling up a map of the town for you." He typed again and said, "Come around to this side so you can see."

Bernie took a few steps around the desk to stand next to Robert. He pointed a stubby finger at the monitor and said, "You see? Here is the train station, and here is the rue du Midi." His breath was warm on her neck and she shivered. She dared not turn her face to his; they were just inches away from each other.

Bernie ducked back around to the other side of the desk and said, "Thank you so much, Robert. You've been very helpful."

Just then there was a loud crash from inside the restaurant, and Robert excused himself. He loped into the restaurant, and Bernie saw an opportunity to leave. She hurried to the elevator and pressed the button. Come on, she implored silently. Come on. And it came. The elevator door opened and she slipped inside. She pressed the number three and waited, hoping the doors would close before Robert reappeared. Bernie knew he was harmless, or at least she believed he was harmless, but she didn't want to give the man any impression that she might be interested in him.

Back in their room, Joan was sitting in the chair by the window, reading. When Bernie stepped into the room, she laid her book on the bed.

"What happened to you? You were downstairs for a long time!"

"The guy at reception was a little...odd. He smelled like smoke." She waved her hand in front of her face. "But he was very helpful." She checked her pocket for the piece of paper and realized she must have left it on the desk. Damn.

"What is it, Bernie?"

Bernie told Joan about the conversation.

"Are you sure you want to find Karl Berset after all these years?"

"I feel...I feel as if there are all these loose ends that need to be tied up. Or cut off. I don't know, Joan, but we're here and I don't know when I'll be back, if ever. I need to say a few things to Karl. Please come with me."

"Of course I'll go with you! Bernie, if you think this is important, I trust you. You know your own heart."

"Robert wrote down Karl's address and I left the paper on the desk. But I don't really want to go back downstairs now. It's okay, I memorized the address. 23 Rue du Midi. I think Robert thought I was flirting with him, and I swear, Joan, I was not flirting with him."

Her aunt giggled and said, "Poor old guy."

"Ha! I'll introduce you if you want. He'll probably be down there all night."

"Don't worry about it. Have yourself a soak in the tub and we'll go out later, whether he's there or not. You've got me for protection," Joan said, making Bernie laugh at the idea of her aunt, a good six inches shorter and twenty pounds lighter than Bernie, as her bodyguard.

The women were able to skirt around Robert on their way out, and he was engaged with other hotel guests on their return. They slept well that night and rose early. As they entered the hotel lobby for breakfast, Bernie saw that Nani was back at the reception desk. She and Joan ignored her and headed into the restaurant.

After they finished breakfast, they were cutting through the lobby on their way out when Bernie heard her name called. "Oh, Madame Maguire! One moment, please." Bernie sighed and whispered to Joan, "Just a second, Joan. Lord knows what she wants now." Bernie forced herself to smile as she walked halfway back across the lobby where Nani stood away from the desk, dressed in a short black skirt and a black-and-gray striped sweater. The girl really favors black, Bernie thought, as she glanced at her feet. High-heeled black boots up to the knee. Bernie raised her eyes.

"Yes, Nani?" Bernie rested a hand on her hip.

Nani smiled sweetly up at her. "When I arrived for work last night, Robert told me you had been here. He helped you to find someone." Bernie frowned at her and the acid burn of bile rose in her throat. Must have been that pastry. Why would Robert talk to Nani about her, anyway?

"He said you forgot to pick up something and asked that I give it to you this morning." She held out the sheet of paper with Karl's name and address on it. "Karl Berset, 23 Rue du Midi, Lausanne. Must be someone very special for you to be seeking him out after all this time." Her flinty eyes glowed black, unadorned by those silly red eyeglasses.

Bernie snatched the paper out of her little hand. The girl's short fingernails were painted black, for God's sake. "This isn't any of your concern, Nani." She whirled away without waiting for a reply and walked purposefully to Joan, who stood waiting by the hotel entrance doors.

"Let's get the hell out of here."

Joan looked back and said, "She's staring after you. What's her problem?"

"Forget it," Bernie said. She stepped outside and Joan followed. A taxi idled in front of the hotel, the driver leaning against his car, smoking a cigarette. Bernie caught his eye and said, "Are you free?"

The driver nodded and extinguished his cigarette. "Where, please?"

"Train station."

"I thought you wanted to walk," Joan said, climbing in after her.

CHAPTER NINE

Joan and Bernie boarded the train in silence. Joan bought an English-language newspaper and a Snickers bar. As the train pulled away from the platform, Bernie finally spoke.

"Joan, I'm not mad at you, please don't think I am. That girl in the hotel, Nani. I don't like her. And I can't put my finger on it, but there's something about her. Something that I don't trust. Something bad. I just wish I could see Michael."

Joan folded her newspaper and laid it in her lap. "Bernie, are you going to tell that young man that you're his mother? After what Hanna told us? You love him, of course you do. But there isn't much time left and you need to decide what to do. Today you're going to face Michael's father. That leaves only tomorrow for you to speak with Michael."

"I know. Time is going by too quickly. He isn't even working today. One more day," she began, and stopped talking.

Joan patted her knee. "You knew he was your son as soon as you saw him. You didn't want to upset him. And I believe you don't want to upset his parents, either."

"That girl Nani..."

"Forget about her, Bernie. Today is Sunday. We leave on Tuesday. That gives you Monday. Michael will be back to work, and you need to think hard about this. If you do say something to him, please just be sure that you're doing what you believe is in everyone's best interest, not just because you think he should know."

Bernie nodded. Joan was right. So much truth and understanding seemed to come on these train rides, she thought.

"Okay, Joan. As usual, your reason prevails. But I still want to see Karl Berset. That's one loose end I need to tie up."

"That's fine. I'm simply wondering what you hope will happen when you see him, when you speak to him." Joan wasn't angry, just curious, Bernie could tell.

"If I see him, and if I tell him, I'm not going to name Michael. But I want him to know that I had a baby and he was the father. I will tell him that I gave up the child for adoption and I don't know where the baby is now. But I want him to know, to know that I went through this myself, that I agonized over the decision, that he treated our weekend together as something disposable."

Joan looked down at her hands, steepling her fingers. "Do you think Karl would ever try to find Michael?"

"No, I don't. I thought about that last night and honestly, I don't think Karl would want to be obliged to someone he doesn't know. Besides, Joan, he wouldn't know if I had the baby here or back home. I'm not giving him any information about it."

The train pulled into Lausanne's train station. Joan tucked her unread newspaper into her bag. The women walked with purpose down the long platform and exited the station to a cold and overcast day.

"23 rue du Midi," Bernie said. Halfway up the Avenue de la Gare, she slowed her pace. "Maybe we should stop for coffee first," she said.

"That's a good idea," said Joan. They ducked into a small café and gave their order to a young man behind the counter. Bernie's French was pretty good, at least she thought so, but he must have detected her accent because he grinned and asked, "Americans?" When they nodded, he said, "I practice speaking English with you, okay?"

"Sure," they said in unison. "What is your name?" Joan began.

"Hi," he said, "my name is Oskar." He extended his right hand to Joan, displaying a forearm covered in colorful tattoos. Bernie imagined the artwork crawled all the way to his shoulder, at least. Both of Oskar's ears were pierced and he displayed a small silver ring over one eyebrow.

"Hello, Oskar, I am Joan and this is my niece Bernadette. We're from America and here on vacation." She pronounced her words carefully, as if speaking to a child, but Oskar had no problem understanding.

"New York?" the little eyebrow ring wiggled slightly as he raised his eyebrows.

Bernie smiled. "Close," she replied, taking the two cardboard cups of coffee to the table. The women spent the next fifteen minutes sipping coffee and helping Oskar to understand American idioms. Bernie bounced her right leg up and down incessantly and checked her watch more than once.

Joan cleared her throat. The cups were empty. "Shall we?" Joan stood up and brought the cups to a trashcan near the door. They put on their jackets and Joan shook Oskar's hand.

"Oskar, which way to Rue du Midi?"

"Rue du Midi? Yes, it's close to here. You turn to the right and walk two, no three streets."

"Thank you, Oskar." Bernie felt as if her internal organs were shifting. She steadied herself on the table. Oskar didn't seem to notice as he wiped down the counter.

"Well, we must be on our way." Bernie took Joan's arm and led her to the door.

Joan spoke up. "Perhaps we'll stop back in this afternoon before we take the train. Then we can speak English some more, Oskar. *Au revoir, merci.*" Bernie was practically dragging Joan out of the café before Oskar could say anything more.

Once outside and away from the café, Bernie leaned against the side of a building, her arms wrapped around herself.

"Can I go through with this, Joan?"

Joan raised her chin. "Yes, Bernadette. You're one of the strongest women I know. Let's just do it." They walked the short distance to Rue du Midi and found number 23.

"I'm ready," said Bernie, only half-believing it.

Joan hung back nearer the street while Bernie counted her steps to the front door. She lifted a shaky finger to press the doorbell and froze. She couldn't do it. Her stomach muscles were seizing and cramping, and the bile burned in her throat. Just as she was turning away, the heavy wooden door swung open. An elegant woman dressed in a pink sweater and tan slacks smiled at Bernie.

"Hello," she said, "may I help you?" Her French was accented, but Bernie couldn't place it. She stared at the woman, whose pale blonde hair swept away from a face that showed little age. Her eyes were so blue, Bernie couldn't believe the color was real. Perhaps she wore tinted contact lenses. Bernie could not say for certain that this was the pregnant woman she'd seen coming out of the hospital on Valentine's Day in 1979. It was so long ago.

In halting French, Bernie apologized and said she must be mistaken, that she had the wrong house. Before Mrs. Berset could close the door, however, there he was, standing behind her. Karl Berset. He looked exactly the same as Bernie remembered, just older, and she tried to swallow, but she felt her heart rise up in her chest, filling her throat, about to strangle all the air from her.

His eyes grew wide in recognition, and his hand held the door open, even as his wife tried to close it. She turned in surprise to look at him, and Bernie knew she had made a massive mistake in coming. She hadn't considered the wife.

Joan called out in English. "Do either of you know how to get to Gruyères from here?" Bernie spun around to look at her aunt, who had opened her map and was frowning at it.

Karl whispered something in his wife's ear and she gave him a hard look, but smiled at Bernie again and turned back into the house. Karl stepped forward. As Mrs. Berset retreated into the inner part of their house, he stepped outside onto the landing and closed the door behind him, never taking his eyes off Bernie. She ran a hand through her hair and shifted her weight from one foot to the other.

Joan took a few steps forward and spoke. "Hello, this is my niece Bernadette. I believe you met her years ago. My name is Joan, by the way, and we don't need directions to Gruyères. But I'm sure you've already figured that out." She took a step back toward the street and bowed her head.

"Bernadette," Karl whispered. Not 'Bernadetta,' the way he used to say her name. Oh, how Michael resembles him, she thought. His hair is mine, perhaps, but the face, it is all Karl. Karl's brown eyes, Karl's forehead, his chin. Bernie could not still her trembling.

"Why are you here, Bernadette?" His eyes that were once so soft, like mink, looked smaller and beadier now. Bernie straightened her spine and took a deep breath. One shot at this, she told herself, get it right.

"I'm visiting Switzerland with my aunt, Karl. Joan is my mother's sister." She opened her mouth to continue the speech she'd been practicing for days when he interrupted.

"I see. And how did you find me?" His jaw was set and his lips, once so kissable, looked thin and dry. The top two buttons of his shirt were undone, and she could see his neck, sagging and crepey. Curly gray hairs were visible, and she imagined his chest, now covered with gray. She felt nothing from the past, no desire, no longing.

"It wasn't difficult at all to find you, Karl. It's actually quite easy these days with the internet." Before he could speak again, she held up her hand to stop him.

"Karl, it was a long time ago, I know. I was young and naïve, and you were my first. We had just one weekend, just one. But I got pregnant. I got pregnant, Karl, and you were gone. I had a baby, your baby." She never took her eyes off him. He tried to keep his face expressionless, but one eye kept twitching. He pressed a knuckle to the corner of that eye and held it there. Bernie took another deep breath and continued.

"I saw you on Valentine's Day in 1979, when you and your wife were coming out of the hospital. You got into a taxi. She was wearing a red dress and was very pregnant. That was your wife, right? The same woman who opened the door, who is inside your house?"

"Bernadette..." He opened his hands and turned the palms up.

"You saw me that day, didn't you? You looked right at me." It was easier now, she thought. I am strong.

"I did not know you were pregnant."

"Of course you didn't. After our one weekend, you disappeared. I walked to the apartment I thought was yours. A stranger opened the door and told me that he lived there, not you. And even if you knew that I was pregnant, Karl, it wouldn't have mattered. You were married. You had left me long before that Valentine's Day. We were done after that one weekend in September, weren't we?"

Karl stared his shoes. Bernie looked down. Those are nice shoes, she thought.

"You have a child, then?" He met her eyes and she saw it. Fear.

Bernie shook her head. "No, I gave up the baby as soon as it was delivered. Adoption." She was careful not to say 'him' or 'her.' He didn't deserve to know.

"So you came back here to find this child? What, twenty-three years later?" There, the mocking eyes. She remembered that look, the same look he gave her the last time they saw each other. Arrogance had replaced fear.

Bernie met that look with one of her own. "I didn't come here to look for him. Or her," she added quickly. "But I wanted you to know. You were my first, Karl." You messed me up royally, she said silently as the tears stung her eyes. "I wanted you to know." She felt her resolve faltering and willed her feet to stay planted.

"Bernadetta..." He extended his arms to her. There it was. With his fucking wife on the other side of the door.

Bernie shook her head. "We have to go now." She raised her face, knowing he'd see the tears streaming down her cheeks. She didn't care now. "Go inside, Karl. It's too cold to be standing out here." She turned to Joan and, linking her arm through hers, they walked away from 23 Rue du Midi.

CHAPTER TEN

Nani and Alain were on their first date. At precisely eleven o'clock on Sunday morning, he arrived at her apartment to take her to Bern. She answered the buzzer immediately and bounded down three flights of stairs to meet him at the door.

"Look at you!" she cried upon seeing him dressed in street clothes. "This is the first time I have seen you wearing something other than your police uniform!" He looked really nice, she thought, in dark gray trousers and a blue sweater. His black shoes were polished. The collar of a white shirt poked out of the sweater at the neck. He carried a black leather jacket over his arm. And he smelled good, too, like the forest, clean and woodsy.

Alain grinned at the compliment.

"You look lovely, Nani, just so pretty." He bent at the waist to kiss both of her cheeks. He straightened up and held out his hand. "Shall we?" She took his hand and was surprised to find it warm and dry, not sweaty as she'd expected. He seemed comfortable, relaxed, confident.

Nani had dressed just as carefully as she suspected Alain had. After all, it was a first date, a chance to make a lasting impression. It had to be something he'd never seen. She'd looked through her closet yesterday morning with exasperation. Each shirt was old, or worn, or boring. So much black. An hour later, she'd tucked a dark pink blouse under her jacket and walked out of the Bellani boutique. She ran all the way back to her apartment, breathless from the run and the sheer rush of stealing something and getting away with it. She'd locked her door and taken out the prize. Pure silk, 229 Swiss francs. Nani loved the way it felt against her skin. She wished she'd picked up a new bra, too, but that would have been too risky.

She paired the new blouse with a short black skirt and her high-heeled boots. Her hair was washed and curled, and she'd applied makeup carefully. Not too much.

Nani looped a long burgundy scarf around her neck and took Alain's hand. Such a big hand, she thought, wondering what those hands would feel like under her new silk blouse. If he cupped his hands under my bottom, she thought, he could lift me up to his eye level and we could have a conversation. But that would have to wait until they were seated on the train; she didn't feel like being carried around on his hand, or craning her neck to yell up to him.

They walked the short distance from Nani's apartment to the train station and waited on the platform for the train to arrive.

"One of my friends told me there's a Greek restaurant in Bern," he said as they settled into their seats for the short ride. "Would that interest you?"

Nani couldn't hide her excitement at the prospect of eating Greek food again. "Really? Yes, I would love that," she said.

Alain slipped an arm around her shoulders and pulled her close. "Good. You will teach me all about Greek food."

I'll teach you everything I know, Nani said to herself and nestled against the big man.

Bruno Eicher helped Klara prepare supper in their kitchen while Lucia rested with her feet up.

"Please, mama, I can help in some way," Lucia called from the living room.

"No, no, we are fine. Almost ready to eat. Will you call Michel?" Klara carried food to the table, which was set with a dark red tablecloth and white dishes. Lucia knew they could eat off the floor if necessary; Klara kept a spotless house. The aromas caused her stomach to rumble. Or perhaps it was the baby, also hungry.

Lucia picked up her phone and flipped it open. She dialed their home number and waited for her husband to pick up.

"Hallo?" He sounded out of breath. Lucia smiled.

"Are you still working on the baby furniture, *amore*? Come quickly, dinner is on the table."

"Okay, coming." He clicked off.

Lucia used her arms to push herself up from the comfortable chair and took a seat at the table. She had not mentioned anything to Michel about the impending conversation, in case Klara and Bruno decided against it, but Klara had hugged her hard when she had entered their house earlier. And Lucia spied her in-laws drinking wine in the kitchen as they cooked. This would not be easy for them, she knew.
Michel pushed open the door to the kitchen and kissed his parents.

"Lulu, I kiss you in one minute. After I wash my hands. *Momento*," he said as he took a few steps down the hall to the bathroom. Klara brought a covered casserole to the table and Lucia caught her eye.

"Okay, mama?"

Klara nodded. She was pale, Lucia thought. She saw Klara look to Bruno, who nodded also.

When everyone was seated, Klara asked Bruno to say a quick prayer before eating. Michel raised his eyebrows to Lucia, who shrugged and looked down as Bruno offered a short prayer of thanks for the meal.

Klara uncovered the casserole of chicken, mushrooms, potatoes and onions and served everyone from her place at the table. Bruno passed a large bowl of steaming hot green beans sautéed with bits of bacon. Lucia watched the three of them from her seat: devoted mother, proud father, loyal and loving son. She said a silent prayer that Michel would take the news he was about to receive with grace and an even temper, no matter how angry it might make him.

"It's good," Michel said through a mouthful of food. "I was hungry!" Klara smiled at her son and speared a piece of potato on her plate.

When all the food was gone, Michel stood to clear the plates. He set a hand on his mother's shoulder, saying "Sit, mama, and rest. I will make coffee." He winked at his wife and disappeared into the kitchen.

Klara looked at Bruno, who nodded, his face set with tension. "Michel, come back in here, please. The coffee can wait."

Michel stood in the doorway, wiping his hands on a cotton towel. His mother gestured for him to sit and the smile on his face faded as concern lined his brow.

"Mama? Everything is okay?" He looked from his mother to his father to Lucia.

Bruno cleared his throat. "Son, your mother and I have something important to tell you, but it is very hard for both of us." Michel's eyes grew wide as he feared the worst and Lucia could see he imagined one of his parents was very sick. She glanced at Bruno and wanted very much to assure him that everything would be alright.

"Jean-Michel, my only son, my lovely boy," Klara began. She twisted her hands together. "You were always an inquisitive little boy. Lots of questions, all the time. Why is the sky blue sometimes and gray at other times? How does the egg come out of the chicken?" She flattened her hands on the table and looked up at Michel. "You remember when your father and I told you about the adoption? When we told you that we had been blessed with you? And you always wanted to know more."

Michel leaned forward, his forearms on the table. His hands were clasped together loosely as he listened. Lucia kept her gaze fixed on him as Klara continued.

"You were still a young boy, only ten or eleven, when you asked about your birth parents."

Michel nodded slowly. "Yes, they died. I remember you telling me. You and papa," he said, glancing at his father.

Bruno coughed. "They did not die, son." Michel snapped his head to his father.

"What?" He stared at the older man.

Klara spoke and Michel snapped his head back to face her. Lucia sat rigid in her chair, unable to move. "Michel, I was very wrong to tell you this. But I was also worried to lose you. Afraid that perhaps you would leave us and try to find them. That you would prefer to live with her, with your natural mama." Klara choked on the words and couldn't continue. She buried her face in her hands.

"Wait, you're telling me that my natural mother and father are alive? Not dead at all?" Michel looked from one parent to the other. Lucia felt a sweat break on the back of her neck, but she was unable to speak. What would she say?

Bruno nodded. He looked at Michel and his eyes were shiny. "We didn't want to lose you."

Michel's voice rose as his face flushed. "Lose me! Why did you think you'd lose me? You're my *parents*. I don't even know who these other people are." He made a fist, two fists. His knuckles were white. "Why are you telling me this now?"

Lucia whispered, "Michel, please. Be calm. This is very difficult for your parents." She reached across the table to hold his hand. It was too far for her; he didn't meet her halfway.

"Calm! Lucia, please. I just find out now that the woman who gave birth to me is alive." His eyes blazed at her and she felt a nausea rise from her belly. Suddenly the baby kicked hard.

"Oh!" She cried out and folded herself in two. Her head bent to the table.

All attention focused on Lucia.

"Lulu, the baby!" Three chairs pushed back from the table in unison.

Lucia's forehead was still on the table. She held up a hand. "Just a hard kick," she gasped. "Perhaps I can lie down?"

"Of course, Lucia," said Klara. "Do you want to stay here?"

Lucia raised her twisted face. "No, I think I go home to my bed. Michel, will you take me?" She tried to take deep calming breaths but she was not calm. The conversation was set aside as everyone stood.

Lucia looked at Bruno first, then Klara. "I'm sorry, I upset everything."

Klara took her daughter-in-law's chin in her hand. "Never, my child. Never. You and the baby are first, okay." She turned to look at her son. "Michel. We did not mean to upset you, or Lucia, or the baby. Please."

Michel kissed his mother on each cheek. "Mama, it's okay. We'll talk later. Tomorrow. Sometime. I'm not angry with you. Or you, papa. Okay?" He looked from one to the other until both nodded. "Come, Lulu, we get you home."

"Maybe I stop by later with some strudel?" Klara asked.

Lucia smiled and nodded. "*Grazie*," she said as they left the house.

Later that night, as Lucia and Michel lay in their warm bed, darkness enveloped them except for the dim light in the bathroom. These days they left a weak light on because Lucia was up two or three times during the night.

"Okay, Lulu?" Michel whispered into her hair. Lucia was lying on her left side, facing away from her husband. It was more comfortable this way, she had told him. He wrapped an arm around her and rested his hand on her stomach.

Lucia turned onto her back. She stroked his face, feeling the scratchy stubble under her fingers. "I'm okay, *amore*, but what about you? That was big news to hear today."

"Yes. I think I can understand why they did it, because I remember being so curious at a young age, and I did ask questions of everything. They must have thought it best to make me think that my natural parents were not alive, maybe better than for me to think they didn't want me, you know? But why this is coming up now, I do not understand."

Lucia wanted so much to tell him. It pulled at her, and she thought perhaps she could smooth out this situation by letting him know, under the warm blanket and comforting darkness. But it wouldn't be fair to Klara or Bruno. She knew that, and yet it tore at her to see her husband so pained. "Maybe because of the baby, it makes your parents think about you."

"Yes, I'm sure that's it," he said softly against her lips. "We should try to sleep, Lulu. It's been a long day."

Lucia kissed her husband. "*Sogno bene,*" she whispered and turned away from him.

"Sweet dreams," he repeated in English.

CHAPTER ELEVEN

On the train ride from Bern back to Fribourg, Nani curled up against Alain. They had walked all around the Swiss capital, poked into little shops, and had the best meal ever at Kalymnos. When the owner learned that Nani was Greek, and came from a village not far from his own hometown, he treated her like family. He provided a bottle of wine with his compliments, and the chef cooked a special meal for the two of them. Nani could tell Alain was enjoying himself, and when he kissed her outside the restaurant after the meal, she felt a surge of desire that she couldn't deny. She even forgot about Michel for a while that afternoon, and she decided to invite Alain back to her little apartment and ask him to stay the night.

He dozed next to her on the train, satisfied from the day and the good food. She looked up at his face while he slept. A strong chin, a full lower lip, straight nose. He kept himself in good shape. She laid her head against his chest and let her hand rest on his thigh.

An annoying little jingle shattered the quiet on the train and Nani groaned. She'd forgotten to turn off her phone. Alain shifted and opened his eyes.

"Damn it," she muttered and fished her phone from her purse. Without looking at the caller ID, she flipped it open and answered. "What," she snapped.

"Nani, this is Robert. At work." She rolled her eyes at the sound of his dull voice and wished she'd never answered.

"It's my day off, Robert," she retorted.

"Well, the boss says he needs you to work tonight. Didier cannot work, he broke his arm."

Nani stretched her legs out from underneath her and pulled away from Alain's warm embrace. "Are you kidding me?" she hissed. "Why don't you just stay and work?"

"Sorry, I can't. You're still the new kid. Boss says you have to come in. Look, I'll stay until nine, but you have to come in."

"Gee, thanks a lot," Nani muttered and snapped the phone shut. Damn it! She stared at the phone and threw it back in her purse. She wanted to throw it out the window of the speeding train instead.

"What's wrong, sweetheart?" Alain leaned toward her. He spoke to the top of her head. She fought back tears. I so wanted us to be together tonight, she thought.

"I have to go in to work," she said without raising her head. She bit the inside of her cheek to try and keep from crying.

"Oh, Nani, I'm sorry." He put his big hand behind her head and turned her face up to his. "We had such a nice day, too. I don't want it to end." He stroked her cheek with his thumb and caught a tear. "Please don't cry." He kissed one cheek, then the next.

Nani rose to a kneeling position and positioned herself on his lap. And ignoring what any of the other stupid passengers might think, she kissed him, hard, on the mouth, and felt him respond to her. Driven by anger at the call from Robert, she kissed him furiously, until he took her face in his hands and gently pulled her away.

"Nani, people are staring," he whispered. She didn't care. She moved her hips in a circular motion to tease him. She walked her fingers all over his scalp, she sucked on his tongue, and she felt him rise beneath her.

The train eased to a stop at the Fribourg station. She leaned back and smiled at him. Wicked, wicked girl, she remanded herself silently.

"Come home with me," she pleaded.

"But you have to work," he said. Passengers were exiting the train and he eased Nani off his lap. Alain grimaced as he stood and ushered Nani off the train to the platform.

"Please," she said, turning to him. "It's only five o'clock now. I don't have to be there until nine. Please, Alain. I need you so much." She pulled him to her.

They hurried out of the station and with the urgency that comes from anticipation of a first time together, the two walked as quickly as they could to Nani's apartment. She fumbled with her key at the door and they raced each other up three flights of stairs, to her small apartment on the top floor. Alain had to bow his head to get in the doorway. Once inside, she locked the door behind her. He removed her clothes with thick, trembling fingers. No words were spoken as she pulled off his belt. They were horizontal in no time. Hungry mouths covered every inch of skin.

As much as Nani wanted it to be special, it wasn't. Maybe it was the rush. Maybe he'd been too nervous, she didn't know. She tried, and she knew he tried, too. She'd never let him know how disappointed she was. Nani made Alain Bouchard believe he was the world's greatest lover. As his breathing grew heavier and rhythmic, she stared at the ceiling and thought about Michel. Michel would have been different, she just knew it. He'd have known exactly what to do; she wouldn't have to fake it with him. She glanced over at Alain, who was snoring, and turned away from the sleeping giant.

At eight o'clock, Nani woke Alain and whispered that it was time to go. He washed in her little bathroom, bent over to keep from banging his head on the low ceiling. He put on the same clothes and used her comb in his hair. He kissed her mouth and Nani tasted garlic and lamb, and it was not as sensual as she'd remembered it earlier on the train. He slipped his hands inside her robe and cupped her small breasts.

"I wish I was working tonight, too. I would come to visit you at midnight and..." He trailed off and wiggled his eyebrows at her.

She resisted the urge to roll her eyes and instead, trailed a finger down his blue sweater to his belt buckle, and smiled shyly up at him. She opened the door to allow him out, but left him to descend the stairs alone.

After scrubbing herself clean in the shower, Nani dressed carefully. Michel would be at the hotel in the morning. She slipped a small bottle of perfume into her purse and left the apartment to walk to the hotel. She loved walking around at night, and on a Sunday evening, the streets in town were empty and quiet. At nine o'clock precisely, she entered the lobby and walked right past Robert, who stood with his coat over his arm.

"Another minute and you would have been late, you know," he chided. She stopped and turned to face him.

"Your shift is done, Robert. You can leave now." Nani glared at him until he looked away. She continued to stare as he put on his coat and that foolish cap.

"Have a good night," he called as he hurried out into the cold night.

Nani had just settled behind the desk with her first cup of coffee when Joan and Bernie returned to the hotel. She glanced up and narrowed her eyes at the two women. They were always so happy, always smiling. Stupid Americans, she thought. And that Bernadette, trying to disrupt Michel's life. How dare she?

She kept her eyes fixed on Bernadette as the women approached the elevator.

"*Bonsoir, mesdames*," she said in a flat voice.

"Hi," said Joan, her eyes darting from her niece to Nani.

"Good evening," said Bernadette. Nani noticed her eyes. Glittery green. Can't trust a woman with green eyes, she thought. She's a serpent, a monster.

"Did you have a pleasant day in Lausanne?" she asked innocently, her eyes never leaving Bernadette's face.

Bernadette turned to Joan and said, "Why don't you go up to the room, Joan." Then she lowered her voice and said something else that Nani couldn't hear. Joan glanced at Nani and entered the waiting elevator.

When the doors had closed, Bernadette approached the reception desk, where Nani sipped her coffee. She sat as tall as she could on her stool and stifled a yawn. If this woman has something to say to me, let her say it, Nani thought. She pretended to be engrossed in one of the hotel's computer applications. Bernadette just stood there, and finally, Nani raised her eyes to the American woman.

"So, you and your aunt leave us on Tuesday?"

"Yes, that's correct, Nani. I'll be sorry to leave." Bernadette stood at the other side of the desk. Nani looked at her hair, dark orange spirals trailing over her shoulders. Ugh, she thought, I'm so glad that isn't my hair. Her long shiny hair was better than Bernadette's, and the memory of it tangled up in Alain's hands made her smile, as if she held a secret.

"Jean-Michel works tomorrow. You'll be able to say goodbye then." She blinked at Bernadette.

Nani watched as a red flush crawled up Bernadette's neck to her cheeks. She sat even taller on her stool.

Bernadette said nothing.

"You and Michel have the same color hair," Nani said without expression. She did not blink.

Bernadette's color deepened as she stared at Nani. "Yes, I suppose we do," she said slowly.

"When did you say you were here as a student? I don't recall the years," Nani said evenly. Each word crept closer.

"I didn't say, at least not to you." Nani smiled again as she spotted a glistening sheen of perspiration on Bernadette's forehead. She traced a finger around the rim of her coffee cup. "I'm guessing maybe late 70's." She locked her eyes on Bernadette's.

Nani heard Bernadette's sharp intake of breath. The space between them had decreased.

"1978 to 1979. You're a smart girl," Bernadette said. "Good night, Nani," she added softly and turned away.

"Bernadette." Nani knew it was inappropriate to call a guest by her first name. She could get in a lot of trouble for doing so. Bernadette turned back to face her.

"What is it, Nani?"

"If you hurt Michel in any way, any way at all, I will find a way to hurt you more. Much more."

Bernadette's green eyes darkened. "He already has a wife, Nani."

"He already has a mother, Bernadette."

CHAPTER TWELVE

Michel trudged into the hotel, ten minutes late for work. He muttered a good morning in Nani's general direction and disappeared into the back room to hang his coat. When he returned to the reception desk, he held a cup of coffee in his hand.

"*Bonjour*, Michel," Nani said, watching him carefully. She slid off the stool and took a few steps backward, still facing him so she could see him as he went through the motions of logging onto the computer, opening the mail that waited for him, sipping his coffee.

He turned his head and looked back at her. "What are you doing here, Nani? You don't work on Sunday night." And as if he didn't care what her explanation was, he turned back to stare at the computer.

Something was wrong here, Nani thought. No smile, no eye contact? She took a step closer. "Didier broke his arm. Robert and I will be working his shift for the next few weeks, I guess."

Michel nodded absently and sighed loudly. This is not my Michel, she told herself. Michel is always happy and positive when he arrives to work. He never showed an angry side, even during the time when she was training with him and made so many mistakes. He always turned it around into something funny, something good. Perhaps he had bad news this weekend, she thought. Perhaps he found out about Bernadette. She had to know.

"Did you enjoy your long weekend?" She moved around behind him, rearranging brochures that were already in straight neat stacks.

"What? Oh, yes, very nice," he replied. His coffee cup sat on the desk. Soon it would be cold, but he didn't even seem to notice it.

Nani hesitated, still behind him. "Um, did you do anything exciting? Take a trip maybe?"

Michel raised his head, twisted around on his stool to look at her, and Nani stepped into his line of vision, smiling. I will raise his mood by being upbeat, she said to herself. Even if it means staying late. Even if she was so tired she could fall asleep standing up.

"We bought baby furniture and assembled it," he said, his voice distant and unfocused. "Lucia and I took the train to Lausanne. We had a nice day." He stared behind her at the wall, where an oil painting of the Matterhorn hung. It was as if he didn't even see her there, right in front of him. And she'd sprayed some of her new perfume just minutes before he arrived.

Wait, he said they went to Lausanne! Nani recalled that Bernadette got an address in Lausanne from Robert. A man, Karl something. Nani presumed it was the man who had fathered Michel.

"Michel, do you know anyone in Lausanne?" She inched closer, standing to the side of the desk where the computer sat.

"No, no one," he said, finally looking at her directly. "We spent the afternoon by the lake on Friday. It's very pretty there, you know. You'd like it." He smiled at her, then turned away, began to type, and turned back again. "You're not in a hurry to leave today," he observed. "And where is Alain? He usually is here by now." Michel looked to the front doors.

"Alain didn't work last night," she replied. "And, well, you just looked...preoccupied this morning. I thought perhaps you needed to talk or something." She was treading on thin ice, she knew. She laid her small hand on his and he didn't pull away. "Can I help with something, Michel?" Nani could barely breathe from the closeness of him. Being near Michel made her light-headed, as if she could float up into the air at any time.

Michel turned toward her and put his other hand over hers, then raised her hand within his two palms, making a kind of sandwich. "You are a good friend, Nani. Can I tell you something, in confidence?"

Nani leaned into the desk for support. "Of course, Michel," she said, wishing she could crawl between those two hands. "You can tell me anything. Anything at all." She glanced around the empty lobby. Those women had better not show up now. It was early; hopefully they were still sleeping.

Michel looked so lost, she thought. This was her moment to be there for him. Her chest lifted as she waited for him to speak.

"I am adopted," he began, his eyes searching hers. She stayed impassive, only nodding to encourage him to keep talking. "And yesterday I learned from my parents that my natural parents, my birth parents, are alive. When I was a boy I was told they were dead."

Nani's jaw dropped. "Why would...I don't understand." She wished with all her heart that it was Tuesday and those women were gone, on an airplane flying somewhere over the Atlantic Ocean. In her mind's eye, she saw the plane doing a nosedive into the icy waters. No, she shook her head, that's bad luck. I don't wish them dead. But I do wish them gone, never to come back to Fribourg.

Michel shrugged. "I'm not angry; I understand why they did it. I was just a boy and they wanted to protect me. But now I wonder. Who is my birth mother? Who is my father? And do I want to try and find them? We have a baby coming soon, and perhaps I should know them, for medical reasons." His beautiful brown eyes were like pools of melted dark chocolate, Nani thought. Like miniature chocolate fondues. She wanted to draw him in her arms and hold him forever.

"They didn't tell you who these people are?" Nani moved her hand from between his to rest on his arm, so strong and firm under starched white cotton. How she wanted to caress that arm.

"Last night, my parents were about to tell me, but Lucia had some trouble. No, no, the baby is fine," he added hastily when he saw her face. "She is fine, but we were unable to finish the conversation. Tonight I think I will learn more."

Just then Nani heard the whoosh of the glass doors parting at the hotel's entrance and Alain's frame filled the entry, blocking all the sunlight. He strode through the lobby to the desk and his eyes stopped on Nani's hand, which was resting on Michel's arm. Nani pulled her hand away when she saw Alain's gaze.

"I came to walk you home, Nani. I was waiting outside the hotel now over ten minutes." He held up his wrist to show her his watch.

"Oh, Alain. You remember Michel. He was just telling me about his wife. She is pregnant. Soon, yes, Michel?"

"Soon, yes," Michel said. Nani watched as his cheeks pinked. "Christmas baby," he said, looking at Alain with a weak smile. Alain extended his hand. Michel stood and accepted the handshake.

"Congratulations. You must be excited," Alain said, pumping Michel's arm up and down.

Even though Michel was tall, he still had to turn his face up to look at Alain.

"Nani is a good friend, a good listener," Michel remarked. Nani let her hand find Alain's back, where she traced her finger in a figure eight pattern. Her thoughts shimmered between the two men she cared most about, one who adored her and one who considered her "a friend."

"She's a good woman," Alain said, casting his eyes on Nani as he held out her coat. "Come on, baby, let me take you home," he said as he wrapped a long arm around her. Nani buttoned her coat and looped her scarf around her neck. She wished Alain hadn't called her baby.

Just before they turned to leave, Nani slung her big purse over her shoulder and said, "So Michel, I will see you on Tuesday afternoon then, yes?" She knew that by then the American women would be gone.

"See you then, Nani," Michel said. He nodded to Alain, and turned his attention to a middle-aged man who had just stepped off the elevator. Nani walked ahead of Alain and burst outside into the damp morning air.

"You don't have to walk me home, you know," she muttered, not sure why she was angry, or even if she was angry. Nani just knew that she wanted to be alone. Alain stopped walking and turned to her.

"Of course I want to walk with you," he said. "Why wouldn't I?" Nani scowled at him and he raised his eyebrows in shock.

"Are you mad at me, Nani?" He looked around for a bench, and finding none, he sat on the edge of the big stone fountain in the square. The ledge was wide enough to sit, and in warmer weather, it would be filled with students and tourists alike. He pulled her to him and she perched on his thigh. Alain took her chin in his hand. He pressed his thumb to her lower lip, and she closed her eyes.

"What is it, sweetheart?" His free hand was on the small of her back.

"Nothing," she replied in a small voice. She leaned against his body, threw her arms around his neck, and buried her face into his coat.

Alain would have to do, she thought. She'd never have Michel, she knew, but it still hurt. Alain was her second choice, and the runner-up wasn't the winner. He stroked her hair, as if she were a child coming down from a tantrum.

"Take me home," she whispered into his ear.

Alain lay next to Nani, his eyes closed, the corners of his mouth turned up. She had made love to him with ferocity, and she knew she'd satisfied him. And she let him believe he'd satisfied her. Perhaps one day she wouldn't see Michel's face above her, feel his lips on hers. One day she wouldn't have to bite her tongue to keep from calling out his name.

She worried about Michel and what might happen while she wasn't at the hotel. By the time she returned to work on Tuesday afternoon, she imagined he would know the truth about Bernadette Maguire. Bernadette would find a way to tell him today that she was his birth mother. The American women were leaving tomorrow morning. Nani's stomach hurt.

"...and then I was thinking I would bring you to my mother's house, would you like that?"

Nani's musing was broken by the sound of his voice. She turned on her side to face Alain, who filled her narrow bed. "What? I'm sorry, I didn't hear everything you said."

"Next weekend, when we both get off work, I want you to stay with me at my apartment, and then I will bring you to meet my mother later in the day. Nani, I want the two of you to meet." He curled a long strand of her hair around his finger.

"Alain, that's a week away," she said. Then, seeing creases of concern on his face, she added, "But of course it sounds wonderful! I would love to meet your mother." He kissed her and buried his hand under the sheet. She emitted a low moan and thought, oh no, not again.

"Sweetheart, I need to get some sleep," she said as she pushed his hand away.

"You're right," he said, kissing her nose. "Let's rest up so we're ready to go again." He turned to his side and was asleep within minutes.

Nani pulled the soft blue blanket up to her chin and stared at the ceiling.

CHAPTER THIRTEEN

At breakfast on Monday morning, Bernie asked Joan how she would like to spend their last full day in Switzerland.

"Joan, I've made all the plans on this trip. What would *you* like to do today?" She looked at the last bite of *pain au chocolat* on her plate and popped it in her mouth. A waitress stopped by the table and refilled their coffee cups.

"Well, we've been to Lucerne, Lugano, Lausanne. All the "L" towns!" Joan laughed. "I'm going to leave it up to you, Bernie. You'll know where we should go today." She sipped her coffee. "I will miss this coffee."

"We'll pick some up," Bernie said, "and pack it in our luggage. If there's any room in there." She savored the chocolate that melted on her tongue and suddenly she knew how they would spend their last day. "Come on, finish your coffee. We're walking to the train station."

They exited the restaurant and Bernie waved to Michael, who was talking on the telephone. He didn't look up. Joan was nearly at the entrance; Bernie hurried to catch up.

"Are you going to keep our destination a secret?" Joan asked. Bernie really loved her, and she was so thankful to have made this trip, this reconnection with her aunt.

"It's a surprise, but you'll like it," Bernie replied. She pulled on gloves. "Maybe it's not the prettiest time of the year, but still, you'll enjoy the views."

"Of course I will! Let's go," she said and started walking faster.

When Karl Berset left for work on Monday morning, his wife Ella still was not speaking to him. He ate corn flakes at the table by himself. If Ella were not angry, she might have cooked an egg for him, perhaps with some leftover ham. He stared down at the now-soggy flakes swimming in milk. Enough, he thought. He stood up, put the bowl in the sink, and walked away. She's home all day; she can clean it.

Karl stood still in the middle of the living room. No sound came from their bedroom; Ella was probably still sleeping. He put on his coat and picked up his briefcase. He had given her everything, this house, the new car, vacations to Capri and Ibiza. He never complained when she arrived home from shopping with boxes and bags. He never said a word about the amount of money she spent at the salon, once a week, every week.

Karl slammed the door on his way out. He and Ella hadn't had an argument like that in years, not since she caught him in a lie about a bank conference that didn't exist. He'd taken one of the young secretaries from work on a weekend escape to Montreux. Karl couldn't even remember anything about that weekend now. Ella had been desperate to reach him after Dani was rushed to the hospital with appendicitis, and when she called his colleague at the bank to get a message to him, she learned that there was no bank conference that weekend. They'd almost divorced then, but the children were still young, and Ella wanted stability in the house. Karl had promised it would never happen again, and he'd kept his word. Not that he wasn't tempted.

Their son Paul was twenty-three now and still lived at home. Karl tried to get him a job in the bank, but Paul wasn't interested. He had eleven tattoos and three piercings, and the money he made from working in a music store would never be enough to support himself. Karl toyed with the idea of throwing him out of the house, forcing him to find suitable work, but he knew Ella would never stand for it. Dani was still his little girl and, at fourteen, was at odds with her mother constantly.

Karl walked two blocks to the Banque Cantonale Vaudoise, where he managed the loan department. He still couldn't believe the visit yesterday; Bernadette Maguire and her old aunt appearing out of nowhere. At his front door! If only he'd been the one to get up first and answer the door. The look on Ella's face when he came back inside the house after Bernadette left convinced him she must have figured out that Bernadette was a past lover. She knew him too well. When she was pregnant with Paul, Ella had accused Karl of being unfaithful. The weekends he stayed in Fribourg, leaving her in Lausanne with his mother. His lame excuses for being away.

As he rounded the corner and neared the bank, Karl replayed yesterday's fight with Ella in his mind.

"Another one from your past, Karl?" Ella had stood in front of him, her hands on her hips, her nostrils flaring as if readying to charge.

"A very long time ago, *cherie*," he replied wearily, and brushed past her. He slumped into his favorite chair and stared at the television. Bernadette had a child, he thought, my child. He closed his eyes. She must have come back to find him. Or her. A child that would now be about the same age as Paul, he mused.

Ella grabbed the remote and turned off the television. She blocked his view and he had to look at her. "How long ago, Karl? Last week? Last month?" Her voice was sharp, like broken, jagged glass.

"A very long time ago. It meant nothing. She wasn't looking for trouble." Karl rubbed his face with both hands.

"Really? But she went out of her way to find you? Why, Karl? Does she owe you money? No, wait, do you owe *her* money?" Ella's hair had come undone, and it fell around her neck. Really, Karl thought, she looked so sexy like that he couldn't help but smile.

"Ella, darling, she was a girl, before we were married, when I worked at the bank in Fribourg."

Ella stamped her foot. Here comes the charge, he thought. I might as well be wearing a red cape. "I don't believe you. A fling from your bachelor days? She showed up at our house, Karl! A girl that meant nothing wouldn't do that! You lie to me, Karl. You lie all the time. And I've had enough." She whirled on her heel and crashed into the bedroom, slamming the door behind her so hard the china rattled in the cupboard.

When he crawled into bed much later that night, she didn't move. He thought she was asleep, until she said in a low voice, "Do not even think about touching me, Karl. Tomorrow you can look for an apartment. I don't want you here."

"Ella, please. Listen to me, *cherie*."

She didn't move but spoke to the wall. "No, Karl. I have listened for twenty-five years. I'm done listening. And I want you out."

Karl walked through the doors at work and nodded good morning to those who were at their desks already. The secretary who had accompanied him to Montreux years ago stood by her desk against the far wall. She was married now, to a doctor, and she kept her distance, as did Karl.

Damn that redhead! She had no business showing up at his home, and after so many years. None of the other American girls had ever pursued him again. When the affair was over, it was over. Most of them were so embarrassed that they avoided his teller window for the remainder of the school year. They made it easier for him. But not Bernadette. And what about this child, he thought. There are ways now of proving paternity. Would he be required to pay, even though the child would be an adult now? She'll be back, he thought, looking for money. It's always about money. Now that she had confirmed his residence, seen his house, she'd be back. He had to find a way to stop her.

At the train station, Bernie spied the mustard-yellow Postbus parked on the side street next to the main building. She smiled. They walked up to the ticket counter and Bernie turned to Joan.

"I've got this, Joan, why don't you stand over there?" She gestured to some photographs on the far wall.

"Oh, you really are planning to surprise me!" Joan clapped her hands together.

Bernie turned back to the counter as Joan walked away to inspect a travel poster of Davos.

"Two round-trip tickets to Schwarzsee, please," she said, handing over her credit card.

"Thank you, *Madame*, the bus is number twelve and leaves soon." He checked his watch. "Six minutes."

"*Merci*." She grinned at the man behind the counter, who replied, "*Merci, au revoir*."

Bernie skipped over to Joan and took her hand. "Come with me," she whispered, as if she were leading Joan to the buried treasure.

Joan followed Bernie out of the station to the waiting bus.

"Where are we going?" Her eyes were filled with anticipation, and Bernie laughed.

"Someplace very special to me. I'll explain on the way."

They climbed aboard the big yellow bus, and Bernie told Joan about a day in late May 1979, a couple of weeks after she'd given birth to Michael, who arrived one month early. Her classmates were all away for the Pentecost holiday, but Bernie had stayed behind in Fribourg. She didn't know how many of the other students had figured out she was pregnant, but in any event, she wasn't comfortable spending three days in their company. She'd bumped into Gary Baptista, a friend she'd traveled with during the year, and they decided to spend the day together in Schwarzsee. Gary hadn't joined the group, either; he was content to be on his own in Fribourg.

"Gary was a friend, not like Timmy Lyon, though. I had feelings for Timmy, or at least I thought I did, but it was always platonic with Gary. He understood me a lot better than Timmy ever did. I was just so caught up in the idea of being with Timmy that I didn't pay much attention to Gary. It was like he knew everything about me, and he still liked me."

"Well, of course he liked you, Bernie! That's silly," Joan said.

"No, Joan, remember, it was 1979. I'd had an affair with a banker, who turned out to be a married man. As far as I knew, my classmates didn't know anything, except for Lisa, but if they had known, believe me, I would have been shunned by some of them. Gary was a good friend. I think he knew about my pregnancy, although he never said. It was just the way he acted. He was kind..." Her words trailed off as she recalled their day together. The bus began its ascent up the hills outside of Fribourg.

Joan patted Bernie's hand. "You don't keep in touch?"

"No. You know, after college, I went to law school. He went to grad school." Bernie scrunched her brow to remember. "I think he was at Rutgers. He might be a teacher somewhere, I'm not sure. He married someone I didn't know. Probably has grown kids by now." She recalled reading something in the college alumni magazine, back when she cared enough to look at her class notes. Was it the late eighties? Something about him being married and teaching.

"Anyway," she said, dismissing the memory, "we had a lovely day at Schwarzsee. It was the first time since coming home from the hospital that I'd ventured out of Hanna's house, where I was living. Of course, it was late May, not early November, but it's a pretty ride. Let's enjoy it."

Bernie and Joan spent the day walking around the village. At 3,400 feet above sea level, both women were conscious of the thin air, and stopped frequently to just sit and look at the beauty that surrounded them. The Restaurant Gypsera was open, and they enjoyed pork schnitzel, served with wedges of lemon and French fries.

"I'll be eating lettuce for a week when we get home," Joan said, plucking the last French fry from her plate.

"We're on vacation, Joan," said Bernie. "No worries until we're home, right?" She lifted a glass mug of beer and took a long swallow. The simplicity of it all was what made her so happy. One café in the village, not twenty to choose from. A lovely meal of fried pork tenderloins and French fries. And a cold beer in a warm café. Perfect, she thought.

"Bernie, it's been just perfect," Joan said, echoing her thoughts. "I couldn't have had a better time, and I wouldn't have wanted to be here with anyone but you."

"I feel the same way, Joan," Bernie said, thinking about Gary Baptista and wondering where he was now. Happily married, kids, a good life, she assumed. My life is so different. Different choices. I made the life I have now, Bernie told herself. In the quiet restaurant, she bowed her head and dissected her schnitzel. Tomorrow at this time they'd be in the air, and Bernie didn't know when she'd be back. When she raised her head and looked at Joan, the tears were streaming down her cheeks.

"Oh, honey," Joan murmured. "It's Michael, isn't it?"

"I don't know what to do, Joan. I want him to know me; I want him to understand why I gave him away. I need him to know that I've thought about him every day, that I remember his birthday every year. Joan, I used to spend every May 18th drinking myself into oblivion, I'd be so sad. My life has been defined by the fact that I gave up my son, my only child."

"I'm sure he would understand why you did it, Bernie. He's a grown man now."

Bernie nodded and wiped her eyes. Their waiter appeared at the table, and when he saw Bernie's tears, he took a step back.

"Something is wrong with the meal?"

"No, no, the food is very good, thank you," said Joan with a wave of her hand. "Really, everything is okay." She waited until he left.

"Bernie, come on. Let's enjoy what's left of this wonderful day, in this beautiful place. I'm so happy you wanted to share Schwarzsee with me. By the way, what does 'Schwarzsee' mean?"

"It means 'black lake' in German. The French call it 'lac noir.'"

They finished their meal, chatting about Joanie and Lou and what they might have missed at home. By the time they climbed the last bus back to Fribourg, the sun was behind the tall pines, and they rode back to town in increasing darkness. Both women dozed on the quiet bus.

At the train station, Bernie turned to Joan. "Shall we walk back to the hotel one last time? Tomorrow morning we'll need a taxi with the luggage."

"Sure, maybe we could stop in every bar along the way." Bernie gaped at Joan, who burst out laughing. "Kidding, Bernie, kidding. You know me better than that."

"Wait, yes, one drink. Come with me," Bernie said as she took her aunt's hand and led the way across the street.

They entered the Eurotel bar, still the dimly-lit place Bernie remembered. Joan followed her to a far corner of the bar, and asked, "Why are we walking to the other end?"

They perched on stools at a high table and Bernie replied, "Because this was the bar where Lisa and I went the night that Karl Berset first professed an interest in me. And we sat at the other end. Some things should not be duplicated," she added with a bitter laugh.

A waitress stepped from behind the bar and greeted them. Bernie and Joan each ordered a beer.

"When I was here with Lisa in 1978, our waitress wore a dirndl skirt and a low-cut peasant blouse,"

Bernie said to Joan. "Like a sexy Heidi." This waitress had short black hair with orange streaks in it. She wore black trousers and a crisp white shirt.

They sipped their beer and looked around. The place was pretty dead except for a few businessmen at the bar. Always the way, Bernie guessed. Men away on business spend their free time in hotel bars; she ought to know, she'd trolled enough of them over the years. There was always someone willing to show her his room. And she had always been willing to see it.

Once the beer was gone, there was no other reason to stay. Bernie paid the tab and they resumed their walk, heading down the rue de Lausanne. Bernie pointed out the building where her friend Lisa had lived, but when they passed the rue Pierre-Aeby, she said nothing. Nothing about Karl's "love nest," where he had brought Bernie. Some things were better left behind.

Back at the Hotel de la Rose, Bernie saw the man from Saturday behind the desk, the man who helped her find Karl's address. What was his name again? Robert, right.

"*Bonsoir*," he called, nodding to them as they crossed to the elevator.

"*Bonsoir*," they replied and waited for the slow elevator to arrive. Please don't speak to me, implored Bernie in a silent prayer; I'm not in the mood for conversation. The elevator door opened and they slipped in.

Back in the room, Bernie packed everything but a tee shirt to sleep in, her toothbrush and toothpaste, and tomorrow's traveling clothes. Joan did the same, and was surprised that everything fit in her wheeled bag.

"Are you alright, Bernie?"

"I think I am, Joan. Yeah, I'm okay. I'm not going to say anything to Michael tomorrow. I wouldn't do that to him, not right before we leave the country. If I couldn't tell him when we first walked into this hotel, then I'll just leave it alone. But I might write a letter to him once I'm home." She looked to Joan for a reaction.

Joan shrugged. "I don't see why not. That's actually a good idea. Give it some distance, then decide."

Just before his shift ended on Monday afternoon, Michel received an email from the boss. There was a meeting in Bern at eight o'clock Tuesday morning and Monsieur Rosolen couldn't attend. Michel was instructed to go in his place. The message included all the information and directions to the office building where the meeting would take place, and the boss concluded by telling him that when the meeting concluded at noon, Michel could take the rest of the day off. He read the email again, then turned to Robert and filled him in.

"Robert, go ahead and call Nani if you need her to come in tomorrow morning. I'll be in Bern all day." No need to tell Robert that the boss had given him the afternoon off.

"Lucky you," sniffed Robert. "No, I'll stay. Nani was pretty steamed about having to come in yesterday, and I don't have anything else to do."

"Okay, well, you have seniority, so you're in charge tomorrow morning," said Michel, straightening up the desk. "The American women in 345 and the couple in 214 are both checking out tomorrow. Anything else you can handle, and just call me on the cell if something comes up."

"Got it," said Robert. Michel always felt a bit awkward giving orders to Robert, who was twenty years older, but Monsieur Rosolen had told him that he'd likely be supervising some older staff, and he'd have to get used to it. Michel knew he was on a fast track to management, and he wanted to prove himself capable. Michel was a leader, his boss had told him. Robert was a follower. Nani, well, he wasn't exactly sure about Nani.

Michel phoned home to let Lucia know he was just leaving the hotel.

"On my way, Lulu," he murmured into the phone, turning his back to Robert.

"Your mother is not feeling well today, *amore*. Just a headache, she said. Would you like to meet me at the pizzeria?"

Michel smiled. He knew it was difficult for Lucia to make supper every night; cooking flustered her sometimes, and she relied heavily on Klara, who usually was only too happy to prepare a meal for the four of them. "I'll meet you there in fifteen minutes, love. *Ciao*."

He bid good night to Robert and walked out of the hotel.

CHAPTER FOURTEEN

Before they headed downstairs for breakfast, Bernie and Joan checked their room one last time, then rolled their bags to the elevator. *Michael will watch our bags while we eat,* Bernie thought. When the elevator doors opened, Bernie was surprised to see Robert at the desk. His chin rested on his chest and his eyes were closed.

"*Bonjour,*" she said loudly.

Robert's eyes flew open and his head snapped upright. "*Bonjour,*" he mumbled and blinked hard.

"May we leave our bags here? We'll be checking out after breakfast," Bernie said as she glanced behind his head. *My Michael must be in the back area,* she told herself.

"Not a problem," Robert said, turning around to follow her glance.

"Where is, um, Jean-Michel?" She kept her voice steady against the pounding of her heart.

"Bern." Robert wheeled the bags to the far corner behind reception.

"Bern? Bern, as in the capital of Switzerland?" She felt nauseated. *He can't be in Bern,* she thought. *He needs to be here, working.* "When, when will he return?"

Robert looked in her eyes and made a fish face with his lips. "He's at a meeting all morning. But he told me that you were leaving today. You and your aunt. Also the couple in 214." Robert squinted at his computer, felt in his breast pocket for his glasses, and cursed when they weren't there.

Bernie pressed her fingertips to her temples. *A meeting all morning?* She turned to Joan, who had heard the same news. Joan signaled with her head that they should go into the restaurant. Bernie followed behind her with zombie-like stiffness. Joan pulled out a chair.

"Sit," she said in a sharp voice. Bernie sat.

"*Bonjour*! Coffee?" The same pretty waitress they always had stood in front of them, a silver pot in each hand to pour *café au lait*.

Bernie nodded dumbly. She rubbed her cheek, as if she'd been slapped, hard. She would not see her Michael again. She simply assumed he'd be at his place, as usual.

"Bernie, come on. Eat. Listen, you weren't going to say anything to him this morning anyway. Just start writing that letter once we're at the airport. I'm going to fill my plate. I'll get what you like, you just sit here."

Bernie's head told her to stop being a fool. Joan was right; it wasn't like she was planning to reveal herself to him at the last moment, then leave Switzerland. She would write to him. Maybe. Right now she just felt sad that she wouldn't see her son before they left.

While Joan was at the buffet, Bernie pulled out a small package from her bag. While Joan had slept, Bernie had unclasped the medal she wore around her neck. A silver medal of Saint Michael that had belonged to her father. After her mother died (was it only last month, Bernie asked herself), Joanie had found it in her jewelry box, and offered it to Bernie. There it was, wrapped in toilet paper.

Bernie took the medal and swaddled it in a clean white napkin. What the heck, she thought, the restaurant will get it back. She wrote a note for Michael on a blank postcard: *This is a medal of Michael the Archangel. May he protect you throughout your life. Bernadette Maguire.* She'd stared at the note. Should she add 'with love'? 'Sincerely'? 'Your mother'? Finally she just left it as it was, with her name.

Before Joan returned with the plates of food, Bernie strode to the reception desk and placed the postcard and napkin in front of Robert. He looked up at her, down at the items, and back up at her. She had tied the napkin corners into a neat little bundle.

"This is for Jean-Michael. Would you please place the card in an envelope and see that he gets it, Robert?" She hesitated, then laid her hand over his.

His head bobbed up and down. "He's not here today. But I will see that he gets it, *Madame.*"

She leaned in close and pressed his hand. His eyes grew wide. Bernie lowered her voice. "You can call me Bernadette, you know. And please, Robert, be very sure to keep it safe until you can give it to him in person. I don't want Na-, anyone else to see it. It is for Jean-Michel only and is *very* important. Do you understand, Robert?"

Again he bobbed his head, unable to speak. She put her lips against his pock-marked cheek and kissed him.

"Thank you so much," she purred and turned back to the restaurant.

After they'd eaten as much as they could, Bernie and Joan stood in front of Robert and expressed to him their thanks for a lovely stay. Robert couldn't stop staring at Bernie. She smiled back at him and just before they left, she grasped his sweaty palm with both hands. The bellhop rolled their bags to the entrance, where a taxi was idling.

"What was that back there?" Joan asked. "Did you and Robert have a moment?"

"Oh, it was nothing," Bernie replied. Glancing up at the sky, she added, "Just Bernie being Bernie."

The rest of the morning was filled with taxis, trains, and the Zurich airport. Bernie felt something pulling at her and realized she wanted very much to drink, but she would say, if anyone asked, that she exercised considerable restraint. A glass of wine in the airport café and another couple of glasses on the plane, just to dull the sharp edges, yes, that would be okay. She wanted to feel some of the pain. She welcomed the ache of missing someone.

Lucia was surprised when Michel arrived home at two in the afternoon. She was arranging bedding and linens in the baby's room, and she didn't hear him come in. She'd been humming a tune from the radio and moving her hips, and when she turned around she was startled to see him leaning in the doorway, hands in his pockets, watching her and grinning. She dropped the little yellow blanket.

"*Amore*! What are you doing home?"

He embraced her and felt her belly press up against his. "The meeting in Bern ended, and the boss let me take the afternoon off."

"Lucky you," she murmured into his neck. "And lucky me. However shall we spend a free afternoon?"

His low groan was the reply she'd been hoping for. He took her hand and led her out of the nursery and into their bedroom. As he emptied his pockets, his phone buzzed with a text message. He rolled his eyes at Lucia and flipped the phone open.

"Hmm," he said, frowning and shaking his head.

"What is it?"

"A message from Robert. Remember the American women who were at the hotel? They checked out this morning, but one of them left a little package for me. The younger one. Robert wants to drop it off on his way home." He looked up to see his wife frowning hard, her bottom lip consumed by her teeth. "I can just tell him to put it in the bottom drawer of the desk at work."

"No, send him a message that he can drop it off here. It won't be for another few hours." He started to type a reply and she said, "Wait!" Michel glanced up from the phone. "Michel, invite him to eat with us. There's plenty of food. If he's coming here to bring you something, he should be invited to eat with us. Your parents are away this evening. He's that older man I met once, right?"

"Yeah, he's okay. A little odd, but he's a good guy," Michel said. "Are you sure about this?"

"Why not? He's all alone. And we have plenty to share. Besides, I want to see what this package contains."

"Me, too," he said, and typed a message to Robert. When he finished, he turned off his phone and set it down. He turned his full attention to his wife, who stood by the bed. In her seventh month, he found her absolutely beautiful: her full breasts, the swell of her belly. He was overcome with desire for her.

"You are my Venus," he croaked, pulling her down with him onto the bed.

Surprising even herself, Nani arrived for work early on Tuesday afternoon. All day long she had thought about what may have transpired that morning, when the American women finally left the hotel. Did Bernadette say anything to Michel? Does he know now that she is his birth mother? She jumped off the bus and ran to the hotel, through the lobby to the reception desk.

"Michel?" she called out.

Robert stepped from the back and grinned at Nani.

"Nope, not Michel. Robert," he said, tapping his name badge.

"What are you doing here? Where is Michel?"

Robert strolled to the computer, logged himself off, and checked his watch. "He had a meeting in Bern today."

Nani felt her pulse quicken. She looked around the lobby frantically. "Did those American women leave?"

Robert looked her up and down. "Yes, they left this morning. Also the couple in 214. Why?" He stuck his little finger in his ear, pulled it out and inspected it.

"No reason. I'm glad they're gone. I didn't like that red-haired woman at all."

Robert stared at her. "Really. I thought she was charming," he said in a dreamy voice. "She seemed to be very fond of me, too."

Nani snorted in disdain. "She was rude and loud. I didn't like her at all. Glad she's gone back to America."

Robert's face lit up all of a sudden. He opened the bottom drawer of the desk and retrieved what looked like one of the restaurant's linen napkins. Nani saw that it was tied at the corners, like a small bundle. He took a long white envelope from the top drawer.

"What is that thing?" Nani stood on her toes and leaned over the counter.

"None of your business," Robert sneered. He seemed to puff up as Nani eyed him. "I'm invited to dine with Michel and his lovely wife this evening, and

I have something to give him. I must be off. *Bonsoir*, Nani." He fluttered his hand in front of her face. Robert took a card and tucked it in the envelope, then placed the envelope and the little package in a cloth shopping bag, the kind Nani brought to the market. He put on his coat and that foolish hat, picked up the bag, and sauntered away.

Nani watched him leave. Her eyes darted around the reception area until she spotted a pen. She picked it up and threw it across the lobby.

"*Salut*, Robert!" Michel opened the door and ushered him inside. "Here, give me your coat."

"It's nice and warm in here," Robert said, handing his coat to Michel, who hung it on a hook next to the door. "Smells like onions." He pulled off his hat and handed it over as well. Robert's hair was full of static electricity and Michel swallowed a chuckle.

"I hope you're hungry, and I hope you like onions," he said to Robert.

"I am and I do. Where is your wife?"

"She's here. Lulu?"

Lucia emerged from the dining room with her hand extended. "Robert, so nice to see you again. It's been a long time," she said. Michel looked on with pride.

"Hello again, Lucia. Thank you for inviting me to your house. Most kind," Robert said with a slight bow.

"It's our pleasure. Now please sit down at the table. We are ready to eat."

The three of them enjoyed pleasant conversation while dining on sausages, onions and potatoes. Robert talked a lot about his cat, Muschi. Michel wished he knew someone he could introduce to Robert; she'd have to be very special.

Lucia cleared the plates from the table. Robert touched his linen napkin to his lips and suddenly cried out.

"Oh!"

Lucia almost dropped a plate of almond biscotti, she was so startled by his outburst.

"What is it, Robert?"

Robert pushed his chair back and ran to the kitchen, where he had left his bag. He knelt on the floor and fished out the package and the envelope Bernadette had given to him that morning. Michel and Lucia stood next to him, waiting. He looked up at Michel and handed the envelope and little napkin-wrapped package to him.

"That nice woman Bernadette, she gave this to me earlier today, before she and the other woman left. She wanted to make sure I gave it directly to you." He stood up from his kneeling position on the floor and held out his hands.

Michel eyed the cloth-wrapped bundle and the envelope that was folded and wrinkled from being stuffed into Robert's bag.

"We could have dessert first, if you want," said Robert, licking his lips.

"Yes, let's have coffee, please," Lucia said quickly. She picked up the plate of biscotti and asked Michel to bring the pot of coffee to the table. "Robert, you drink coffee?" She poured a cup for Michel and held the spout over Robert's cup until he confirmed that yes, he did like coffee, with cream and lots of sugar.

"Here, take two," she said, passing the plate of biscotti to him. He took just one, smiling, and dunked it in his coffee.

Michel stared at the little bundle on the table and glanced at his wife. What had Bernadette done, he wondered. Perhaps it was something from America, something to thank him for his hospitality? But it seemed odd for her to give him a gift; they weren't friends.

"So, how was work today?" Michel asked as he picked up his cup. He considered bringing out a bottle of brandy, but was unsure if Robert drank, and decided to leave it in the cupboard.

"Good, good. Nothing unusual. Four new rooms today, one for a week. How's that for November?" He stopped, and stared at the biscotti he still held between his fingers. "Nice lady, that American."

"Robert?" Lucia asked.

"The one with the red hair," he said. "Bernadette. I wish she could have stayed. I think she liked me," he said. "Although she didn't give me a gift," he added, turning to look at the little package that waited, inert, at the other end of the table.

Michel winked at his wife. Good old Robert. Bernadette Maguire must have shown him some extra kindness, and now Robert was smitten. And she was gone, back to America.

"They were very nice women," Michel agreed as he poured more coffee.

"She said to be sure to give that to you," Robert said, pointing with his fork at the napkin bundle. "I didn't peek, honest, but I wanted to."

Michel set the coffeepot on the table. "Well, let's have a look, shall we?" He glanced at Lucia, whose mouth was open. She raised her cup to her lips.

Michel reached for the package and untied the corners of the napkin. He lifted out a silver medal on a silver chain. He squinted at the medal and frowned.

"I don't understand," he said, and handed it to Lucia.

Lucia looked closely at the medal and let out a sigh. "It's Saint Michael. The archangel." She raised her eyebrows to her husband.

"Perhaps the note has an explanation," said Robert, who helped himself to one more biscotti.

"Ooh," Lucia murmured. Michel jerked his head to her and saw her hand pressing in her stomach.

"Lulu?" But she waved her hand.

"Just a little kick. I'm fine. Read the note."

Michel slipped the card from the envelope. It was a postcard from Morcote, of all places. He looked at Lucia and showed her the picture. She grinned, remembering their first meeting in the lovely town. Michel's eyes widened as he read what Bernadette had written in her neat handwriting. His voice was clear and strong as he said aloud, '*This is a medal of Michael the Archangel. May he protect you throughout your life. Bernadette Maguire*'

Michel stared at the postcard for a long time. No one spoke at the table, not even Robert.

Finally Robert said, "Well, that was very nice of her. Didn't I tell you she was a nice person?" He picked up his biscotti and resumed dunking.

Michel caught Lucia's eye and mouthed "I love you" to her. She mouthed the same words back. He cut his eyes to Robert, who was busy eating. Michel made a fist and bounced it off his heart twice while gazing at her.

Finally, Robert said he must go home to tend to his cat. Michel breathed a sigh of relief to himself. Lucia wrapped up the rest of the biscotti for him to take home, and he put the small package in his bag. As he slipped on his coat, he held up a finger to Michel.

"That napkin has to go back to the restaurant, you know."

Michel suppressed the urge to laugh, and with a serious face said, "I'll have it with me tomorrow morning. Thank you, Robert, for bringing this to me." He shook Robert's hand.

They waved goodbye to their guest and watched him lumber away up the street to his own small apartment in a house not far from theirs.

Michel exhaled. "Well, that wasn't too bad, was it, Lulu?" He encircled his wife in his arms. As she rested her head against his shoulder, he added, "But I have to say that was a strange gift to receive. There was no box, so I'm thinking perhaps it belonged to Bernadette. What do you make of it?"

Lucia twisted gently from his embrace and took her husband's face in her hands. Her touch was soft and warm against his skin. She used her fingers to make circles on his temples and said, "Come sit, my love. There is something I need to tell you."

CHAPTER FIFTEEN

Bernie and Joan passed through customs at Logan Airport and heard their names called. Bernie spun around looking – where were they? The crowd parted and she saw them. Joanie and Lou, grinning with arms outstretched to welcome them home. Joan ran to Joanie, and Bernie accepted Lou's awkward hug. After switching, Joan asked, "But where are the girls?"

"They're home with my parents. You'll see them; I told Mom and Dad to bring them by the house later. Lemme just call to let them know you've landed." Lou turned away and pulled out his phone. Bernie wondered what everyone did before cell phones. She glanced around the arrival area. Not a pay phone in sight. Sometimes it was good to be unreachable, she thought, happy to have left her own cell phone at home.

Joanie fell into step with Bernie as they walked through the open doors into the cold air of a November afternoon in Boston. "Do you want us to drop you off at your place or are you coming to Mom's house for the night?"

Bernie thought about her apartment in Providence. Funny, but she wasn't quite ready to go back. "I think I'll stay at Mom's tonight. Joan can drive me back tomorrow, right, Joan?"

"Are you kidding? I can't stand to be with you for another day!" She laughed out loud. "I'm kidding!" She turned to her niece. "I couldn't have had a better traveling companion." She grabbed Bernie's arm and held it.

Back at Acorn Circle, the women rolled their bags into the house and left them by the door. Joanie started a pot of coffee and Bernie dug out the gifts they'd purchased. Plenty of Swiss chocolate, a pretty scarf for Joanie and a tee shirt for Lou. Joan had selected some earrings for the twins.

Joanie called out from the kitchen. "There's a stack of mail on the table by the door. I saved all the sympathy cards for you to look through. Bernie, one envelope came addressed to you here. I didn't open it," she added. The smell of coffee brewing filled the air as Joanie continued to clink around in the kitchen. Bernie picked up the stack of mail and brought it to the table. She handed half of it to Joan. They opened one sympathy card after another: kind words from old friends, an effort to comfort the bereaved. Mass cards and spiritual bouquets from the Catholics. Bernie spotted a pale yellow envelope and drew it out.

It was addressed to her here at Acorn Circle, and showed a return address in New York. She looked up at Joanie, who was setting coffee and pie on the table. "Do we know anyone in New York City? West 23rd Street?"

"I don't," Joanie said with a shrug. Lou shook his head, as did Joan.

Bernie pursed her lips and opened the envelope. Inside was a standard "With Sympathy" card. Daffodils on the front, a short message inside: 'May memories comfort you at this difficult time.' She skipped past the handwritten sentiment to see "Gary" at the very bottom. Gary Baptista, wow. As she read the words he'd written, she felt as if her body had been turned inside out. As if all her internal organs were visible, unprotected by skin. He'd written in small, straight handwriting: "Dear Bernie, Tim Lyon told me about your mom, and I'm so sorry. I didn't find out until after the services or I'd have come up. I think of you often and wish you peace. Love, Gary"

Bernie rested her elbow on the table and the heel of her hand made a little shelf for her chin. Gary Baptista. She felt three pairs of eyes on her.

"Gary Baptista from college." She licked lips that suddenly felt very dry. "I haven't heard from him in years. Timmy told him about Mom." She read his note again and blinked hard.

"The Gary you mentioned when we were in Schwarzsee? Oh, that was just yesterday, wasn't it? Well, wasn't that thoughtful of him." Joan cut slices of pie for everyone. "Did you make this, Joanie? It looks delicious."

It was odd though, Bernie thought, to be living in New York City with a wife and kids. Not that people didn't do it all the time, but she was sure she'd read in that alumni magazine that they were in Connecticut. One of those nice towns on the rail line, like Stamford or Greenwich or Cos Cob. Yes, Cos Cob, she was sure they lived in Cos Cob. Usually you didn't move your family from Connecticut to Manhattan, although she assumed it could happen. Maybe he's not married anymore, a small voice inside her head whispered.

She slid the card back into its envelope and tucked it in her purse. Joan stifled a yawn.

"We'd love to see the girls before Joan here nods off," Bernie said. "We're still on Swiss time, and it's one in the morning for us." As soon as the words were out of her mouth, the doorbell rang and everyone laughed.

Angela and Amanda, Lou and Joanie's twin daughters, tripped into the house ahead of Lou's parents. There were hugs all around and Joan pulled extra chairs to the table. Bernie looked at the girls as if she hadn't seen them in years. In fact, she realized, she hadn't been present in their lives for a long time, and she hoped it wasn't too late to make up for the time she'd lost. They were smart and beautiful girls, and she was but a distant aunt to them.

After an hour's visit, Joanie glanced over to see her aunt nodding off.

"Come on, everyone, we're going home. Our world travelers need to sleep."

The girls thanked Joan and Bernie for their gifts, Lou's parents were happy with their chocolate, and Bernie hugged her sister and Lou.

"Thank you both so much for picking us up, for everything," Bernie said at the front door of her mother's house, now Joan's house. "I know it's only nine o'clock, but we'd better get some sleep." She made a slight movement with her head toward Joan, who was curled in a corner of the sofa with eyelids as heavy as the bags they'd carted home.

Joanie hugged her sister and whispered, "Glad you had a good time. You look...rested. Better."

Bernie pulled away slightly to look down at her older sister's face. "I am better, Joanie. Really. Thanks again." She kissed Lou on the cheek.

"Joan'll drive me up to the apartment tomorrow. We might wake up at four, you know, until our bodies adjust to the time difference. But I'll see you soon, okay?"

They waved goodbye and Bernie closed the door after them, clicking the deadbolt in place.

"Joan, come on, we need to sleep. Do you want me to help you unpack?"

"Tomorrow, Bernie. I have an old tee shirt here. Good night." She kissed Bernie and closed the bedroom door behind her. Joan slept in Mary Maguire's old bedroom now; her sister, Bernie's mom, had lived in Joanie's old room for the last months of her life, in a hospital bed. Bernie peeked into the room and saw that the bed had been removed and the room was empty but for a dresser and chair. Joanie took care of everything, Bernie thought; she always did. I was never really around, but Joanie was a mainstay, there for Mom, there to take care of this house along with her own.

Bernie entered her old bedroom and blinked at the familiarity: the narrow bed, the white bookcase still filled with Nancy Drew mysteries and the novels she'd read in college. Tomorrow she'd go back to her apartment and her law practice. She really needed to take charge of her life. Everything had been unraveling slowly, like a ball of yarn on a soft downward slope. Bernie had tried to keep it together for a long time, for years actually.

Now, she'd made peace with Timmy, and she probably had him to thank for letting Gary know. She shook her head in wonderment. Gary Baptista. What a good friend he was to her after her father died unexpectedly. She even suspected that he knew about the baby, but he never said anything about it, no hint, no judgment. She would write back to him, send him some chocolate. She saw his kind face as she drifted into sleep.

CHAPTER SIXTEEN

It was Saturday, December 14, and the hotel Christmas party was in two hours. Lucia lay in bed, curled up on her side, and cried uncontrollably. She knew how much Michel wanted her to be with him at the event, she understood it was important for him and for his career, but she couldn't go to a fancy party when she looked like a cow. She would be out of place and a source of laughter. And she had nothing to wear.

She'd tried to be attentive to her husband in the weeks following "the revelation," as she referred to it now. She'd been watchful of any change in his demeanor ever since the night she took her husband by the hand, led him to the sofa in the living room, sat down next to him and told him that Bernadette Maguire, the American redhead who stayed not once but twice at his hotel during late October and early November, the woman who cried when she first saw him, the woman who left behind a silver medal of Michael the Archangel, was his birth mother.

She told him this because she knew that Klara couldn't bring herself to say the words, as much as she may have wanted to. She told him because he needed to know. And, as expected, it was a lot for him to absorb. He had been quiet that night, very quiet. Lucia watched her husband struggle with his emotions. That night neither of them slept much. In the early morning hours, Lucia, still awake, observed her husband, twitching as he dreamt. The next morning, when he trudged off to work on too little sleep, she ventured next door to visit with Klara, and told her everything. They both cried, naturally, but

Lucia could tell that Klara was relieved. And that evening, when the four of them gathered around the table to eat, Lucia offered a prayer of thanksgiving. Michel took his mother's hand in his own, and grasped his father's hand with his other, and told his parents that they would always be his parents, no matter what. He told them what he believed: that Bernadette Maguire must have been very afraid, but very brave to make her decision, and that he was the lucky one, to have been adopted by two such caring and loving people. He made his parents cry and laugh, and it had been a very good night.

Now, five weeks later, Lucia was supposed to be getting dressed for this Christmas party. Michel was out of the house, getting a haircut, and Lucia's thoughts turned to the event at the hotel this evening. Really, she thought, why am I crying? It's true I don't want to go, but it won't be that bad. Michel even said we don't have to stay for long. She figured it was her hormones causing this ridiculous crying, and she rolled off the bed. I will make myself as presentable as any woman just two weeks away from giving birth can manage. No reason for him to see me this way, she reasoned, as she splashed cold water on her face. It was too early to dress. Maybe just a snack to hold me until the meal, she thought. She wiped her face and waddled to the kitchen.

Lucia opened the refrigerator and found some leftover ham. She grabbed it along with a chunk of cheese. There was some bread from the morning; she cut two thick slices and spread one slice of bread with mustard and layered two slices of ham and two slices of cheese on it, then topped it with the other slice of bread. Her sandwich was about three inches thick. Lucia pulled a bottle of Rivella from the cabinet and opened it. There. She took her snack to the table and began eating. She felt much better.

So, I'll finally meet this girl Nani who works with my Michel. She knew Robert, and she'd met Didier, but had not had the pleasure of meeting Nani. She'd asked her husband about her once, and he shrugged. "She's Greek," he said through a mouthful of food one night at supper. "And short," he added, his hand indicating that she was about two feet tall. A short Greek girl. Lucia told herself that she had nothing to worry about, but still. She wanted to see the short Greek girl for herself.

Lucia finished her sandwich and cleared the plate and glass, placing them in the sink. She turned away, then turned back and washed them, dried them, and put them back in the cupboard. No evidence. Dr. Schmidt told her that she'd gained twenty-one kilos during this pregnancy. That was a lot of weight, and she wondered if she could lose it all after the baby was born. She told me to be careful about gaining too much, but I can't help it if I'm always hungry, Lucia said to herself. And it wasn't like she was eating chocolate, or French fries. Lucia craved real food. Besides, she didn't want to eat a lot at this party, or everyone would notice. With a little sandwich in her stomach, she wouldn't be so hungry.

The door opened and Michel breezed in, bringing a wave of cold air with him. His orange hair was clipped close again, and he smelled like after-shave, sandalwood and amber.

"And look," he said, holding up his hands. "Marco's daughter was there and gave me a manicure!" His short nails were perfectly trimmed and buffed.

"Marco's daughter Elina? She always had a thing for you," Lucia muttered, turning away.

"Oh Lulu," he crooned into her ear as he caught her in the middle of the kitchen. "It's you, only you," he sang to her until she laughed and pushed him away.

"You want to take a big cow to this party, do you?" She bowed her head, feeling the pressure in her eyes that signaled more tears. Oh, he must be so tired of my tears, she thought.

"You," he said, lifting her chin with his fingertip, "will be the most beautiful woman there. You always are, wherever we go, Lucia." He nuzzled her neck and she felt his smooth cheek against her skin. "Perhaps we have time to rest a little?" His lips kissed her neck, traveled up to her ear, but she shook her head.

"Maybe after," she whispered, and touched his cheek. "I cannot right now." She really didn't want to make love anymore; it was too uncomfortable. But there were other options for pleasuring a spouse, and Lucia knew and understood her husband's needs and desires.

"Okay, Lulu, it's a shower for me then. Cold, cold shower," he said, making his sad puppy face. She laughed again.

"Okay, I join you in the shower. But the water must be warm," she said as he took her hand and led her down the hall. This night would be fine, she told herself.

Bernie dressed for her date. It had been twenty-two years since she and Gary graduated from college, and she hadn't seen him once since then. She'd written back to him almost immediately after receiving his card, sending him one of the postcards from Schwarzsee and a bar of milk chocolate with hazelnuts, his favorite, as she recalled. She'd included her phone number and email, and he'd called her.

Their first phone conversation lasted two hours. Gary was divorced now, as she'd guessed. His wife Roxana, who he married in 1982, had met someone else, an investment banker on Wall Street. Their two children lived with her: Justin was seventeen and Nicole was fifteen. Roxana still lived in Cos Cob, in the house they'd bought back in 1983. Gary lived in a small apartment in Chelsea and was a full professor of German Literature at NYU. He spoke about his marriage without bitterness, but it was clear to Bernie that he missed his kids.

Bernie told him about her mother's illness, about the trip to Switzerland with her aunt Joan, and about her law practice. She wanted to tell him about seeing Michael, but that was better left for a conversation in person. She also left out telling him about all the bad choices she'd made over the past twenty years.

And here she was, applying a second coat of mascara. Gary had offered to take the train up to Providence so they could see each other. He'd booked a room at the Marriott for the night and was planning to return to New York the following afternoon.

Bernie's bed was layered with just about every item of clothing in her closet. Gary told her he'd made a reservation at the new Riverwalk restaurant after Bernie couldn't think of a place to eat. It was embarrassing; she lived in Providence and couldn't even suggest a restaurant. She didn't want him to know that she rarely went out to nice restaurants. For the past couple of years, her social life had consisted of sitting on a barstool at the Drop-Off, talking to Norm, and occasionally leaving with someone in a well-tailored suit with a nice haircut. She prayed that it wasn't too late to change her life around. Bernie glanced at the clock on the wall: six-ten. She had twenty minutes, because Gary would be on time, she just knew it.

"Maybe something not black for once, Bernadette," she said aloud. She hadn't owned colorful clothes since the early nineties. But it was two weeks before Christmas, and everyone would be looking so damn festive. She walked back into the big closet and pulled a string to turn on the light at the very back. There was a dress with the tags still attached. She grabbed the hanger and walked out of the closet to look at it. She couldn't remember buying this dress, but obviously, she'd never worn it. It was the color of burnished copper with tiny beads that reflected light, and it had a matching cropped jacket. Where did this dress come from, she wondered, shaking her head. It didn't matter. She clipped the tags and tried it on. Checking her reflection in the full-length mirror, she had to admit that it really did look nice. Complements my hair. Now, what about shoes. She found a pair of heels that worked, and heels were fine with Gary, who she remembered was at least six feet tall. She slipped the heels on and turned in front of the mirror.

Quickly, she hung each piece of clothing back in the closet. Funny, a few months ago she would never have gone on a date without downing a few drinks beforehand. Not this time. She smoothed out the quilt on her bed.

With five minutes to spare, she gargled, spit, wiped, and reapplied lipstick. There was a knock on the door and she opened it to see Gary Baptista standing there, holding flowers. They hadn't exchanged pictures, so seeing him, twenty-two years later, was something of a surprise. Gary was still

Gary, but without the beard and shaggy hair from Fribourg. He looked clean and neat. And handsome.

"Come on in," she said, swinging the door wide open. "It's warmer in here."

"These are for you," he said, handing her a paper-wrapped bouquet of red roses and white carnations.

"They're lovely, thanks," Bernie replied, setting the flowers on the table. She opened her arms and they embraced, not with passion, or even with love, not yet. Her hands reached around his broad back and up to his shoulders. She smelled the cold air on him, and peppermint. His arms were around her waist and she wanted to lift off the floor, just for a moment. He let go of her and let his hands fall to his sides.

"Bernie, you haven't aged at all. How did you manage that?"

She laughed. "That's very kind, but there are days I feel even older than I am. I can't say you haven't changed, Gary. The long hair, the beard, the aviator glasses? Where is that boy?"

He smoothed back his thinning hair. "Sometimes I wish I could be that boy again. I grew a beard once, when we rented a cabin in New Hampshire one summer, and Roxana said she'd leave me unless I shaved it off." He hunched his shoulders and dropped them. "I shaved it off and she left me anyway." His smile faded and he shifted his weight.

"Let me just get these into some water. Can I get you something to drink?" Bernie pulled a square glass vase from the cupboard under the sink, ran tap water into it, and arranged the flowers. She could tell he was staring at her, so she took her time arranging the flowers.

"There!" Bernie stood back to admire the arrangement, which complemented the few Christmas decorations she had placed around the apartment. Not much, really, just a miniature tree and a pewter angel and a string of white lights on the mantle to make the place look festive. Joan said she wasn't going to put up any decorations, but would help Joanie and Lou at their house. Joanie at first was against it, saying it was too soon after Mom's death, but Joan prevailed, reminding her that it was important, that Mary would have wanted them to celebrate. Bernie brought her head back to the present.

"It's amazing, Bernie. You really do look the same as you did in college." Gary stood still in the middle of her apartment, filling the space. She tilted her head at him and he looked down as his face reddened.

Bernie realized that even if they both looked as good as the other said, or thought, there were years to span. Each of them had lived a life. Bernie's was full of regret and she didn't necessarily want to share much of it with Gary, and least not tonight.

Gary checked his watch. "We should go," he said, extending his hand.

"I'm starving." Bernie picked up a small brown clutch purse from the table and took his hand.

Gary stopped. "What about your coat? It's freezing outside."

"Oh, right." She turned back from the door. Her leather jacket wouldn't do. Neither would the ski parka, or the trench coat. She made a face. "I'll be fine," she said. "It's not like we're going for a walk in the park." She locked the door behind her as they ran to the car. "You have heat in here, right?"

CHAPTER SEVENTEEN

The restaurant at the Hotel de la Rose was closed to the public for the evening; a sign on the entrance door to the hotel stated that there was a private party in the restaurant for hotel employees and guests. Everyone who was booked into the hotel, and there were forty-eight guests that weekend, was invited to attend the party if they wanted. All of the hotel employees, and there were twenty-one, plus their spouses or dates, were invited as well.

Seventy-seven people filled the hotel's restaurant, which was decorated with fresh bayberry, bright red winterberries, and tiny white lights. From the massive oak bar at the back wall to the windows looking out over the square, nothing was left bare, and Michel whispered his approval to Lucia as they stepped into the restaurant. He offered his elbow and she linked her arm through his.

Michel wore a dark gray suit, a new white shirt, and a festive red tie with green holly on it. Lucia wore a new dress, one she'd never wear again, a long dress of dark green velvet with a high scoop neck. Klara had lent her pearls, and Lucia wore flat black velvet slippers on her swollen feet. She'd carefully applied makeup and perfume and Michel had told her three times already that she looked beautiful.

"You two look like the Winter King and Queen," said Monsieur Rosolen, owner of the hotel. He kissed Lucia's cheeks and kept his hands on her shoulders. "You are the picture of beauty, my dear," he told her. He looked like Santa Claus, plump and jolly, with twinkling blue eyes and thick white hair. All he needs is a beard, Lucia thought. In the taxi on the way to the hotel, Michel had told her that Monsieur Rosolen often dressed up as Santa at the hospital, visiting all the children and handing out toys he had purchased.

"The room looks lovely," said Lucia, her eyes wide like a child's on Christmas morning as she took it all in. Michel had brought her to the hotel nearly a year ago, and she'd remarked to him then what a grand old place it was. She knew he was happier working in an old hotel than for one of the big hotel chains, with concrete blocks in the major cities. No charm, no character there.

"Enjoy the party," said Monsieur Rosolen, bowing to Lucia as he moved toward another couple.

"Would you like something to drink, Lulu? Orange juice?" Michael kept his arm around her and led her to the bar, where Jorge stood waiting, ready to fill their order. Michel said, "Nice hat," pointing to the red cap with white fur trim atop Jorge's head. Jorge shook his head and a little bell jingled. "Now I never be lost," he said in heavily accented English.

"Orange juice, please. Small one," Lucia said to Jorge, who nodded and looked at Michel.

"And you, sir?"

Michel hesitated. "I don't want to drink too much this evening; after all, it's still a work event," he said.

"But is also a celebration," Jorge countered.

"Okay, give me a Sonnenschein whiskey. Plenty of ice." The bartender poured out a generous shot for Michel and placed the two glasses on the bar.

"All drinks free tonight," he said and grinned at Lucia with big teeth as white as paper. Michel put a five-franc coin on the bar and pushed it to Jorge.

"Thanks," he said with a smile and took Lucia's arm again. "Shall we sit?" He gestured to an empty table where they could watch the people come and go. In a low voice, he identified each of the employees to Lucia as they entered the restaurant.

"There's Robert," he said as the odd man entered the room. Robert wore a suit that could not have been his. The trousers were too short, Lucia noticed, and the jacket didn't match. But he looked happy to be a part of the festivities. "Shall I call him over?" Michel looked at Lucia and sipped the whiskey.

"Not yet, my love. Let me enjoy these few moments, before I must share you with your adoring fans."

"My fans! You are a funny woman," he said, leaning in to kiss her lips. "You smell like Christmas," he said and when she raised her eyebrows, he added, "Vanilla and cinnamon and mistletoe," and kissed her again. "And you taste like sugar."

Lucia leaned back in her chair and relaxed for the first time that evening. Michel slid an empty chair closer to her so she could elevate her feet under the table. She would be happy to sit here for the entire party. Her baby would be here soon, in two weeks. A Christmas present for us all, she thought with a smile. "*Salut!*" Lucia heard a female voice call from behind her. Twisting her head around, she saw a tiny woman lurch forward, followed by an exceedingly tall man. Michel stood up. "*Salut*, Nani," he said, and extended his hand.

"Happy Christmas!" she slurred and reached up to hug him. Lucia gaped as Nani hung her arms around Michel's neck and her feet lifted off the floor. Michel kissed her cheeks awkwardly and pulled her off him, then shook the hand of the tall man behind her.

"Alain, good to see you again," he said, then turned to Lucia. Her eyes immediately went to the bright red mark of lipstick on his cheek and she felt as if a big hand was squeezing her heart. Michel laid a hand on Lucia's back and made the introductions. "Nani, Alain, this is my beautiful wife Lucia. Lulu, Nani and her boyfriend Alain."

Lucia stayed seated but held out her hand to Nani, who gazed down at her with glassy black eyes. Her gaze traveled to Lucia's swollen belly and back up to her face. Obviously, this girl was drunk and Lucia imagined it wouldn't take much liquor to affect someone so petite. And the boyfriend seemed very uncomfortable with the whole situation.

"Finally I meet the woman who has Michel's heart," she said. Nani's eyes were rimmed in black, her hair was piled high on her head, and the smell of wine emanated from her. Lucia fixed a smile on her face and said, "Nice to meet you, Nani." Before Nani could say anything further, Lucia turned slightly to extend her hand to Alain, who was so tall, Lucia found herself staring at his belt buckle. She tilted her head back to look in his face. To her surprise, Alain crouched down next to her to be at eye level. His voice was low and silky. "It's a pleasure to meet you, Lucia, and I wish you and Michel every happiness as you welcome your child into the world."

"Alain, stand up," Nani barked. "Let's get a drink," she added and turned to Michel. "Can we get you a drink?" She swayed in front of him and Lucia thought she might fall off those dreadfully high heels.

"No, we're fine, Nani, thank you. You go ahead, we'll be sure to catch up later." As the couple turned toward the bar, Michel sat down and rolled his eyes at Lucia.

"Well, now you have met my co-worker Nani." He shook his head. "She should remember the boss is around tonight."

Lucia rested her hand on her husband's arm. "It isn't your concern, *amore*." She took the paper napkin from under his drink and wiped the lipstick from his cheek. His eyes met hers.

"That girl certainly likes to leave her mark on you, doesn't she?" Lucia folded the napkin and laid it on the table.

"Lucia, she is nothing, you do know that, don't you?" Michel's brown eyes looked so soft and warm. "I do know that, yes. But be careful. She is a woman in love."

"In love with Alain, you think?"

"No, Michel. She is in love with you."

It was a short drive to the restaurant, and Gary told Bernie about the ride up from New York on the train.

"The city can be crazy this time of year. Actually, it starts well before Thanksgiving now. And the day after Thanksgiving, forget it. Penn Station was a madhouse," he said.

"Are you happy living in the city?"

He stared straight ahead as she directed him down the street. "Well, I'm closer to NYU. And I guess it's better to be living alone in Manhattan than it would be in Cos Cob."

"Yeah," she murmured, not knowing what to say. Bernie pointed out the sign indicating valet parking and Gary pulled up, handing the keys to the attendant as he unfolded his long legs from the compact car. He put a hand on Bernie's back as they hurried from the cold air into the restaurant.

Bernie took a deep breath once they were inside. Her nostrils took in the tantalizing aroma of oregano and garlic, and she couldn't wait to eat. The restaurant was warm and a low candle flickered on each table. Gary handed his coat to a sullen girl who sat just inside a small coatroom, and took the small plastic ticket she held out to him. A young man at the front of the restaurant led them to a table near the back. Bernie passed couple after couple. No kids, she thought with relief. Children don't belong in a restaurant like this. That's what Applebee's is for.

Gary held Bernie's chair until she was seated, then took his place across from her. The candlelight illuminated his face, danced in his eyes, and softened the laugh lines around his mouth. She hoped it had the same effect on her.

"So tell me what went through your mind when you saw Fribourg, Bernie. Did it transport you back in time?" Gary's eyes had flecks of gold in them, she noticed. Or was it a trick from the candle?

"It took me back, yes. How could it not? So much of the town is exactly the same, Gary. Things don't change the way they do here. And I guess I was looking for things to be the same. You know, I could point out to my aunt some of the same places we'd been to. She wanted the grand tour," Bernie said with a laugh, recalling Joan's curiosity about everything that had to do with her life back then.

"What about our café?"

Bernie shook her head and leaned back. "Gone. A jazz bar now. I couldn't bring myself to go in." She looked away for a moment, remembering times good and bad spent in that café.

"I'd love to go back sometime," he said. "Where did you stay?"

Bernie was about to respond when a waiter appeared at their table with menus. In a low monotone, he recited some specials, took their drink order, and walked away.

"We stayed at the Hotel de la Rose. Remember how grand it looked? I'd always thought that would be a great place to stay. It hasn't changed; well, not that I was ever inside except for Christmas dinner. The Eurotel is still across from the train station," she said, thinking how she'd never stay there, since she associated it with Karl Berset. "Fribourg isn't like the major cities, which all have chain hotels now. So we checked in there the day we arrived, after taking the train from Zurich." She wiped her palms on her thighs under the table. "And when we got there, I walked up to the front desk." She felt her throat constricting and blew out a breath. Where is that drink, she thought.

The waiter returned and set drinks in front of them. Gary raised his glass and said, "Here's to you, Bernie." She responded with "Cheers, Gary," and took a drink. Oh, vodka. She closed her eyes. He didn't say 'Here's to us.' But then why would he? We're not an 'us,' Bernie thought.

"Are you okay?" He was staring at her.

Bernie picked up her glass again, looked at it, and set it down. She pushed her hair back from her face and just blurted it out.

"Gary, I had a baby in Fribourg. I don't know if you knew, maybe everyone knew. Timmy knew, I mean, Timmy found out. I had an affair with the guy who worked in the bank, the teller there, and I got pregnant. I was pregnant practically the whole time we were there. And I had a baby, in May, and Mr. Gordon had moved me after my father died, and I was living with Dr. Schmidt, Hanna Schmidt, his girlfriend, who was an obstetrician, is an obstetrician, and…"

"Bernie, stop." Gary put a hand over hers. "Stop. It's okay. You don't have to tell me everything now." Bernie heard her own breathing and tried to quell it. "Yes, I knew you were pregnant, or I should say, I guessed you were. I think a lot of the other kids were so wrapped up in their own little worlds and dramas that they didn't notice. Either way, no one ever said anything to me about it, including Tim." He turned her hand over so the palm was facing up, and he laid his palm against hers. "I want to hear your story, if you want to tell it to me. But don't feel you have to pour everything out right now. I'm a happy man, sitting across from my college friend who looks even more beautiful than she did when she was twenty years old."

"Wow." The word wasn't meant to be spoken, but it escaped Bernie's lips before she knew it. She stared at Gary, who looked so different than he did in 1979, and yet, still Gary. Clean-shaven, no glasses, crinkles around the eyes and mouth, a little gray at the temples. Professor of German literature at NYU. And his wife left him. Why?

"Why did your marriage end?" Bernie saw the waiter approaching the table and waved him away.

Gary glanced at the waiter as he walked away. "Well, it was complicated. I guess it always is." He lifted his glass and took a long swallow. "I think I never lived up to the expectation she had of me."

Bernie watched him as he spoke.

"You don't have to tell me everything either, Gary. I shouldn't have asked."

"It's okay. I'll give you the Reader's Digest version. Roxana worked when the kids were very young. We needed two incomes with the house and the life that went with it in that neighborhood. In the beginning, we both enjoyed living well. But there's always something more, you know? The neighbors have a better car; maybe they just bought a time share in the Caymans. The kids got bigger, and then there were tennis lessons, violin lessons, whatever the neighbors were doing, Roxana felt we had to do it, too. Or more. At one point, I remember we were at this house party, and one of the guys who lived a few houses down, he worked on Wall Street. He suggested a few of us all pool our money and buy a limousine. A limo, Bernie!"

"Buy a limo? Why?" She was hungry but didn't want to interrupt Gary to bring the waiter back over. She sipped her drink and hoped for a bread basket.

"The idea was to use it to commute into the city during the week, and rent it out for events on the weekends. The guy said it would pay for itself in no time. This was the 80's, remember. But I think it was around twenty thousand or something that each of us would have to put up. Anyway, Roxana was all excited about it, giddy about the idea of her husband traveling to work in a limo, with the investment bankers. And I was content to take the train. I could read and correct papers. More importantly, I didn't want to spend our money that way." Gary stopped talking and focused on Bernie. "I'm sorry, Bernie. I didn't mean to go on and on like that."

"Don't worry about it, Gary. I'm the one who asked the question." She caught the eye of the waiter and nodded.

"Would you like to order?" There was no inflection in this waiter's voice, Bernie noted. Like he'd rather be anywhere else than here, taking their dinner orders.

"Yes, please. I'll start with a cup of lobster bisque, and I'd like the seafood risotto." Bernie gave the waiter her best smile. Nothing.

Gary chuckled and Bernie shot him a glance. "What?" she said.

He looked at the waiter. "Same thing she's having," he said and Bernie laughed out loud.

The waiter looked from Bernie to Gary and said, "Okay."

"And a bottle of the Albola Pinot Grigio," Gary added. The waiter nodded and walked away.

Bernie was still laughing. "Did you copy me on purpose?"

"No, it's really what I had in mind. But the waiter was not amused." Gary shook his head.

"Well, he can't mess up the order, can he?" Bernie felt her entire body relax, probably for the first time that evening. She was enjoying herself.

"Tell me about your kids. Justin and Nicole, right?" She wanted to know about them, wanted Gary to know she was interested, and yet, Bernie felt a detachment as she listened to him describe his children. She'd never be connected with them, she thought. Bernie heard Nani's sharp retort in her mind: 'He already has a mother, Bernadette.' Gary's children already have a mother. She forced herself to focus.

"Justin is seventeen. He's a junior in high school and just learned to drive." Gary rolled his eyes. "He loves soccer and the Yankees. And Nicole is fifteen. She's on the gymnastics team, does ballet. They're good kids. Neither of them has ever given us any trouble." Gary rapped his knuckles on the tablecloth.

"That's really wonderful, Gary," Bernie said quietly.

"It is," he said, then quickly added, "I'm sorry for the kids. Our marriage ended because Roxana wanted out, but I knew the love was gone. I'm just sorry they got caught in it. I'm trying to be dad, but I can only be dad every other weekend. Roxana, she's getting remarried in February." When their eyes met, Bernie saw no flecks of gold, no flicker of candlelight in them.

The waiter appeared with the lobster bisque; his timing was perfect, thought Bernie, as she was at a loss for words. If she asked him how he felt about Roxana getting remarried, she might not want to hear his answer.

They ate. The seafood risotto was magnificent, and paired well with the wine. Bernie sipped hers as slowly as she could, allowing Gary to refill his glass while hers was still half full. Trying to keep the conversation light over dinner, she chattered on about Switzerland and the towns she and Joan had visited: the old wooden bridge in Lucerne; the lake in Lugano; and, of course, the visit to Schwarzsee.

"It hasn't changed much, Gary, after all these years."

"What a relief," he said as he pierced a scallop with his fork. "Wasn't it a beautiful place, Bernie?"

Bernie nodded. "I found the spot where we sat that day, remember? Under the yellow umbrella? And we thought the skies would open before the bus headed back to Fribourg."

"You remember all of that," he said.

"That was one of the best days I had all year," Bernie said softly. "You appeared when I needed a friend. You just listened, Gary. You were..." she looked away for a moment to steady herself and when she turned her gaze back to him, his eyes were shiny.

"You were, too," he said.

"Nani is not in love with me," Michel protested. "She knows I'm married! And I'm in love with you."

Lucia's smile was tight. "A woman knows her competition, my love."

"There is no competition, Lulu. I am yours, only yours." He took her hand and pressed a kiss to the back of it.

The quartet in the far corner of the restaurant played a swing version of the American song "Winter Wonderland." Michel stood and held out his hand. "Would you dance with me, Lucia?" His brown eyes, unblinking, beseeched hers.

"Please no, Michel. I cannot go out there in front of everyone." She saw the light fade from his face as he nodded.

"It's okay, Lulu. I'll be right back." He looked at her empty glass. "Another orange juice for you?"

Lucia shook her head no. She had just turned down her husband and she wanted to disappear under the table. This is his party, and he wanted to dance with me, she thought. And I am such a hippopotamus that I cannot dance with him. Everyone will laugh at me. She laid a hand on her big belly and fought back tears.

She dabbed at her eyes, careful not to smear the makeup she'd so carefully applied. Looking toward the bar, she saw Nani and Alain there. Nani perched on a stool and Alain leaned against the bar next to her. Lucia watched as Nani reached a hand out and rested it on Michel's shoulder. She seemed to turn all her attention to Michel, Lucia observed. Alain pulled a cell phone from his pocket and took a few steps away from the bar to answer it. Lucia watched the scene unfold from her table. Alain snapped his phone shut and returned to the bar. He bent at the waist and said something in Nani's ear. She turned on the barstool and her hands flew up in the air. He leaned over to kiss her cheek and she swatted him away. Alain shook Michel's hand and walked out of the restaurant with his head down. Didn't Michel say he was a policeman? He must have been called away, Lucia thought. She turned her attention back to the bar, where Nani was now standing in those ridiculously high heels. The band was playing another song now. She recognized this one as "Jingle Bells," a jazzed-up version. Lucia stared as Nani pulled Michel onto the dance floor, far away from where she was seated. They joined a few other couples who were swaying to the music. Michel looked as if he was trying to talk to her. She took his hands and began swinging them with hers. Then Nani drew closer, closer. Her arm reached up to his neck. In those shoes, she almost could reach it.

Lucia couldn't watch any more. She pushed up from the table and made her way out of the restaurant into the lobby. She saw the sign for the ladies' room and headed toward it. I will just lock myself in there until this miserable night is over, she told herself. That woman, Nani, and her red lipstick. Michel was a fool. Any idiot could see what she was doing. And Lucia did not wish to continue witnessing Nani's drunken attempts at seducing her husband.

She took her time in the sanctuary of the restroom, but knew she had to return to the restaurant. When she entered the festive room, the band had stopped playing. She saw her husband back at their table, standing, looking all around the restaurant. From the corner of her eye, she noticed Nani toss back a shot of something at the bar.

Lucia caught her husband's eye. She held up her hand and he rushed to her, past the tables and candles and greenery.

"Lulu," he exclaimed, "I couldn't find you. I was so worried. I asked Nani to find you." He glanced behind her.

"She's still at the bar. I was in the ladies' room. Will you take me home? I'm so tired, Michel."

"Yes, yes, of course, honey, of course. Come, we'll get a taxi now." He waved goodbye to Robert, who was seated at the table. Robert waved and grinned back, his mouth ringed with confectioner's sugar.

Just before they walked out of the restaurant, Lucia turned toward the bar and made eye contact with Nani, who slid off her stool at the bar and was looking around the restaurant. Lucia lifted her chin to the girl and turned to Michel. Knowing she was watching, Lucia took Michel's chin in her hand and pulled him to her. She gave him the most sensuous kiss he'd ever received.

"Amore," Michel groaned, gasping.

Lucia cast one last look at Nani before turning to exit the restaurant. The couple climbed into a taxi as snow flurries began to fall.

CHAPTER EIGHTEEN

The listless waiter brought coffee to Gary and Bernie.

"You're sure you don't want to split a dessert?" His eyes sparkled at her.

"I wish I could, but there isn't any room," Bernie said. She was warmed by the wine, and satisfied by a fine meal. Conversation with Gary had been easy all evening, even the topics that were difficult to broach.

"Well, I wish we didn't live so far away from each other," he said, reaching for her free hand.

"Me too, Gary."

Bernie sipped her coffee and peeked at him over the rim of her cup. He pulled out his credit card and slipped it into the leather folder containing the bill.

"Thank you," she murmured. "This was a perfect meal."

He traced a fingertip across her hand. "Can we talk some more, at the hotel?"

She looked down and nodded, then realized with panic that she didn't have any extra clothes with her, in case he asked her to stay. Was he asking her to stay? Or just to visit, and he'd drive her back to her apartment later? I won't stay with him tonight, it's too soon. Wow, that's really a new Bernie, she thought.

"Um, let's go back to my apartment instead." Seeing the confused look on his face, she added, "It's just more comfortable. I can make coffee, or drinks. We could stay up all night talking."

"Do you have any chocolate?"

"You can't be hungry!" She shook her head and giggled. "But, yeah, I always have chocolate."

"I had a feeling you would," he said.

Back at her apartment, Bernie changed clothes in the walk-in closet, switching the gorgeous dress for jeans and a sweatshirt. She slipped thick socks on her feet and took her stash of Swiss chocolate, in the old Tupperware container, from the cupboard above her kitchen sink. She brought it to the coffee table and set it down.

"There should be something here to satisfy you," she said, fully aware of the double entendre. Bernie sat close to Gary on the sofa and tucked her feet under her. He had taken off his jacket and tie, but still looked uncomfortable.

"I have another sweatshirt, it's really big. Would you rather wear that?"

"Yeah. You don't have any really big sweatpants, too, do you? I'm not used to wearing suits."

Bernie laughed. "I don't think I can help you with that, but wait a sec." She jumped up from the sofa and walked back into her big closet.

"Don't get lost in there," he called. Bernie reappeared with a dark green hooded sweatshirt and tossed it to him. Gary stood up and began unbuttoning his shirt. His eyes met Bernie's as he removed his shirt and he grinned at her. She could see a muscular build under the white tee shirt he wore. He took the sweatshirt from her outstretched hand and pulled it over his head. His hair was mussed up now, and Bernie thought he looked even better. Gary lowered himself back to the sofa, and this time when she crossed the room to join him, he captured her in his arms.

"I think I've waited long enough to kiss you, Bernadette," he whispered.

Bernie parted her lips and kept her eyes open as Gary brought his lips to hers. He began by just touching his lips to hers, then increased the pressure and the urgency. As he slid into a horizontal position, he pulled her on top of him, lips and hands finding their way around each other, charting new territory. When they stopped for a moment to breathe, Bernie raised her head and looked Gary in the eyes.

"Gary."

"Bernie."

"Are you okay with this?"

"Okay with kissing you? Yeah, I'm okay with it." Before he could kiss her again, she hoisted herself up to a sitting position, straddling his knees. Gary raised himself up on his elbows.

"What is it, Bernie?" He reached out to stroke her hair, gathering it in his hands, pressing his fingers to the back of her neck.

"This has to mean something." Bernie swallowed hard.

"Why wouldn't it?"

She hesitated and looked away. "Because many times for me, it hasn't. And this time, it does." She swallowed again and brought her eyes back to his. "Does it for you?"

He kissed her again, soft, light. "Bernie, I couldn't wait to see you this weekend. Our phone conversations, the emails, all of it reminded me why I liked you so much in the first place. We can't bridge twenty-two years in one night. I don't expect us to. But tonight? Tonight I'm here with you, and you are beautiful, and very desirable, and I care for you. I'm not going to hurt you. I'm not going away."

She brushed her fingers along his cheek, traced his jawline to his chin. This was Gary. It was different with him.

"Please stay," she whispered.

The Christmas party was winding down; it would end officially at eleven o'clock, but Nani's shift began at ten. Michel and Lucia had left at nine, and Nani hadn't had anything to drink since then except coffee. She slouched on the stool behind the reception desk, glaring at couples as they floated out of the restaurant with their arms linked, laughing, cooing. It made her sick.

Stupid Alain had left as soon as they'd arrived, and he hadn't even sent her a message since then. He knew how important this night was for her. He knew she'd spent a lot of money on a new outfit. And Michel! First so attentive to her, then all he cared about was that fat cow. He would never be as happy with Lucia as he would be with her, she knew it. How could he not see what was so obvious? No one would ever love him more than she did. No one. She grabbed a piece of paper from the copier. Back at the desk, she found a stack of plain white envelopes in a drawer.

Nani bent over the paper, carefully printing in block letters "I KNOW WHO IS YOUR REAL FATHER. AND I WILL TELL YOU SOON." She folded the paper and slid it into an envelope, then used the same block lettering to print Michel's name and address. She rummaged around in the drawer until she found a sheet of colorful stamps and carefully tore one away from the sheet. She affixed it to the upper right-hand corner of the envelope and pounded it with her fist.

Before she had time to second-guess her actions, Nani walked to the small postbox next to the elevator and dropped the letter inside. There, it would be picked up on Monday and delivered to Michel. She would see him on Tuesday and would be the only one to comfort him, as he would undoubtedly be very upset by the news.

The hotel lobby grew quiet as the guests all returned to their rooms, filled with sandwiches, pastries, and free liquor. Most of the employees had all gone home. Nani wondered if Alain would stop by tonight. She wanted to make him pay for deserting her.

"I have to be out of the room by eleven," Gary said, stretching his long legs next to Bernie's. His bare feet played with hers.

"What time is it," she asked, squinting at the clock. Eight-thirty. They'd stayed up until four, talking, laughing, crying. Well, she cried. Bernie told him all about seeing Michael at the hotel, about Hanna's intervention, and Nani's interference. Told him she left behind the medal for him on her last day, but that she hadn't heard a word from him since. Gary held her close as her emotions washed over them both. They didn't make love, both knowing the timing wasn't right, and it left Bernie wanting him even more. Now, lying next to him in her bed, both of them in tee shirts and Bernie in her yoga pants, she hated that he had to leave.

"Let's shower and dress, then head back to the hotel so I can get my stuff. Is there someplace we could go for brunch?" He raised himself on one elbow and tangled his fingers in her hair.

"There's a Cuban restaurant not far from the hotel. I think they serve brunch."

"Great," he said, rolling out of bed. Gary stood and peeled off his tee shirt. Standing in his boxers, he looked totally at ease. Would he be comfortable standing there naked? Were all guys like that? Were all women so insecure, especially after forty? He wore a devilish grin and said, "We could save water, you know."

"I know," Bernie murmured. "Rain check?" She knew her face was pink from the warmth she felt.

Gary laughed and walked back to the bathroom.

Bernie heard the shower and slid out from the warmth of the covers. When Gary emerged from the bathroom with a white towel around his waist, she hurried in to the steamy shower, giving him time to dress. Bernie had piled her clothes on the floor just outside the door. There was plenty of time for them to be naked together, she reasoned, but it wouldn't be today.

They drove back to the Marriott, where Gary checked out of a room he didn't use. They ate plantain omelets and drank good, strong coffee at Cuban Revolution. Bernie had never felt so at ease in the company of a man, especially one with whom she'd just spent the night. She felt as though she were living inside one of those giant soap bubbles, and that it would pop at any moment.

"You know, Christmas is in ten days," he said as he ate. She watched his long fingers as he held his fork, scooping up the last bit of egg on his plate.

"What are you getting me?" Bernie's eyes danced as she teased Gary.

He grinned. "You may have to wait a week. Would you be able to come to New York for New Year's? I want to spend it with you, Bernie." He set down his fork and wiped his mouth on a napkin. "Please say yes."

She held her coffee mug in both hands, clinging to the last warmth of the cup. "I want to spend it with you, too, Gary. Will you see your kids at Christmas?"

He nodded. "I'm having them the weekend before, and Christmas Eve on Tuesday. They'll go back to Connecticut on the first train Christmas morning."

Her eyes searched his. "I'm really looking forward to meeting them." That wasn't exactly true, but Bernie could be convincing. And she knew it was important.

"Me, too. They'll like you, Bernie."

"God, I hope so," she said without thinking. Seeing his surprise, she added, "I really want them to like me, Gary. I just haven't had much experience around teenagers."

"You'll be great," he said.

Bernie set down her mug and traced her finger around its rim.

"Michael's wife is having a baby. Any day now. Hanna sent an email." She tried so hard to smile. It was happy news, after all. Gary pulled her finger from the mug and held her hand.

"I hate to leave you."

"I know, I feel the same." They stared at each other for a long time, as the coffee turned cold.

Robert's voice was unnecessarily loud. "*Bonjour*, Nani!" He lumbered through the hotel lobby with that idiotic grin on his face, looking like he'd just won the lottery.

"*Salut*, Robert," she muttered, closing her eyes. She looked at the cup of coffee on her desk. What was that, the fifth? Sixth? And still this headache wouldn't go away.

"Did you have a good time at the party, Nani?" Robert shrugged off his coat and pulled that stupid red hat from his big dumb head. He disappeared into the back.

Nani squeezed her eyes shut and tried to remember. Did she have a good time? No, she did not. Alain left her early on, and he didn't even come to visit her during her shift, although he sent a message to her saying he was on assignment and would see her in the morning. This morning. She opened her eyes and saw the yellow postbox that was affixed to the wall next to the elevator. Her eyes grew large as memory came rushing in like a burst dam. The letter. Oh dear God no. The letter to Michel. It would sit locked in that box until tomorrow. And there was nothing she could do to get it out.

"I made a new pot of coffee," Robert shouted as he walked back toward her. "In case you want some before you leave. But if you're going home to sleep, don't drink coffee. Hahaha."

Nani slid from the stool and stretched. One shoulder forward, then the other. Up on her tiptoes, then down. Neck roll to the left, then to the right. Her head felt like there was an iron clamp on it, slowly turning and squeezing her temples together. Screw Alain, she thought. I'm not going to wait for him. It would serve him right.

"Nani, you have to log off," Robert said. "What's wrong with you today, anyway?" He peered at her face and his forehead wrinkled into three horizontal lines.

"Just tired, Robert," she replied in a weary voice. "Really tired, that's all."

She went behind the reception area to get her coat. The snow flurries from last night hadn't accumulated into anything. She'd take the bus back uptown to her apartment, where she would crawl into bed and sleep the day away.

"Goodbye, Robert." She patted his back as she passed him.

"Bye, Nani!" He called after her as she reached the entrance.

Just as she was stepping through the doors, Alain appeared from around the corner. Nani twisted her scarf around her neck.

"*Salut*," he said, bending low to kiss her.

"*Salut*, Alain," she said to the ground. She began walking to the bus stop.

"Nani. Wait." She walked a few more steps and finally turned back to him.

"What is it, Alain?"

"I thought we would visit my mother this afternoon."

"I'm really tired, Alain. I need to sleep. I don't know if it's a good idea." She hunched up her shoulders against the cold.

"Nani, I'm sorry I had to leave the party last night. It couldn't be helped. There was a very important matter at work, and I can't even speak about it. Are you angry with me because of that?" His hands hung limply by his side. He has the biggest hands I've ever seen, Nani thought.

She shook her head. "Don't worry about it. I'm going home to sleep."

The bus pulled up and Nani boarded. Alain climbed aboard after her. She found a seat next to a window, and Alain folded himself to fit in the seat, but his long legs stuck out into the aisle.

"Nani, please. I'm sorry if I made you sad." He turned in his seat to reach for her hand, but they were deep in her pockets and she kept them there.

She looked into his eyes. So blue, so warm, but everything inside her felt frozen. "I just need to be alone, okay, Alain? Okay?" She signaled the driver to stop and stood up. So did Alain, to let her out. She gave him a tight smile and got off the bus without looking back.

CHAPTER NINETEEN

On Tuesday, Klara helped Lucia with her housework; actually, Klara did all the housework. Lucia just couldn't be of much use anymore. She apologized over and over to her mother-in-law, who finally sighed and said "No more apologies, Lucia! I am happy to do this for you. Soon the baby will come and everything changes."

"I wonder if it will arrive on Christmas," Lucia said in a quiet voice. She stroked her belly, thinking about the precious new life inside. Lucia was anxious about the birth; her mother had told her to expect a great deal of pain. Lucia wanted to talk to Klara about it, but Klara had never given birth, so she wouldn't know. And Dr. Schmid had just smiled and said there were plenty of drugs for her when the time came.

"It's possible. But whenever the baby comes, the house will be ready, so you rest and let me take care of everything." She had prepared a casserole of chicken, rice, and mushrooms, and it was ready to go into the oven an hour before Michel came home. Klara would do this every day for her son and his wife. Sometimes she would make enough food so that she and Bruno could join them; other times she left it for the couple to enjoy and returned home to feed her husband.

Lucia lay back against the cushions on the sofa and allowed her heavy eyelids to close. She was just so tired all the time now, likely from not sleeping well at night. Anytime now, baby, she whispered to her stomach, anytime now.

She felt Klara lightly rub her shoulder and opened her eyes to see her mother-in-law standing over her.

"I made tea. And the mailman was early today," she said, holding a few items. She handed them to Lucia, returned to the kitchen, and came back with two mugs of hot tea. She set them down and seated herself.

Lucia surveyed the pieces of mail. Michel took care of the bills. One flyer from a local carpet cleaning company for a discount. And here, what was this? A plain white envelope addressed to her husband in bold black letters. No return address. She held it up to show Klara, whose eyes narrowed.

"What is that?" Klara took the envelope held out to her by Lucia.

Lucia shrugged. "No idea," she said. Klara turned it over in her hands. Very strange, but it was addressed to Michel. Well, he would know soon enough. She replaced it on the table with the others.

As soon as Klara had finished her tea, she stood.

"Dear, I'm going to leave now. Michel will be home soon. I'll put the casserole in the oven, and when he arrives, it will be ready." She bent down to kiss Lucia's forehead and smoothed her hair back in a loving gesture.

"Thank you, mama," Lucia responded, looking up and smiling. "Thank you for everything."

Klara knew that Lucia would doze until Michel came home, and she was happy that her son had no worries about his home or his wife. Klara would see to that.

Nani had not seen or spoken with Alain since Sunday morning. He had called her twice, but when she saw his number on her phone, she didn't answer. He left two messages, one on Sunday, one on Monday, pleading with her to call him. Good, let him beg, she thought. She would call him today, before she went to work, before she saw her darling Michel. The memory of the letter she'd sent still felt like a spiked ball in her stomach, but there was nothing she could do about it now. Besides, she tried to think that something good would come of it. Let it happen, let him tell me about it, so I can comfort him. I have the power because I have the information, she told herself.

She opened her phone and punched in Alain's number.

"Oh, Nani, I've been so worried about you," he said, the words spilling out of him in a rush.

"I'm sorry, Alain. I was not feeling well at all and spent the past two days in bed, just sleeping. I suppose it was some exhaustion from all the extra work at the hotel. But I feel much better now."

She heard his sigh of relief. "Will I see you tonight? Are you going to work?" The urgency in his voice delighted her. Alain was in love, she knew it.

"I hope to see you," she crooned into the phone, using her sultriest voice, knowing the effect it would have on him. "Will you come by at midnight?"

"Yes, Nani, I will see you then. Put a scarf around your neck, please. It's very cold outside."

She cut off the call before he could tell her he loved her, as she knew he was going to do. She slipped the phone back in her purse and looked at the clothes hanging in her closet. What to wear, she mused. This would be the first time she'd see Michel since the party. She recalled being a bit flirtatious with him, especially on the dance floor, but he seemed willing. He danced with her, even held her hand, in spite of his fat wife sitting across the room. Given the right opportunity, Nani had no doubt they would be together. She decided to wear something other than black today. Her fingers flitted through blouses and tunics. She frowned. A sea of black clothes stared back, inky and mournful. Like the old widows back in the village, she thought. Once a widow, always in black. She plucked a pair of soft brown slacks and threw them on the bed. Next, she opened a drawer and found a pale blue sweater folded at the bottom. A gift from her parents, yet she'd never worn it. Hated the color. Well, today she would wear the pale blue sweater. She pulled it over her head and it felt creamy and warm against her skin. She stepped into the slacks and slipped her feet into her brown boots. A thin silver belt around her tiny waist – perhaps it would make Michel think of his wife's enormous belly. Nani patted her flat stomach. I will never have children, she promised herself as she turned sideways and smiled.

Nani surveyed herself in the mirror. She wished her breasts were bigger. Cupping her hands under them, she lifted them high and squeezed them together. She dropped her hands and the little mounds bounced back into place. She opened a carved wooden box that held a few pieces of jewelry and pulled out a silver chain with a small turquoise star attached. She fastened it around her neck.

"Maybe blue isn't so bad," she said. Her shiny black hair fell around her shoulders, curling at the ends.

No red lipstick today, she decided. Just transparent lip gloss and a little mascara. She would look more like Lucia, the innocent. Nani snorted at the memory of Michel's wife, wearing that giant velvet tent at the party, drinking orange juice.

She was ready for work. Nani pulled on her black coat and scarf and locked the door behind her. Today she would walk; it would do her good to be out in the air.

Michel had his coat on when Nani sauntered through the hotel doors. He gathered his things and stuffed them into his messenger bag as she approached him.

"*Salut*, Michel!" She was quick to take off her coat so he could see her sweater. She smiled with her shiny lips and casually tossed her hair over her shoulder.

"Nani, *salut*. Listen, sorry to rush away but I must go. Have a good night," he called over his shoulder as he ran out the door.

Nani stood frozen, her coat on her arm. What just happened here? Not even two minutes for a little conversation? She stamped her booted foot and threw her coat over the copier.

Why the rush? She pouted and glared at the entrance. A thought entered her mind and she felt a pain in her stomach. Was it the letter? Today is Tuesday, she told herself, and the letter should arrive today. Perhaps Lucia called him at work to tell him?

"Calm down," she whispered aloud, then quickly looked around to see if anyone was there. A young couple sat together in the lobby, unaware of her presence.

Lucia anticipated the arrival of her husband, as she did every evening during the week. Until he was in the house, she felt incomplete, just half of a whole. She was grateful for all of Klara's assistance these past few months, but if she were honest, this baby couldn't come soon enough. She was tired, and tired of being pregnant.

She turned off the oven but left the casserole inside. Michel liked a glass of wine with dinner; well, she did, too, but she would not drink during the pregnancy, even if some of the older women told her it was okay. Her mother said she drank wine every day when she was pregnant, and there were no problems with either Lucia or her brother. Still, Dr. Schmid advised her to stay away from alcohol, and she did. She wanted to have the healthiest baby possible.

She sat at the table and waited. Last night, Lucia had dreamt about that girl Nani. In her dream, Michel arrived home with his face covered in bright red kisses, and no amount of washing would get rid of the lipstick. It was as if those kisses were tattooed on him. Nani had branded him, marked him as hers. Lucia wanted to believe that her husband was as faithful to her as she'd always been to him. She'd never wanted anyone but Michel.

As she drummed her fingertips on the tablecloth, she reflected on the conversation they'd had about Bernadette Maguire. Lucia had told him about his birth mother because Klara could not do it.

"Bernadette Maguire?" he'd asked, his eyes wide with amazement. "The woman who stayed in the hotel?"

"The red-haired woman, yes, Michel," Lucia had replied.

"It seems too strange to be true." Michel shook his head from side to side. He brushed a hand over his short hair.

Klara had cried. Bruno, too. And the following evening, with Dr. Schmid a guest for dinner, it was all confirmed. Later that night, in bed, she fingered the silver medal around her husband's neck.

"She must have been very frightened, so young, all alone," Lucia murmured. "I can't imagine going through this pregnancy without you."

"Dr. Schmid said she didn't know who my natural father is," Michel said, lying on his back. "But I'm sure Bernadette knows."

Lucia rested her hand on his chest. "You know who your parents are, *amore*," she said.

Michel turned on his side to face her. "Yes," he said. He chewed on his lip.

Lucia knew her husband; she could tell what he was thinking. "Write to her. She's probably waiting to hear from you."

"She didn't leave an address, Lulu."

"She stayed in your hotel, Michel." He had nodded and turned on his back.

The sound of the door opening brought Lucia back to the present. She waddled into the kitchen to greet her husband.

"I couldn't wait to get home to see you," he said, wrapping her in his arms. Releasing her, he shrugged off his coat and hat and hung them next to the door. He pulled off his boots and slid his feet into slippers.

"Your nose is red," she said with a laugh, cupping a warm hand over it.

"I'm hungry," he growled at her, pretending to bite her neck.

"Okay, okay, can you take the casserole from the oven then? Here, use these, so you don't burn your hands." She passed him two oven mitts and Michel lifted the blue ceramic dish from the oven.

"Look at that bubbly cheese!" he exclaimed. "What treasure lies beneath?"

"Chicken and mushrooms," she said. "Thanks to your mother, of course."

Michel bent his head and took a deep breath.

Lucia nudged him with her hip. "I'll do this, *amore*. You sit down." She spooned mounds of chicken, mushrooms, rice, and cheese onto the plates and carried them to the table, where her husband sat waiting.

As he dug into his meal, she said, "A strange letter arrived for you today with the mail. I set it aside."

He looked up at her. "Okay, but first we enjoy this nice food." Lucia poured a glass of wine, and took a small sip before passing the glass to him. She closed her eyes and smiled.

Once supper was over, Michel relaxed on the sofa and Lucia wrapped the casserole with aluminum foil. There was enough food for another meal, and Michel didn't mind leftovers. Thank you, Klara, she said to herself before joining him on the sofa.

"Okay, let's see this mystery letter," he said. Lucia handed him the plain white envelope. Without looking at the front or back, Michel slipped his index finger under the flap and opened it easily, then pulled out the single sheet of paper and unfolded it.

Lucia watched her husband's face drain of color. His muscles tightened and his jaw set.

"What, Michel?"

He handed her the sheet of paper. Lucia gasped and looked at him.

"Where is this coming from?" She stared at the paper again.

Michel balled his hands into fists and looked to the ceiling. "I don't know, but I don't like this at all. I don't care who my natural father is! I don't care! I have a father. His name is Bruno Eicher. My mother is Klara Eicher. The woman who gave birth to me is named Bernadette Maguire. Someone is trying to cause problems for us, Lulu, and I won't have it." The veins in his neck stood out. "Who would do this?"

Lucia took the envelope and held it close to her face. "It's postmarked from Fribourg, yesterday. It didn't come from Bernadette, she's long gone back to America." She shook her head.

Michel grunted. "She wouldn't do that, anyway."

One thought entered Lucia's mind, one name. She would not speak it aloud, though. She closed her teeth over her tongue and stayed silent.

"I have an enemy, Lulu. Plain and simple. Someone is trying to hurt me."

At five minutes before midnight, Alain's large figure appeared in the doorway and Nani walked slowly to the front to let him in. He towered over her, his face a combination of concern and desire.

"Oh Nani, you are beautiful in that color," he groaned, reaching out to take her in his arms. Nani jumped up to grab him around the neck, and her legs wrapped around his waist. She knew there was no one to see them, and she didn't care, anyway. They stood there like that, in the empty hotel lobby, and he kissed her hard. Nani moaned softly into his mouth and kissed him back with an urgency that surprised her.

"I want you so bad," she whispered. "All I could think of was you these past few days. You're everything to me, do you know that, Alain? Don't ever let me go."

With her legs still wrapped around him, Alain walked back to the reception area, where he set her on the desk. Now their faces were nearly at the same level, and he kissed her again, his hungry mouth on hers.

Nani was lost in him. He was Michel to her. As long as she thought only of Michel when they were together, everything would be fine. She desired him. She loved him.

Alain covered her small breast with his massive hand. "I wish I could take you right here on the desk," he muttered. "I need you, Nani. I need you so bad."

"We can't, my love," she said softly. "Not here. Your wife—" Her eyes flew open.

"My wife? You know I don't have a wife, Nani." He pressed his body against hers.

"No, I meant to say someone might come downstairs." She kissed him again and made him forget all about her little slip-up.

"I'm taking you home in the morning. Nani, I want to give you everything." He cupped her chin in his hand and searched her dark eyes. "I'm so in love with you, Nani."

"I'm in love with you, too," she said. Michel. I'm so in love with you. "Alain."

They kissed again, and exercised remarkable restraint on the reception desk at the Hotel de la Rose. When Alain left a half hour later to return to work, Nani waved goodbye and drew little hearts all over the magazine in front of her.

Karl Berset telephoned an old friend. Henri Rutz was retired from the Fribourg police department and now worked as a private detective. He and Karl became friends when Karl worked at the bank in Fribourg, and they usually met once a month for drinks. The two men shared similar interests: single-malt whiskey, downhill skiing, and pretty girls.

"Karl! *Salut*, old buddy. How's everything?"

Karl didn't tell Henri that he'd taken a small apartment, leaving Ella and the kids in the house. He still wasn't welcome there, according to Ella.

"Not bad, Henri, not bad. Er, well, I do have a small problem, and I'm hoping you can help."

"Sure. Anything, Karl, what do you need?"

"Can you meet me for a drink this evening? There's a café inside the train station, the Express."

"Six o'clock? I'll see you there."

"Thanks," said Karl, snapping the phone shut.

At a few minutes after six that evening, Karl sat with a tall glass of lager in front of him, his third. He spotted Henri as he approached and stood to shake his hand. Henri sat across from him, pointing to the beer when the waitress walked over.

Henri Rutz was the kind of guy who blended into backgrounds very well, which was necessary for undercover work and surveillance. Even if someone noticed him, there was really nothing that person would remember about him later. Medium build, dark hair. No distinguishing features. Karl looked at Henri and almost laughed.

"What's funny, Karl? Thought you said you had a problem." Henri tugged on his lower lip.

Karl sucked down half of his beer and wiped his mouth. The smirk disappeared. "I do have a problem." He took a breath. "Many years ago, I had an affair with an American college student."

Henri laughed loudly. "You had an American girl every year! So what?"

"So one of them got pregnant. I never knew; I cut off the affair after one weekend. She was, I don't know, she wasn't someone I wanted to continue to see."

Henri nodded. "You conquered her and moved on?" Now it Henri's turn to smirk at his friend.

Karl looked away for a moment. "I guess. Anyway, I never saw her again." He snapped his fingers. "Wait, yes I did. I was with Ella and I did see her, but I didn't speak to her." Karl finished his beer and suppressed a burp. "That was in 1979. She showed up at my house last month."

Henri perked up. "What? What do you mean, showed up at your house?"

"She showed up! Twenty years later, she's on my doorstep! She must have found me, found my address. You know how that is," he said with a dark look. "She told me she had a child, my child, and she said she gave it up for adoption."

"Wait, you said the girl was American."

"She was here on vacation, I don't know. Had an old lady with her, an aunt or something."

"You think she came back to find the kid?" Henri took a long drink.

"Maybe. It's a fucking nightmare right now." Karl picked up his empty glass, looked around for the waitress and, not seeing her, set the glass down.

"So this American girl, this woman, shows up at your house twenty years later and tells you she had your baby? Was Ella there?" Henri's dark eyes locked on Karl's face, and Karl knew Henri could always spot a lie. Besides, this was his old friend, and he had to confide in someone.

"Yeah. She opened the door. The girl, uh, the woman pretended to be lost. She asked for directions from Ella. I was behind Ella and as soon as I saw her, I recognized her."

"Even after all this time?" Henri saw the waitress and signaled for two more beers. This was turning out to be far more interesting than he'd expected. He rested his stubbly chin in his hand and waited for Karl to continue.

Karl cut his eyes to the side, remembering. "Her hair, it was this coppery red. Great body. Very memorable," he added, smiling. "I was speechless, Henri. Yeah, I'd had girls back then, you were right, but none of them ever came after me. When I was done with them, I moved on. Funny, but I don't think I can even picture the other ones. But this one, I remembered her right away."

"And Ella?"

Karl raked his hand through his thinning hair. "Not good. Her patience ran out, I think. Whatever I tried to say to her, it didn't matter." He exhaled loudly. "I'm not living at home these days."

Henri lowered his voice. "What can I do for you now, Karl?"

"The girl, her name is Bernadette, she said she gave up the child for adoption. That baby had to have been born here. I remember we were together shortly after the students arrived, sometime in September. I want to find out where the child is. Bernadette didn't say if it was a boy or a girl. It would be the same age as my son Paul, twenty-three."

Henri pulled a small notebook from the pocket of his jacket. "Her name," he said, his pen hovering over the paper.

"Bernadette Maguire. M-A-G-U-I-R-E. Good thing my memory is still sharp."

Henri nodded. "Where does she live now?"

"The States, I would imagine. I don't know where."

Henri scribbled. "And you think the baby was born in Fribourg? At the hospital?"

Karl nodded. "Yeah. Ella was with Dr. Hanna Schmidt at the hospital in Fribourg. Bernadette may also have gone to her."

"Okay, so the baby was born in...1979? I'll start with that," Henri said, tucking the little notebook away. "I'll find your child, Karl. But be sure you want to find him. Or her. Are you sure?"

"Yes," said Karl. I can get to Bernadette though this child, he thought. She had no right to do this to me. His eyes darkened again. "Yes, Henri. And thanks." The men stood and shook hands again before Henri disappeared into the crowd.

CHAPTER TWENTY

Bernie spent Christmas Day at Joanie and Lou's house, with Joan, the twins, and Lou's parents. Family members on the DiGenova side of the family stopped in throughout the day. After a quiet Christmas Eve by herself, she was happy to be in the company of others. She and Gary had talked on the phone around midnight, after his kids had gone to sleep. He was going to put them on the early train to Connecticut in the morning.

"If I had a car, I could drive down to see you," she said to Gary.

"I know you, Bernie; you'd rather ride the train." She laughed. "I guess you're right about that. Can't wait to see you, Gary. You know."

"I know, and I feel the same way. Counting the days."

Joanie loved a house full of people. There were eight for dinner, and Joanie had outdone herself, again. With help from Joan and Connie DiGenova, there wasn't an inch of table or counter space that wasn't covered with food: turkey, a small ham, lasagna, countless side dishes, trays of decorated cookies. Bernie looked at the spread and felt guilty; her contribution had been beer, wine, and soda, even as she'd promised herself to take it easy on the alcohol consumption.

Once they were all seated around the table, Joanie stood. Bernie saw tears in her eyes and prayed that her sister wouldn't lose it right before Christmas dinner.

"A toast to all of us," she began, then fixed her eyes on her younger sister. "And to our parents, who are looking down on us from Heaven," she pronounced in a shaky voice. She raised her wine glass.

"Cheers," everyone replied in unison. Even the twins were permitted a little wine this year.

"So I hear you're spending New Year's Eve in the Big Apple," he said on the drive from Cranston to Providence. Lou always brought Bernie back to the city. Joan had asked her to stay the night, but Bernie wanted to be in her own bed. And she wanted to talk to Gary in the privacy of her own place.

"Yeah, an old friend from college invited me down," Bernie said. The highway was deserted. Everyone was where they were meant to be, she supposed.

"That's what Joanie said. The guy who sent you the card, right?" He glanced at Bernie. She grinned at Lou.

"Yeah. Gary Baptista. We kind of found each other after all these years, I guess."

"Glad for ya, Bernie. Hope it all works out." Lou kept his hands on the wheel just the way they'd been taught when they were teenagers. Ten minutes to two.

"Thanks, Lou." Bernie stared down at her lap.

Lucia went into labor at eight o'clock on Christmas night, but she didn't deliver until the following day at nine in the morning. A boy, weighing six pounds and eleven ounces, with jet-black hair and perfect little features, was born on the feast of Saint Stephen. Michel sat in a chair next to his wife's bed and watched as she nursed their son. She knew she'd made him very happy. Both sets of parents were waiting outside the hospital room, waiting to greet their new grandson.

"So, Lulu, have you decided on a name yet? The nurses were asking." Her husband's wide grin split his face in two.

She looked at him with her light blue eyes and said, "I think Jean-Bernard. That is his name. Jean-Bernard." Her eyes held his. Michel looked down and his shoulders shook.

"*Amore*, what is it?"

He raised his head. Fresh tears lined his cheeks. "I couldn't be happier than I am right now, Lulu. We are a family."

The baby finished nursing and a nurse appeared in the doorway. Lucia touched her husband's arm.

"You should write to her and let her know. We can have someone take a picture of the three of us. But you should write to her, Michel." He nodded through his tears.

Not that it mattered much, but Bernie closed down her law practice for two weeks, from before Christmas to after New Year's. She didn't have much work these days, and she'd tied up the loose ends before going to Switzerland with Joan in October. Once in a while she'd get a good case, or at least someone who could pay her, but she began to question the whole notion of running her own practice. The question was, what would she do? She was forty-four years old with a law degree and a less-than-stellar resume. It wasn't like her phone was ringing with offers.

She took a taxi to the train station on New Year's Eve. The cab dropped her off in front of the entrance, and when she stepped out of the cab, she was looking directly at the Drop Off. It was too early; they'd open at eleven and likely would be packed until closing. Bernie reflected on past New Year's Eves, when she'd spend hours on the same barstool, her barstool, drinking vodka tonics, chatting with Norm, surveying the men who entered. She didn't care if they were married or not; they filled some kind of emptiness inside her, but it was always temporary. The married men left right afterwards. They had somewhere to go. The single guys, mostly losers, wanted to stay longer than she could stand having them there, whining about their exes and how much they were costing them. Bernie closed her eyes for a moment and she couldn't see any of their faces. All those faceless, nameless men. When she opened her eyes, she turned away from the bar and walked purposefully into the train station.

She bought a ticket at the Amtrak window and descended below ground to the tracks. Cold and gray, concrete and steel. Her train arrived on time from Boston, and she climbed aboard, finding an empty seat next to a window. The train would arrive at Penn Station just before two. Gary had sounded so excited on the phone last night and Bernie smiled at the memory. He'd convinced her to stay until Friday, so she could meet his kids before she returned to Providence. She'd assured him that she wasn't interested in doing touristy things, which was true. This was their time, a chance for them to see what it was like to be together for an extended period of time. It was important to Bernie to see how they got along under regular, normal circumstances. Gary was special, she knew. She also knew they were both flawed, both damaged. She stared out the window at the platform, and the people there: passionate kisses, friendly hugs, handshakes. Coming and going. She wasn't sure where she was going, but she felt more hopeful than she had in a very long time.

The seats filled quickly and the car was alive with excited voiccs. Of course, it was New Year's Eve, and people were heading to Times Square. Bernie looked around and realized that most of the passengers on the train were easily twenty years younger than she was. She remembered the anticipation of travel, and being young enough to not care about all the comforts of home. There was a time when she would crash at someone's apartment and sleep on the floor. A time when she would wear yesterday's clothes and not care, when she could subsist on beer and bread if she had to.

"Is this seat free?"

Bernie turned at the voice and looked up into the face of a young man of maybe twenty, no doubt a college student. She smiled and nodded and he hoisted his backpack to the shelf above, giving her a glimpse of a chiseled abdomen with just a trace of dark hair marching south from his navel. She looked away and rummaged through her bag, feeling the heat on her face. He fell into the seat beside her and brushed against her arm.

"Sorry!"

Bernie looked into a pair of crystal-blue eyes. My God, he looks like Jake Gyllenhaal, she thought. Her breath got stuck in her lungs for a moment. He grinned at her, showing a brilliant smile, and said, "Hey, I'm Tyler." Tyler. Of course you're Tyler. Good Lord, you are indeed Tyler.

"Bernadette," she said quietly. Her name sounded better when spoken in a quiet voice, she'd decided long ago. She could feel the blood pounding in her temples. Good thing Gary and I have decided to have sex this weekend, she thought. I'm probably old enough to be this kid's mother, she told herself. Well, sure, if Michael is twenty-three, then yeah, I could be his mother.

"You heading to Times Square?" Bernie glanced at his thighs, straining against faded denim. There was a small hole in the fabric just above his knee. She willed herself to stay focused and look in his eyes, not at his thighs.

"Um, no. I'm going to visit a friend for a few days," she managed to say. She wanted a drink in the worst way. Gary. Gary. Gary. She forced herself to picture Gary. Gary's face on Tyler's magnificent, young body.

Bernie flashed back to New Year's Eve in Fribourg, when she took the train to Bern by herself and saw that cute guy, the one she fantasized about until he was met on the platform by his wife and son. She remembered the one night with Timmy Lyon, when her hormones simply couldn't be controlled. What is it about New Year's Eve, she asked herself. Nothing's going to happen with this boy, it wasn't even a possibility. She just liked to remember. I'll save it all for Gary. I'll be a tiger with him tonight.

"You look happy," said Tyler. He smelled delicious, all citrusy and virile.

Bernie turned her forty-four-year old face to Tyler and said, "It's New Year's Eve, who wouldn't be happy." Then she gave him the kind of smile a mother would give a son. Close the door on that fantasy, Bernadette.

"Cool beans," he said, and plugged his earphones into his ears. Bernie pulled a book out of her bag and stared at the words on the page.

Alain proposed to Nani on New Year's Eve, catching her way off guard. Earlier that afternoon, she'd met his mother, an imposing woman whose face remained impassive during their entire fifty minute visit. Nani had turned on the charm, and Madame Bouchard smiled back at her, until Alain left the room. Then she scowled at Nani and said nothing until he returned. Nani wondered if perhaps Alain had told her about the impending proposal. She was sure Madame Bouchard would not have approved.

After they'd left Madame's big, cold house, Alain brought Nani to a pretty place outside of Fribourg, a little park overlooking a lake. No one was around on such a cold day, and Nani wished they were someplace warm instead. She was just about to complain to Alain when he dropped to one knee in front of her. Surprise turned to shock when he held out a small velvet box.

Only a week ago they'd spent Christmas Eve together. Alain had presented Nani with a thin gold bracelet, and she was ecstatic.

"Oh, Alain!" she'd cried out when she saw the bracelet. She slipped it on her little wrist and admired it. She regretted for a moment that she'd bought him only a scarf, but the guilty feeling passed. "Nani, I want to cover you with gold. You are a princess," he said to her as she nestled in his lap.

She gave him the scarf. "This is for when I cannot be there to wrap my arms around your neck," she cooed into his ear.

Maybe she should have realized that the bracelet was kind of a rehearsal gift. She reacted to it the way he wanted, so he forged ahead with his plan. And here she was, freezing her ass off, while he knelt before her like some medieval prince. She took the little box from his outstretched hand and lifted the top. The ring took her breath away. She stared at the flawless round diamond set in gold. It was huge.

"Nani darling, you would make me the happiest man on earth if you would say yes." She pulled her eyes away from the sparkling ring to meet his. "Be my wife, Nani."

She knew the seconds were ticking by and he was waiting. Say yes, she told herself silently, you can always back out later.

"Yes!" she blurted, startling herself.

"Yes?" Alain stayed in a kneeling position and she nodded.

"Yes, Alain, yes. I will marry you." She swallowed down a strange taste that had risen in her throat.

He plucked the ring from the box, and pulled the glove from her left hand.

"Your fingers are so tiny," he murmured, "like a child's." He slipped the ring on her finger. It dominated her little hand. Alain gathered her into his arms and pulled her close. As she wrapped her arms around him, she gazed over his shoulder at the ring, and wondered how much he'd paid for it.

They walked to a small bistro where Alain said he knew the owner. At the entrance, Alain whispered something to the man, whose fat face beamed. He leered at Nani.

"Congratulations, Alain!" He slapped Alain on the back and thrust his sweaty, pink face at Nani. "And aren't you the perfect little specimen," he purred. "Ripe for plucking, eh?"

She wanted to kick him in the balls. Fat pig, she thought, he's not coming to the wedding. The owner led them to a private room in the rear of the restaurant.

"The chef has made a special meal for us, sweetheart," said Alain, holding Nani's chair for her. "Roasted lamb with rice pilaf and root vegetables. To celebrate our engagement."

Nani gave Alain a quizzical look. She bent her head toward him and said in a low voice, "You were sure of my answer then, Alain?"

He reddened and took a sip of water. "If you had said no, I would have called him to tell him," Alain stammered, much to Nani's amusement. Alain's friend brought a bottle of champagne to the table and winked at Nani. She glared at him. With a flourish, he popped the cork and filled glasses for both of them.

"Keep refilling her glass, Alain," he said with a nudge. God, he was obnoxious, Nani thought.

Alain raised his glass just as a waiter appeared with plates of Greek salad. He paused until the waiter set the plates down and left.

"A toast to us, my love. To a long future together, and a house filled with children!"

His smile faded as he looked at her face. She tried to smile, but it was futile, she knew.

"What, Nani? You do want children, don't you?"

Nani squirmed in her seat and looked at her ring again. "Of course, sweetheart. But not right away," she offered. Her eyes met his and she batted her thick dark eyelashes at him. That usually worked.

"No, that's fine, dear. Not immediately. But you know, I'm almost thirty years old, so we shouldn't wait too long." His enormous hand slid across the table toward hers. Quickly she picked up her glass with her right hand and slipped her left hand under the table.

"As long as I have some time alone with you," she whispered. "I wish it was just us in this restaurant right now." She held his eyes and he blinked rapidly.

Stretching her leg all the way out, she trailed her boot up his leg under the table and watched his eyes widen. Her foot would only reach midway up his thigh. She grinned wickedly at him, enjoying his embarrassment.

"Let's eat first, shall we?" He cleared his throat and dug into his salad.

The owner approached their table, carrying a bottle of red wine.

"From my special collection, a gift for the happy couple," he said, placing the bottle on the table. "Alain, if you can't drive back to Fribourg, I'll arrange for a ride. Don't get into trouble tonight if you drink too much. They won't care that you're a police officer."

Turning away from Alain, he smiled at Nani, and when her eyes met his, he ran a chubby tongue over his greasy lips.

Michel was on leave until January 4. Jean-Bernard was a good baby, and there was no shortage of love and attention given to him. Klara was all too happy to help, and it warmed Michel's heart to see his wife and his mother get along so well. Klara had never known the pain of childbirth, and she wept for Lucia's ordeal, but both women were overjoyed with the tiny life that now completed the family. Lucia's mother had only stayed for a day, then made an excuse about having an important meeting in Milano. Michel sensed she wasn't comfortable around babies, especially since Lucia had confided that she and her brother were mostly raised by a nanny.

While mother and baby slept, Michel sat at his desk and pulled paper from a drawer. He didn't want to send an email to Bernadette, even though it would have been easier. He wrote out what he wanted to say to her, checked his English, then copied it onto the stationary in neat, cursive handwriting.

Dear Bernadette,

Lucia and I want you to know about our new baby. Jean-Bernard Eicher was born on December 26, 2002, at 9:02 a.m. He is a healthy and beautiful boy as you will see in the photograph.

I'm sorry I haven't written to you earlier. I know that you are the woman who gave birth to me in 1979. And I understand why you didn't tell me when you were here, but now I also understand better your tears and emotions upon seeing me for the first time at the hotel. You did a very selfless thing at what must have been an extremely difficult time, and Lucia and I decided to name the baby in your honor.

Someday perhaps we can all meet. My parents are wonderful people, and my wife would very much like to know you. If you decide to return to Switzerland, please let me know. You will be my guest at the hotel.
Sincerely,
Jean-Michel

P.S. Thank you for the medal of Saint Michael, which I wear on my neck all the time.

Michel read over what he had written and was satisfied. He knew some of it was a bit formal, but he was writing to his birth mother, after all, and letting her know that he knew about her. She would no doubt be very surprised to read that.

He slipped a photograph of the three of them into the envelope and sealed it. Lucia was right, he was able to find her address from the credit card receipt, and he printed it on the face of the envelope.

The post office would be open until noon. He'd be sure to mail the letter today.

He turned the envelope over in his hand and thought about the strange note he'd received a couple of weeks back. Someone had information about his natural father. Michel frowned. Did he want to know who had fathered him and abandoned Bernadette? He could ask her; perhaps she would tell him, if she knew. Maybe she'd had a brief fling with someone, a stranger. Do I really need to know, he wondered. Dr. Schmidt had said she didn't know who the father was. He shook his head; the last thing he wanted to do was to upset his family. He opened his bag, where he'd placed the anonymous letter. Pulling out the envelope, he squinted at the block lettering. What was it about this envelope that seemed familiar? It was a plain white business envelope, like any other. The lettering was indecipherable. He couldn't figure it out, so he replaced the envelope in his bag.

"Are you sure you don't want to go to Times Square? Watch the ball drop?" Gary's eyes were sparkling with merriment.

"Quite sure," Bernie replied. "I am very happy to stay right here with you." She wrapped her arms around his waist and pressed closer. His shirt was soft against her cheek, and smelled like clean laundry. She breathed in deeply.

There were two white bags from Dean & Deluca on the counter, filled with their New Year's Eve feast. Bernie had stressed she didn't want to go out, so Gary had picked up roast chicken, salads, crusty bread, and a couple of bottles of wine. They spread the food on the low table and sat on the floor.

Gary's apartment was really small, but Bernie didn't mind. She was used to living in a compact space, and she was so comfortable with Gary that the close quarters worked to their advantage. When the kids came to stay, one of them took his bed, one slept on the futon on the alcove, and Gary kept an inflatable mattress handy, he explained.

They watched television in bed, made love twice that night, and slept until noon on New Year's Day. Over coffee and bagels, they filled in more of the gaps of twenty-two years. Lives lived and mistakes made. He talked about his children a lot, and Bernie could tell he missed having them in his life all the time.

"Justin's a mature kid. There were some anger issues when Roxana and I first split, some acting out in school, you know, getting into fights, that sort of thing, but he's seventeen now and it seems that he's really grown up in the past year. I know he doesn't like her boyfriend, and I think he can't wait to go away to college next year. From some of the things he says when we're together, I know he still has some resentment."

"Toward you?" Bernie spread cream cheese in a thin, transparent layer on half a toasted sesame bagel.

"Toward both of us, I think. He sees divorce everywhere, Bernie. Most of his friends don't live in what we would have considered a traditional household. Families are defined in all sorts of ways. His friend Alex has two dads. Nicole's best friend Lola has two moms. A lot of kids have one parent living at home, or two adults living together, with kids from other relationships." He stared across the room. "Whatever the child understands as normal is what they want to continue. Do you know what I mean?"

"Yeah, but kids are resilient. They can bounce back more easily, right?"

Gary rubbed his eyes. "I'll always be their dad, and my job is to make sure they know that. That they can come to me for anything and I'll still be their father. But Phil, that's Roxana's boyfriend, Phil's going to be a part of their lives, too." He smiled at Bernie. "You'll meet them on Friday. That's why I wanted you to stay 'til then. They're coming in on the train, about an hour before you head back. We'll have a chance to spend some time together."

"I don't want to think about heading back just now," she said, tracing her index finger along his shoulder.

He bent his neck to kiss her, and licked a bit of cream cheese from the side of her mouth.

"As much as I would like to take you back to bed, Bernadette, I'm a little worn out from last night. How about a walk through Central Park?"

She grinned. "Perfect. And it's not too cold today, either."

"No, but dress in layers. Once the sun goes behind the buildings, it does get cold." He brought the plates to the sink and swept crumbs from the table.

"Gary?"

"Yeah, babe." His back was to her as he washed the mugs and plates and set them on a drying rack. She crept up behind him.

"Best New Year's ever for me." He turned, his hands dripping with soapy water.

"For me, too," he said in a soft voice. She took his wet hands and led him to the shower.

CHAPTER TWENTY-ONE

Nani had a wedding to plan. She called her parents to tell them the good news. She could picture the two of them, both trying to listen in on the one telephone in the house.

"We have not met him," her mother complained. "You cannot marry a man we haven't met."

"I will not permit it," her father bellowed into the phone.

"What is his last name?" her mother inquired.

"You cannot marry a policeman," her father shouted.

"French? Oh, Nani," her mother sighed. "It will never work."

She ended up yelling back at them and ended the call abruptly. Then she fell on her bed and cried. Why was her life so difficult? Why could her parents not be happy for her? She sent money home to them every month. She wanted more from life than to live in the same backwards village as her family had for countless generations. These days, most of the young people were leaving, and all that was left in the village was to wait for death. Nani refused to be part of it. Switzerland offered her hope, an opportunity to work, to advance, to make money. Alain wanted to marry her, and even if she didn't love him as much as he loved her, she would marry him. And not in Greece, either; they would marry here, in Fribourg, as soon as possible. Perhaps she would send a note to her parents after the wedding. After it was all over.

She would talk to Alain. He would take care of everything. Nani turned over to lie on her back and stare at the ceiling. Perhaps she could love Alain in time. She would try. He was a good man, honorable and decent. Perhaps in time she would stop thinking about Michel every time they made love.

Michel was still home with the new baby. He had emailed a photograph to the staff, and Nani saw the happy threesome smiling on the computer. Someone, probably that idiot Robert, had printed the photograph and hung it next to the coffeemaker, so every time she refilled her cup she had to look at them. The little baby was very cute, she had to admit. They named the baby Jean-Bernard, it said in the message. Interesting, Nani thought, to include Bernadette Maguire's name in the baby's name. So then everyone must know that Bernadette had given birth to Michel, and they were all fine with it. She grimaced at the memory of the anonymous letter she'd written the night of the Christmas party. Nani stretched her arms toward the ceiling. Michel had never said a word about the note she'd written when she was drunk and jealous, and Nani assumed that his wife had intercepted the letter and destroyed it. Better that way, anyway, she told herself. I will not interfere with their happiness. I will create my own happy life.

She wore a dark red tunic over black leggings. Little by little, Nani was adding color to her wardrobe. Can't always wear black, she thought. It's 2003, a new year. Let it be a new start for Alain and me. I will make him happier than any man could possibly be.

The diamond sparkled on her finger, and she reveled in all the attention she'd received when she showed up for work the first night. She wondered what Michel's reaction would be when he saw it. Surprise? Relief? Perhaps both.

Lucia opened her eyes and squinted at Michel, who was standing next to the bed, smiling down at her.

"Where are you going so early in the morning?" she whispered. The baby slept soundly in the crib next to the bed. "You don't go back to work until tomorrow."

"Migros," he replied. "I want to get the grocery shopping done early today. Maybe I will even cook tonight!" He leaned down to kiss his wife. "Go back to sleep, Lulu." He stopped to lay a finger on his baby's tiny head, then headed out of the bedroom.

Michel hopped the bus and rode into town. He wanted to do something for his wife, and also for his mother, to show his appreciation for all the help she'd given since the baby was born. Klara had been doing everything for the past two weeks, and tonight Michel would invite them to dinner. At the same time, he knew he wasn't much of a cook, so he wanted to find something easy to prepare. Maybe a shrimp curry with rice. Migros stocked plenty of ready-made food.

He held a basket in his hand as he navigated through the market aisles.

"Michel!" He turned at the sound of his name and looked up as the towering figure of Alain Bouchard approached. Michel stuck out his hand and Alain grabbed it, pumping hard.

"*Salut*, Alain!" Michel wished him a Happy New Year and told him about the new baby.

"Yes, Nani said you emailed a picture, and she said the baby is very cute," Alain said. He stuck his hands in his pockets and scuffed his shoe on the floor.

"Tomorrow I go back to work. It's been good to be home with Lucia and the baby, but today is the last day." He gestured to his empty basket. "I'm cooking tonight, but trust me, I'm going with prepared food!"

Alain cleared his throat. "Um, have you spoken with Nani?"

"No. Is she okay?"

"Then you don't know?" Alain rocked back and forth on his heels.

Michel's perplexed look fueled Alain.

"We're engaged to be married!" When Alain grinned, which wasn't often, Michel could see all the way to his back teeth. He looked like a horse, a very happy tall horse.

Michel shook his hand again. "That's great news! Congratulations, Alain. When will you marry?"

"Very soon, I hope." Michel averted his eyes and Alain added quickly, "No, she's not pregnant."

"No, I didn't..." Michel faltered and felt stupid. "Of course not, Alain. Either way, it wouldn't matter."

"We just have to clear the paperwork. It will be a small wedding. Um, Nani's family is in Greece and cannot travel here for the ceremony. So we'll marry in Fribourg, maybe travel to her home one day." He looked off in another direction.

"Well, that's excellent news. I will be sure to tell Lucia." Michel turned to leave, then stopped. "Alain?"

"Yes?"

"Maybe you could help me with something, since you're a police officer. I, well, I received an anonymous letter a few weeks ago."

"What?" Alain seemed to grow a few inches with this news.

"There was no return address, but it was postmarked from Fribourg. It wasn't a threatening letter, but indicated that someone had information I might be interested in. That's all I ever heard since then, nothing more. I was just wondering if there was a way to find out who sent it."

Alain rubbed his hand against his cheek. His eyebrows became one as he thought.

"Hmm, that would be difficult, Michel. If no one made a threat to you or your family, the police department probably wouldn't get involved. And there was no extortion, right? All kinds of fingerprints would be on it by now."

"No, no request for money, no threats. It was just weird. Well, thanks anyway." Michel picked his shopping basket up off the floor.

"The only other way would be to get DNA from the stamp. You know, the person licks the stamp and leaves DNA on it. I saw that on a television show. I watch those American police shows a lot."

Michel tried to keep a straight face. That method may work on a television show, but trying to get DNA from a stamp? Who would do it? Alain had already said the police wouldn't get involved.

"Okay, well, thanks again. Like I said, it's no big deal."

"Well, if anything else happens, if you get another letter, you be sure to let me know."

"I will. See you, Alain."

"See you, Michel."

Michel was still chuckling to himself when he reached the cashier. She looked at him and smiled, a big gummy smile. "Well, aren't you in a good mood today!" She batted her eyelashes at him. There was a tiny diamond stud on the side of her nose and a large pimple on her shiny chin.

Michel smiled and used his left hand to place items on the belt, so she could see his wedding band. "I'm a new father," he said, trying not to look at the pimple.

"Great," she muttered, ringing up his purchases as quickly as she could. He grinned at her anyway.

Bernie awoke on Friday morning with a sense of dread, then realized it was because she would return to Providence on the evening train. She didn't want to leave Gary. As she lay in his bed, listening to his even breathing, she thought back. Her life had been non-stop, out of her control, it seemed, since her mother died. October brought the wake and funeral, the reappearance of Timmy Lyon after decades, truth and tears, recrimination, and finally, some peace. Then, after a couple of weeks, it was off to Switzerland with Joan. Seeing Michael, tamping down emotions. An unresolved desire to be closer to her son, and the realization that she couldn't trespass in his life, his world. Back home in November and the beginning of this thing with Gary. This thing! This relationship. Bernie closed her eyes. She wasn't used to having relationships; she had affairs, flings, one-night stands. Gary, who'd been such a good friend to her while she was focused on the likes of Timmy Lyon and Karl Berset. Bernie recalled thinking of Hanna Schmidt as her safe harbor while she was pregnant. Now she thought of Gary that way. Gary was shelter, a place where she could stay anchored. She wanted to be by his side.

She was nervous about returning to Providence. Her law practice was limping along; she could pay the bills but hadn't saved much money over the years. And she had no real girlfriends. The past twenty years had been all about Bernie, and the men who slithered in and out of her life. Lisa, her best friend from college, had her own life out west with Maggie, and the little girl they'd adopted from China a couple of years ago. Bernie had mended her relationship with Joanie, somewhat, but they would never be best friends.

"Morning," Gary murmured. He rolled toward her and draped one arm over her stomach. His fingers tickled her bare hip.

Bernie turned to him and pressed as close as she could. "Tell me it's not Friday already."

"I wish it weren't," he whispered back. "Bernie, I don't want you to leave. But for now, it's what we have. I was hoping the idea of practicing law in New York might have entered your mind." His eyes locked on hers. There were tiny flecks of gold in his irises. His eyeglasses lay on the table next to the bed; Gary was blind without them. Though he wore contact lenses most of the time, she liked him in his German professor glasses, as she referred to them.

Bernie swallowed back emotion and looked away.

"What is it, honey? What is it?" Gary's finger touched the outer corner of her eye.

She buried her face in his neck. "I have thought about it. I don't want to go home."

He pulled her even closer and turned her face up to his.

"I remember when you said that to me in Schwarzsee. Bernadette, this much I know. I love you. I do. I loved you way back in Fribourg, but I didn't have the courage to tell you, and besides, I don't think you were open to it then. But I loved you."

His words pierced her heart. She never gave him a chance to show her back then, but he loved her. All those years ago.

"Gary, I have a lot of regrets." He put a finger to her lips to stop her from saying anything more.

"No looking back, unless there's a lesson to be learned from it. Go back to Providence tonight. I'll come to you next weekend, okay?" She nodded and held on.

Was this crazy? They were so comfortable together, so normal. This was only five days, though. Not long. Her time in New York had passed so quickly. If she could just keep herself busy for the week, he'd come back to her.

Gary's body shifted against hers, and she responded. She made love to him as if she might never see him again.

CHAPTER TWENTY-TWO

Nani was lying on the sofa in the back room when she heard the front doors open. She checked her watch – it wasn't even seven o'clock yet. But then she heard him call her name. It was Michel. Why was he at work on this Friday, she wondered. He wasn't due back until Monday.

She stayed where she was and kept her eyes closed. Wouldn't it be wonderful if he crept in and kissed me in my sleep, she thought. I am Sleeping Beauty and he's my handsome prince. Nani allowed herself to indulge in the fantasy for a minute more. She heard him tapping on the keyboard out front and sat up. He's not coming back here to kiss me awake, she conceded.

Her hair was a mess. Nani tried to untangle it with her fingers. She used some of the mouthwash that was kept in the little bathroom and gargled, then freshened up her makeup and smoothed out the creases in her clothes. She'd been on that sofa since four o'clock, and it showed.

Nani peeked out from the back.

"*Bonjour*, Michel!"

He swiveled around and jumped off his stool to greet her.

"Happy New Year, Nani! Um, what's new?" He grinned and turned his palms up.

Nani wiggled her left hand in front of his face and delighted in his reaction to the big, sparkly diamond.

"Wow, that's quite a ring." He opened his arms to embrace her. "I'm very happy for you and Alain."

Nani pressed close to Michel, breathing in his scent. She could have stayed like that for the next hour.

"Is there coffee?" Michel pointed to a white box on the counter next to the computer. "I brought croissants."

Nani smiled. "I'll make a fresh pot. Why are you here, anyway? You weren't supposed to work today." Her voice trailed off as she disappeared in the back room to start the coffee.

Michel raised his voice so she could hear him. "Big group arriving today. Boss called me and asked if I'd come in to help. I didn't mind; it's just one day, anyway. Oh, here it is. Twenty-four guests arrive this afternoon. You must have logged this one in, Nani. 'Wedding Keubel/Heinz, Rooms 320-333.' Good job."

Nani scooped out coffee and filled the basket. She drew fresh, cold water from the tap and slowly poured it in the coffeemaker. She was elated to see Michel, and to have this time together before her shift ended. And he seemed genuinely happy about her engagement. Perhaps she and Alain would end up being friends with Michel and Lucia. She imagined dinner parties, evenings at the movies. Maybe she and Alain would even baby-sit for the little one sometime. Eventually she'd have to get used to being around a baby.

It was quiet out front. Michel must be working on the big wedding party that was arriving that afternoon. She pulled a long serving tray down from one of the shelves and took two plates, napkins, cups, spoons, sugar, and cream and arranged everything on the tray. I wish there were fresh flowers around, she thought.

Nani carried the tray to the front, where Michel sat motionless before the computer.

"I have everything for a nice breakfast," she announced.

Michel nodded and sighed heavily. His whole demeanor had changed from the time he first walked in.

"Michel? Something is wrong?" She stood next to him and looked at his face. He was holding a sheet of stamps, a commemorative of the centenary of Swiss railways. Twenty stamps, five by four. Blue, brown, yellow, and green, each depicting a Swiss train. One stamp was missing.

Nani lowered her gaze from his face to the desk and saw the envelope, the one she'd addressed in plain black letters, with no return address, and a stamp, a blue stamp of a Swiss train on it. Suddenly she recalled a time when she was caught stealing a chicken from the neighboring farm. She was eight years old and thought it would be fun to steal a chicken. The farmer caught her and dragged her by the hair to her house. She couldn't sit down for three days after her father's beating. Why she was thinking of that incident now, she didn't know.

"Oh, I forgot the coffee," she exclaimed, and hurried to the back to retrieve the pot. Her hand was shaking as she lifted the heavy coffeepot, and she was sure she'd drop it before she brought it back out. She took one deep breath after another, trying desperately to calm herself.

When she returned to Michel, he had put everything away. The stamps and the envelope were gone. Perhaps it is nothing, she told herself. She smiled broadly, showing her teeth.

"Nice to have a few minutes to catch up, Michel. Thank you for sending the picture of the baby. He's very cute." She fidgeted around him, straightening files that were already neat.

"He looks like his mother, fortunately." Michel's smile faded. "Nani, I need your opinion on something very serious."

She pulled up a stool and sat with her knees touching his. Could he hear her heart pounding? It sounded like a tympani in her ears.

"Anything, Michel."

"I don't want to turn this into a long boring story. Nani, I am adopted. I've known it for many years, and I love my parents very much."

Nani wished the stools had back support; this one was very uncomfortable.

"They must be very happy about the baby. And how is your wife doing?"

"Everyone is fine, Nani. Please, let me continue." Michel grasped her wrist and Nani flinched. She pulled her wrist away and rubbed it.

"I have to get going, Michel." She stuck her hands under her thighs and knew she should sit up straighter.

"Your shift isn't even over yet. Nani, please, as my friend, just listen to me."

Nani took a deep breath and waited.

Michel cleared his throat. "I know who my birth mother is, but I don't know who is my natural father."

"Let me pour some coffee." Nani pulled her hands out from under her legs and poured coffee for each of them. She didn't touch her cup, though.

"Last month," he continued, "I received an anonymous letter, sent to my home, from someone who said they know who my father is. Of course, it was very distressing to me and to Lucia. I had only just learned the identity of my natural mother."

He took a small apple-filled croissant from the open box and placed it on his plate, then slid the box closer to her. Nani stared at the golden croissants in the box. Three of them, all perfect in shape.

"I mean, why would someone do that?" He looked into her eyes, and she did her best to mirror the look on his face. He took a bite and licked the apple filling that had spilled out the side.

"I don't know, Michel," she whispered. She watched his lovely pink tongue and wished she was that croissant.

"Anyway, I saw Alain yesterday," he continued.

"Alain?" Her voice cracked and she coughed. "My Alain?"

"Yes, that's how I knew about your engagement. I asked him if there was a way to track down the sender."

Each word was like the sting of a slap on her bare skin. She tried to breathe normally and found it difficult.

"And what did he say?" Nani gripped her hands together in her lap and willed her body to stay still.

"Well, listen to this. He said we could get DNA from the saliva used to lick the stamp! Isn't that funny?! Your fiancé watches a lot of police shows from America, Nani." He shook his head sadly. "No, I'm afraid I know who did this."

Nani was a statue as she waited for the final, fatal blow.

"I think Robert did it."

The bus carrying Justin and Nicole was due to arrive at the Port Authority at four-thirty. Gary suggested they eat at a restaurant close by. When Bernie learned the kids were coming in by bus, she decided to take the bus back to Providence.

"Don't you already have a ticket for the train? It's no problem, Bernie. We'll get to the station."

Bernie cast her eyes down. "I bought a one-way ticket down here," she said quietly.

Gary laid his hand against her cheek. "I knew you'd never want to leave me," he teased, but his eyes were serious.

Bernie shrugged a shoulder. "I wanted to keep it open-ended," she muttered.

Gary laughed out loud. "In case you couldn't wait to get away!" He hugged Bernie hard. Her hands clutched his shoulders.

"I hope your children don't hate me. You know, I'm the girlfriend," she said, feeling a tightness in her throat that no amount of swallowing would clear.

Gary let go and placed his hands on her shoulders. He backed her up a step but held on. "Don't worry about it, honey. They're teenagers. I haven't introduced anyone to them, so this is something new. It's why I thought it best for you all to meet this way. We'll have something to eat, get comfortable..."

"And then I leave," Bernie finished. She smiled. "It's okay, Gary, and it's a good plan."

"Come on," he said, taking her hand. "The bus is here."

They walked to where the bus was disgorging its passengers: students covered in faded denim, couples coming to the city for the evening, and Justin and Nicole. Bernie stared at the miniature Gary and a wisp of a girl with pale skin and a brown ponytail. Neither child was smiling, but both faces brightened as soon as they saw their father.

"Daddy!" Nicole jumped into Gary's arms and he lifted her off the ground. She couldn't weigh more than ninety pounds, Bernie thought. Justin was tall and gangly, still a skinny kid, all arms and legs, with a mop of light brown hair. Once Gary had set Nicole back on the platform, he and his son did that half hug thing men liked to do.

"Guys, this is Bernadette," he said.

Bernie stuck out her hand and said, "Bernadette or Bernie, I answer to both."

The kids shook hands awkwardly, but were polite. Good manners, Bernie thought, even if they don't like me.

"Hungry?" Gary looked at each of his children.

"Yeah, I am," Justin mumbled. Nicole bit her lower lip and played with her ponytail.

"Okay, well, let's go then." He threw an arm around Nicole and walked ahead. Bernie fell into step with Justin. Oh God, she thought, what do I say to a teenage boy?

"You like New York, Justin?"

He walked with his hands in the pockets of jeans that were too big for him. Without looking at her, he said, "Yeah, it's great. There's so much here. I'd never get tired of it."

"So you're a junior? Are you thinking about college?"

"Yeah, maybe NYU. Or somewhere in the city."

"Good idea," Bernie said. I am so lame, she thought, staring ahead at Gary and Nicole. Girlfriend can't compete with daughter, she reminded herself silently.

They exited the Port Authority, and Gary signaled that the restaurant was just ahead. Bernie was relieved.

They entered a medium-sized bistro, the kind of place with food for everyone, catering to tourists in and around the theater district.

The interior was dark wood and polished brass, and filled with middle-aged women wearing sneakers and fanny packs. Bernie didn't care. A young woman in a black leather miniskirt led them to a booth. Nicole slid in on one side, and Justin was about to slide in opposite her, but Gary held his sleeve. With a motion of his head, he directed his son to sit next to his daughter, then held his hand out for Bernie to slide in on the opposite side. He joined her, and pressed the length of his thigh against hers. She felt some of her tension subside and she pressed back.

"I wanted you guys to all meet, before Bernie heads back to Providence," Gary started. He was interrupted by a waiter in a white-blond crew cut who appeared at the table to take drink orders. Gary ordered a Diet Coke, so Bernie did the same, as much as she longed for something stronger. Justin asked for a regular Coke and Nicole wanted water with lemon. She really is a mite, Bernie thought. I suppose all the girls are like that now, she told herself. They all wanted to be a size zero thanks to Ally McBeal, aware that her own jeans were snug after five days of feasting with Gary. I'll just watch what I eat when I'm not with him, she promised silently.

Gary took Bernie's hand and continued. "She's very special to me." He turned to look at her and she felt her face get warmer.

"Have you been here all week?" Nicole's voice was high-pitched and a little squeaky, like a mouse in a cartoon.

"Since New Year's Eve," Bernie said.

"Did you guys go to Times Square?" Justin asked. Neither of them seemed particularly concerned that she'd shacked up with their dad for the past few days.

No, we stayed in the apartment and acted like horny teenagers, Bernie thought, pressing her thigh hard against Gary's. He pressed back.

"Are you kidding? I wouldn't go near Times Square on New Year's Eve," Gary said. "No, we watched movies and ate popcorn," he added. Bernie watched the kids' impassive faces. They weren't dumb, they could figure things out. Please don't hate me for screwing your father, she prayed silently. I do love him.

"What are you guys planning to do this weekend?" Bernie glanced at the menu, pretending that it didn't matter what they would be doing. She'd be back in Providence, trying to figure out what came next.

"Hairspray," replied Nicole as she squeezed lemon into her water. Bernie felt a drop hit her face, just above her eye.

"I wanted to take them to a show for Christmas, and we were able to convince Justin to see 'Hairspray' with us," Gary said. "Right, Jus?"

Justin made a big show of rolling his eyes, then laughed. "How bad can it be, right?"

Bernie really liked Justin. He was genuine and well-mannered. The jury was still out on Nicole, who ordered a salad. Gary and Justin wanted bacon cheeseburgers. Bernie chose the chicken quesadilla.

I suppose she doesn't like the idea of sharing her father, Bernie thought, and decided she wouldn't try too hard. Fifteen is fifteen. Well, fifteen when I was fifteen is not like fifteen today. I'll be leaving in another hour anyway, she told herself. Let them get used to me gradually. I'm planning to be around for a long time.

"What do you do?" Nicole was staring at her. Her light brown eyes were huge on such a tiny face, and she wore just a bit of makeup. Seriously, she looked like a child, Bernie thought, not a teenager almost old enough to drive. Her thin eyebrows were perfect arches and she had gorgeous cheekbones. A little china doll.

"I'm a lawyer," Bernie said. She sipped her drink and set it down. "Do either of you have any interest in the law?" It was a question she asked in a bright voice, but fell flat on these kids.

"Do you handle divorces?" Nicole looked up at her as she moved her salad around on her plate. Bernie noticed that the young girl moved her food around, but hadn't yet eaten it.

"Not very often," Bernie said, pressing her thigh against Gary's again. Be here to support me if I need it, her thigh said to his. "I do a lot of probate work." Both teenagers looked at her blankly, and she decided it was a good time to eat her quesadilla.

"Bernie has her own law practice, so I guess you could say she does a little of everything."

Gary slipped his left hand under the table to rest it on Bernie's thigh. His fingers traced a random pattern of circles and squiggles. She sighed and found Nicole staring at her again. The girl's eyes darted to the edge of the table and back to Bernie. Bernie shifted on the banquette, causing Gary to remove his hand.

"Honey, you've barely eaten," Gary said quietly to his daughter. It was true; Bernie hadn't seen her lift that fork to her mouth once. Meanwhile, everyone else's plates were clean, except for some fries on Bernie's plate.

Nicole shrugged her narrow shoulders. "I wasn't that hungry," she squeaked.

"Okay," Gary said. "Well, there's plenty of food at the apartment."

Bernie checked her watch and turned to Gary. "I'd better get going," she said, hoping he wouldn't mention that she still had another thirty minutes. He nodded and held her eyes with his. She gave him her best smile and said, "This was great. I'm glad we met," looking first at Justin, then Nicole.

Gary signaled the waiter and handed him a credit card. The young man bounced away and returned immediately with the bill. Gary signed the slip, took the duplicate, and pulled a ten-dollar bill and two ones from his wallet.

"Why didn't you just add the tip onto the bill, Dad?" Justin asked.

"I'd rather he get the tip in cash," Gary said. "That way he gets to put it in his pocket. I know what it's like to wait tables and rely on tips. Always tip in cash if you can." He raised his palm as if making a solemn proclamation. The kids both rolled their eyes.

"Good point," Bernie said. Gary nodded. "I'll do it from now on," she added, reaching under the table to stroke his thigh one last time. She didn't care if Nicole knew, dammit.

They slid out of the booth and walked back to the bus station. Bernie stopped to buy her ticket, then turned back to the Baptista clan.

"Get going, you three," she said with the widest grin she could manage. "And I'll see you next Friday," she said to Gary, while the children flanked him silently.

He embraced her. No sloppy wet kisses in front of the kids, she thought, but he said into her ear, "I miss you already, my love."

Bernie went soft in his arms and whispered back, "I love you." He pulled back and grinned at her.

"Have a good trip back."

Bernie waved to them and turned on her heel. She didn't know if they were watching her, and she didn't turn around, in case they weren't, but she practically skipped to the bus.

"Does Robert work tonight?" Michel stirred his coffee and looked at Nani. She chewed the inside of her cheek and looked to the ceiling.

"Think so," she said.

"What's wrong, Nani?"

She pulled her eyes from above and snapped her fingers. "You think Robert sent you an anonymous letter because one of your stamps is missing? Oh, Michel, I am so sorry. I took one of those stamps back in October, and it's my fault I never replaced it. I didn't realize they were yours, and a special set, or I never would have taken it." Her heart was about to beat out of her chest, and when she finished talking, she held her breath, waiting.

He stared at her. "You took one of these stamps?" He pointed down at the now-closed drawer.

She nodded. Just keep talking, Nani, a voice inside her instructed. "I didn't realize they were special. I thought I had some stamps in my bag, but I didn't, and I had a letter that needed to be sent that day, and Michel, I'm so sorry." She tried to slow her words down, but they were like the waterfalls in springtime when the mountain snows melted. "Don't blame Robert for this. It was me, Michel. If I had known, I would never have borrowed the stamp. Perhaps I can purchase another commemorative set for you. A full set."

Michel eased off his stool and stood. "No, it's okay, Nani, you didn't mean it." There was a deep crease between his eyebrows.

"It's true, I didn't mean it." She couldn't feel her feet and her head was like a balloon about to pop.

"You should go; it's nearly eight. Take the croissants with you." He picked up the box of pastries and held it out to her.

"No, leave it here for everyone." She tried to laugh. "I don't want to be a fat bride." She disappeared to the back and returned with her coat over her arm.

"Here," said Michel, helping her with her coat. "Go home and sleep. And congratulations on your engagement, Nani." He surprised her by kissing her temple.

"Thank you, Michel. Thank you." She turned away and walked across the lobby to the door, and never looked back, in case he was watching her.

CHAPTER TWENTY-THREE

Bernie was on a mission. When she returned to her office on Monday, the first thing she did was find out about sitting for the bar in New York. Well, better to find out, right? Next, she pulled up her client list and reviewed each case. The ones who owed her money, which were many, the ones who needed to settle their cases, which were few. She made notes next to each one and prioritized them.

Next up was her lease. John Bagini, the owner of the building, had always given her a break on rent, but it came with a price. He'd usually send flowers to her office, which served as a signal that his wife was out of town. That evening, he'd show up at her apartment. He never called first. Last time she'd seen him was at the end of the summer, and she knew he'd be sniffing around soon. She needed to end it, even if it meant losing her lease. She opened a drawer in one of two tall filing cabinets and found the lease agreement. Of course, the language was vague; he'd probably had some family member draw it up, or he'd looked online for a generic document form. As far as termination, it basically said nothing. Great. She would let him know that as of the end of January, she was moving out. It didn't matter; she could work from home, or from her mother's house. Joan wanted to stay in the house and was willing to buy it from Joanie and herself. There was no mortgage, and both Bernie and Joanie agreed to sell it to Joan for a dollar. Keep it in the family. Their mother had left behind some family money; her daughters would never be rich, but they'd never be poor, either.

Bernie decided to start moving things out of the office each day; with any luck, Bagini wouldn't be around. She knew that she wanted to be with Gary, and only Gary. It wasn't like she needed to be married, but she wanted the stability that he offered. There had been plenty of men over the past twenty years. Too many to count, she had to admit, as she stared out the office window at the highway. Gary had probably only really loved Roxana, although he said he loved me when we were in Fribourg, she thought. How could she have not seen it? Because she could see only Timmy Lyon? When Gary was right there?

She and Gary were rooted in their friendship. Bernie had never been friends with the men she'd known. Once the relationship was over, it was over. They either went back to their wives or found someone else, but she did not keep in touch with them. She realized how alone she was. No wonder I bounce from one man to another, she thought.

She'd make this work. And she would find a way to make it work with his children, too. Justin was fine; next year he'd be preparing for college. He'd mentioned to Bernie that he wanted to attend school in New York, which made Gary happy. Nicole was another issue. Gary didn't seem too concerned about the fact that the girl didn't eat, but Bernie noticed. She wasn't the girl's mother, but she could ask Gary if Roxana was aware. She just had to step carefully. She didn't want to alienate anyone, not at such an early stage.

Bernie was bent over, riffling through the files in the drawer when a hand on her bottom made her jump.

"What the hell!" She whirled around to face John Bagini. He was tanned, probably from Christmas in Aruba.

"Hey, sexy," the old man said in his low, guttural voice. His flinty eyes raked her up and down and she wished she'd worn her old jeans and a baggy sweatshirt instead of the purple silk dress and heels. He was dressed all in black, the buttons of his shirt straining against a belly fattened by excess. John Bagini was in his late sixties and dressed as if he were Tony Manero, ready for the disco. Bernie stood her ground, hands on her hips. In her high heels, she had a good five inches on the wizened little pervert.

"John, what a surprise. I never see you around here."

"Yes, well." He glanced around the office, up to the ceiling, out the tall windows. "Happy New Year, Bernadette." He leaned in for a wet kiss and she deftly maneuvered to peck him on his leathery brown cheek.

"Happy New Year, John. Actually, I'm glad you're here. Please, sit." She would control this visit.

He lowered himself to the slippery leather loveseat and slid forward. Bernie tried not to laugh as she perched on the edge of her desk. He stared at her long legs.

Before she could speak, he held up a hand, and then pointed a long bony finger in her direction. "We've had a good arrangement, you and I." He winked and she felt a wave of nausea wash over her. "But it's a new year, and I'm afraid I'm going to have to raise your rent. Everything has gone up, Bernie. Heat, electricity, insurance. I hate to do it, but perhaps we could work something out." When he smiled, he showed a mouthful of teeth yellowed with age and cigars. She could not have been more repulsed. What the hell had she been thinking, allowing him into her bed? Of course, she'd always drunk enough vodka to blur everything with him.

Now it was Bernie's turn to hold up a hand. "Well, John, I guess our timing is excellent." Seeing his raised eyebrows, she continued. "I'll be moving out at the end of the month. I reviewed my lease for cancellation provisions, and there are none, so since it's nice and early in January, I'm letting you know that I'll be out by the thirty-first." She uncrossed her legs slowly and slid off the edge of the desk. She walked over to the leather sofa and stood with her legs apart. "No more arrangements, John."

His smile disappeared and she saw in his eyes the icy hardness that must have made him a successful CEO. When he stood up, there was barely an inch of space between them. "Moving on to another sugar daddy?" He smelled of overpriced cologne and tobacco.

Her hand twitched, but she would not slap him. Bernie was smarter than that. "Good-bye, John." She slammed the door after him and turned the deadbolt.

Nani rushed out of the hotel and into a stinging wind. Tiny pellets of ice hit her face and ran down her cheeks. The scene in the hotel kept replaying in her head as she hurried up the street. Did he believe her? Michel is smart, but Nani could not let Robert take the blame. As much as she disliked the quirky old man, she couldn't do it.

That damned Bernadette Maguire! She blew into town and upset everything. Before she and her stupid old aunt arrived, things were fine. Now, Nani reflected, her parents weren't speaking to her. Michel was upset. If Alain knew about the letter she'd sent, he'd break off the engagement. She trudged up the hill and stopped in front of the Tilleul Tea-Room on the rue de Lausanne. Lured inside by the smell of buttery croissants, she entered and heard the familiar "*Bonjour*!" from one of the women behind the counter.

"*Bonjour*," she mumbled. She found an empty table along the back wall and slumped into a chair. Her clothes were damp and heavy. A young girl brought coffee to her table, and she nodded her thanks. She stirred sugar into her coffee and sipped. It seemed she lived on coffee all the time. Nani hated working nights. She longed for a more normal life, and if that meant marrying Alain, fine. Maybe it would be best to find another job. She liked the Hotel de la Rose, and she loved seeing Michel, but perhaps it would be better to look for a job where she could work during the day and be away from him. Alain would always work nights, he said so himself. He enjoyed it. And perhaps that was the way to make this marriage work: Nani working days, Alain working nights.

Nani stared ahead, ignoring the activity and noise around her. Alain would be at the hotel now, asking Michel why she'd left and not waited for him. And what would Michel say? Would they continue their discussion about DNA on stamps? Maybe she should just send Michel another anonymous letter with the name and address of the man in Lausanne. She still had the scrap of paper from the day Robert found the address for Bernadette. I hate Bernadette Maguire, Nani said to herself. Her phone vibrated in her pocket, but she ignored it. I hate everything about that woman, from her red hair to her green eyes to her stupid aunt. The only good thing she ever did was bring Michel into the world.

An idea came to her at once, and she picked up her big bag. Rummaging around inside, she found the scrap of paper. She looked at it for a long time as she chewed her lip. He should know, she said to herself. They should both know. She finished her coffee and walked to the counter. Pointing to a large croissant, she had the girl put in a paper bag. She laid money on the counter, took the bag, and rushed out of the tea-room before anyone could say, "*Au revoir! Merci!*"

At the Fribourg train station, Nani kept looking behind her, half-expecting Alain to be there. She checked the schedule and walked quickly to platform two. The train to Lausanne should arrive in four minutes. She would do it. He may not be home, but she would find out where he worked. She only wished she had a picture of Michel with her.

The recorded announcement came over the speaker. Here comes the train to Lausanne. Not stopping until Romont. Please get on board. Nani climbed the steps and found a seat next to the window. Her phone vibrated again and she checked. Alain. No, she would speak with him after this was done.

The train pulled away from the station and gained speed as it sailed through the countryside. Farms rushed by in a blur until the stop at Romont, where a few passengers got off and a few got on. Within a half hour, the train arrived in Lausanne. Nani stepped off the train and took a deep breath. The air was cold and she filled her lungs, feeling energized about her plan. She pulled the paper out of her pocket and looked again at the address. 23 Rue du Midi. She asked at the train station for directions. Not far, she was told. Good, she thought, she couldn't spend the day traipsing all over the city. As she neared the Rue du Midi, she stepped in the path of a well-dressed man walking toward her. He appeared to be in his late forties or early fifties, and wore black-rimmed eyeglasses. His face was soft and saggy. This could be Karl Berset!

"Pardon, *monsieur*, but I am looking for someone. I have his address, but I'm afraid he must be at work this morning. Do you live on this street?" She gave him her prettiest smile.

The man's face lit up. It must not be often that a young woman stops to talk to him, Nani thought. She tossed her hair and batted her eyelashes. "His name is Karl Berset. I have an urgent message for him."

The man looked behind him and pointed. "He lives there," the man said, "but you're right, he is likely at the bank now."

"Do you know which bank?" Nani dared to lay one gloved hand on the fine wool sleeve of his well-made coat. He looked down at her tiny hand and his lower lip fell.

"Yes, he works at the Banque Cantonale Vaudoise, next to the train station. Miss, would you like to have a coffee? I have time." His eyes, a watery grayish-blue behind thick lenses, held hers and she had to look away.

"I am so sorry, *monsieur*, but this is an urgent matter. I must meet Karl Berset and then return to Romont. But perhaps you will visit me there? My name is...Simone Marceau."

And before he could ask for her telephone number, Nani rushed away. Banque Cantonale Vaudoise, near the train station. She heard him call, "Simone!" but she didn't turn around. She only hoped he didn't also work in the same building.

Alain usually waited outside for Nani, but because of the harsh wind and sleet, he entered the hotel to wait in the lobby. He saw Michel at the back desk, staring into a cup of coffee, so he made his way toward the reception area.

"Michel! *Bonjour*!" He clapped him on the shoulder.

"Oh hi, Alain." Michel didn't look up.

"What's the matter? Missing the little one?" He laughed at his joke. "Speaking of little ones, where is my little Nani?"

Michel raised his head. "She left about fifteen minutes ago."

"She did? That's strange, she knows I come here to pick her up." He pulled his phone from his front pocket and dialed her number. Michel did not look up as Alain waited, with the phone pressed to his ear. Finally he clicked it off and slid it back into his pocket.

"Michel?"

"Hmm."

"Was Nani okay this morning?" Michel glanced up to the tall man. "I mean, was she troubled about anything? The wedding?"

Michel rubbed his cheek. "Remember when we saw each other yesterday and I mentioned about the letter I received? The anonymous letter?"

Alain rested his elbows on the desk. "Sure. Did you find more information?"

Michel dropped his chin into his upturned palm. "I still don't know who sent it. But I noticed that one of my stamps was missing." He pulled the drawer open and retrieved the stamps. "You see? One was taken." He held up the stamp set so Alain could see it.

"Ah, yes, the commemorative edition. I remember those," Alain noted.

"I told Nani all about it. I thought it must have been Robert who works here, you know? He is strange sometimes. But I couldn't understand why he would send me a letter saying he knows who is my birth father. Then Nani said she had taken the stamp, to use for a letter. Way back in October, and she forgot to tell me about it. And that's fine. So, now I know why the stamp is missing, but I still do not know who sent the letter."

"And the letter says that someone knows who your father is?"

Michel flinched. "The man who fathered me, yes. Bruno Eicher is my father." He set his jaw.

"Yes, yes, of course, Michel." Alain and Michel both rested their chins in their hands and pondered the situation.

"Do you want to know who this man is, Michel? Your birth father?"

"I don't know. Maybe not." He turned to Alain. "Perhaps it is someone here in Fribourg, someone I know. It could be anyone, I suppose."

Alain's dark eyebrows joined together as he concentrated. "Michel, if your, if the man who fathered you knows that he fathered you, I would think he'd have come forward by now. If this man does not want to know you, maybe it's best to just leave it, unless you receive another letter."

"I'm sure you're right."

Alain stretched his back as he stood tall. "Well, I should be off. Perhaps I'll go to Nani's apartment. See you, Michel."

"See you."

As Michel watched Alain's back retreating, a thought crawled into his mind. Snake-like, it wormed its way into his consciousness, wrapping itself around his brain. He shook his head from side to side to dislodge it, but it stayed.

CHAPTER TWENTY-FOUR

Bernie decided to work from home. After the scene with John Bagini, she didn't want to run into him at the office, not today. She'd need to call someone to help her move her stuff out of there. Even with a few weeks to go until the end of the month, even with a deadbolt lock on her office door, she didn't trust the old man. He'd been rejected, and he was angry. And she didn't want to find out how vindictive he could be.

She worked all morning, straightening out closets, cupboards, and using her laptop to contact old clients. Around noon she stopped working, sat back and raised her arms over her head. She needed to walk. Fresh air, maybe some Thai food. Bernie pulled her hair back into a ponytail, grabbed an old ball cap from a hook inside the closet, pulled on her coat, and opened her door.

"Oh!" She jumped, startled. The mailman stood at her door, and looked up with a grin.

"Sorry, did I scare you?" He held a stack of mail in his hand.

She laughed. "Well, I wasn't expecting you. Happy New Year."

"Same to you," he said, handing her the mail and continuing down the street.

Bernie looked at the seven or eight letters in her hand. Now or later? Later, she decided, as she tossed them on a table just inside the apartment and locked the door behind her. She pulled the cap down over her eyes and headed to the Thai restaurant a block away.

Nani stood in front of the Banque Cantonale Vaudoise and listened to the voices in her head. One told her to hurry up and open the door, find Karl Berset, and tell him everything she knew. The other told her to slow down and think about what she was planning to do, what lives would be affected by her actions. She loved Michel more than anything or anyone. She'd been able to lie her way out of a potentially sticky situation, and she felt confident that he believed her story about taking the stamp. Michel would never suspect Nani of sending that letter, but she couldn't let Robert take the fall, either. And she believed that Michel had a right to know his birth father. Plus, she wanted to get back at Bernadette Maguire somehow, and this seemed to be the way to do it. Expose that woman for what she was, and if it upset things, well, maybe Michel would want nothing to do with her ever again.

She stood on the mat and waited for the glass doors to part. Inside, she blinked against the harsh fluorescent lights and noticed an older woman sitting at a desk, front and center. The woman's head was bent low over a pile of paperwork on her desk.

"*Bonjour*," Nani said in a tentative voice. The woman looked up and lowered her eyeglasses. She smiled in that courteous, professional way Nani recognized from waiting on guests at the hotel.
"*Bonjour, mademoiselle*. May I help you?"

Nani looked around the office, at desks and file cabinets and copy machines. "I'm looking for Karl Berset." She hoped the woman couldn't see her shaking.

"Do you have an appointment with him?" Her eyes stayed on Nani's face, and Nani tried her best to appear calm and impassive.

"No, I'm sorry, I do not. But I can wait if he's busy. It's very important that I see him." It's now or never, Nani thought. She took a deep breath and exhaled through her nose.

"One moment, please," the woman said, picking up her phone. Nani glanced at the desk and saw a name plate. *Mme. Grancy.* "You may sit over there." She pointed with the telephone receiver to an area with chairs. Nani nodded and walked away.

She opened a magazine but preferred to watch people move about the office and wondered what it would be like to work in a place like that. Certainly there were some nice-looking men here, all trim and sharp. She was so busy following one of them with her eyes that she jumped when a man said, "Hello? May I help you?"

Nani looked up and into the face of Michel's father. Of course, she could see it. She pulled off her eyeglasses and rose to her feet.

"Karl Berset?" She kept her face composed but blinked rapidly in his presence.

"Yes," he replied, holding out his hand. "I understand you're here to see me."

"May we speak privately?" She glanced about the office area.

Karl stared at her and his jaw slackened. "So you are the girl," he whispered.

"Pardon?"

"Please, come into my office." He guided her to his office along the back wall. Once inside, he closed the door. Standing behind his desk, he picked up his phone, waited a moment, then said, "Please, no calls, no interruptions." He motioned for Nani to sit on the opposite side of his desk. She could see sweat glistening on his forehead.

"Are you all right?" she asked as she loosened her scarf.

Karl dropped into his chair and pressed a handkerchief to his sweaty brow. "This is just a surprise. Henri didn't call."

Nani frowned. What the hell was he talking about? "I'm sorry, I don't know Henri," she said, watching him carefully.

"No, no of course not, um...I'm sorry, I don't know your name." He smoothed back his thinning hair and Nani saw a thick gold band on his ring finger.

She regarded him with suspicion. Her name? "Simone," she replied. "Simone Marceau." She smiled at him. Perhaps when he sees his neighbor, they will talk about the lovely Simone Marceau.

"You're a beautiful young woman," he said. "Dark and beautiful."

She narrowed her eyes. "Listen, there is something we need to discuss," she began. The sooner she did this, the better.

"I know. I know, *cherie*. Please." His eyes darted around the office as she continued to stare at him. She wouldn't take her eyes off his. He brushed a hand across his forehead. "Do you need money? I can give you money."

Money? Why is he offering me money, Nani wondered. He doesn't even know why I'm here. She straightened her shoulders and leaned forward.

"You and Bernadette Maguire..."

"Yes! Yes, I know!" He stood up suddenly, thrashing his arms about. His face looked like a ham, all pink and moist.

"You know?" Nani was confused. Bernadette must have told him.

"I'm sorry!" He whirled around from behind the desk and stood facing her. He dropped to his knees and held out his hands. "I'm so sorry," he sobbed. He hung his head and his forehead hit her knees.

Nani looked up to the ceiling. What the heck is going on here? She put her hands on his head. Even his scalp was sweaty. Gently, she pushed him away and rolled back in her chair until she could stand up.

"I should probably go," she said in a near-whisper. This was getting ridiculous. Karl Berset was a nut.

"Wait," he cried, and ran behind his desk. He pulled a key from his pants pocket and opened a drawer. As he fumbled behind the desk, sniffling, Nani fastened her coat buttons and retied her scarf around her neck. Karl thrust a large manila envelope into her hands. "Please," he said in a strangled voice. "Please, Simone, take this," he whispered.

Nani grabbed the envelope and hurried out of the office, past the surprised woman at the front desk, into the street, and she didn't stop running until she reached the train station.

Bernie returned to her apartment in the afternoon and filled the teakettle with water from the faucet. She turned the burner to high and set the shiny copper kettle on the blue flame. Shrugging off her outer clothes and boots, she picked up the pile of mail from the table next to the door and plopped onto the sofa. She lifted her feet to the coffee table and leafed through the mail. Electric bill, cable bill, a sale at Macy's. And a pale blue envelope from Givisiez, Switzerland, addressed to Ms. Bernadette Maguire. She fingered the envelope for a minute before opening it, caressing the stamp, running her index finger along the edge. Finally she slipped her finger under the flap and opened it.

Dear Bernadette,

Lucia and I want you to know about our new baby. Jean-Bernard Eicher was born on December 26, 2002, at 9:02 a.m. He is a healthy and beautiful boy as you will see in the photograph.

I'm sorry I haven't written to you earlier. I know that you are the woman who gave birth to me in 1979. And I understand why you didn't tell me when you were here, but now I also understand better your tears and emotions upon seeing me for the first time at the hotel. You did a very selfless thing at what must have been an extremely difficult time, and Lucia and I decided to name the baby in your honor.

Someday perhaps we can all meet. My parents are wonderful people, and my wife would very much like to know you. If you decide to return to Switzerland, please let me know. You will be my guest at the hotel.
Sincerely,
Jean-Michel

P.S. Thank you for the medal of Saint Michael, which I wear on my neck all the time.

The teakettle whistled, but Bernie didn't hear it.

CHAPTER TWENTY-FIVE

Nani finally listened to the three messages Alain had left on her phone, each one with increasing alarm. Once she was back in her apartment, she called him.

"But where were you, my love? I was worried sick. Michel said you'd left the hotel in such a hurry, and you weren't at your apartment. I was so worried, Nani."

"I'm sorry, Alain. There was something I wanted to do...in anticipation of the wedding. It's a surprise. I didn't mean to worry you." She'd come up with 'the surprise' later, she promised herself.

He sighed. "As long as you are all right," he breathed into the phone. "Nani, we should set a date for the wedding. There is paperwork. I will take care of all of it, but tell me when. Springtime? Summer?"

Nani stared at the manila envelope resting on the bed next to her. She hadn't opened it until the train was pulling away from Lausanne, en route back to Fribourg. Then, she'd taken it into the bathroom and looked inside. Bundled packets of Swiss franc notes. Twenties, fifties, hundreds. She'd counted twenty thousand Swiss francs in total.

"Nani?"

"Yes, Alain," she answered in a thick voice.

"What do you think about a wedding in May?"

"Lovely," she replied.

"Okay! I will start the process. I know some people at the registry office, so it should be no problem. We will begin to count the days, sweetheart."

"Yes, Alain," she said, fingering the bills as if they were made of the finest silk.

By the end of the week, Bernie could think of nothing but Gary's arrival. She'd spent the week working from home, although shc'd stopped into her office early on Thursday morning, earlier than anyone else, just to make sure nothing had been damaged. The office looked the same, and she picked up a few more files to carry home.

On Friday, she walked down the hill in the late afternoon. The days were getting longer, she thought, which was one good thing about January. Gary's train arrived at six, but she wanted to be early. She found herself standing in front of the Drop-Off. Since last October, since the day her mother died, Bernie hadn't been inside what was once her favorite bar, her other home.

She pulled on the door and felt a warm rush of air greet her as she stepped inside. The place was packed on a Friday night, and she was glad. She edged her way in to the bar. There was one empty seat, but where was Norm? Bernie slid onto the stool and nodded at the guy next to her, but she didn't make eye contact. Down at the other end, a young man jogged back to his place behind the bar. He had model looks, almost like a Ken doll. Perfect cheekbones, brilliant smile, blond hair all neat and groomed. Where's my Norm, Bernie thought. The bartender slid her way and caught her eye.

"Hi there! I'm Ryan. What can I get for you?" he asked. He grinned and showed off perfect white teeth. Blue eyes sparkled against a lightly tanned face. Had to be a spray tan, she thought.

"Uh," Bernie stammered, "actually I was looking for someone. He used to tend bar here, a few months ago. Norm?" She searched Ryan's eyes.

His face fell just a bit, but he recovered quickly and was perfect again.

"Oh, Norm is no longer with us," he said, making a very pretty pouty face.

Bernie stared. "What? Did he...die?" Oh no, she thought. Please don't say that he died.

Ryan tossed his head and giggled. "No! He isn't dead! He retired at the end of the year. Said he wanted to spend more time with his grandkids. Now," he said, striking a pose, "what can I get for you?"

Bernie squeezed her eyes shut. "Actually, I probably don't have time. I have a train to catch. But thank you anyway." She got off the stool and pushed through the crowd to the exit.

Back on the sidewalk, she gulped the cold air into her lungs and ran her hand through her hair. Oh, Norm, I'm sorry I didn't say goodbye. Seems I never get to say goodbye to the people who mean the most to me. She bowed her head for a moment and pictured a smiling Norm surrounded by little children.

She walked the short distance to the train station. I don't want to miss this chance for happiness, she thought. Gary makes me happy. I think I make him happy. She sat on a bench and sipped hot coffee, waiting for his train. People passed through the large waiting area, checking schedules, talking on phones. A big man in a trench coat stopped just in front of her and checked his watch. As he turned his face, Bernie realized she knew him and quickly, she buried her face in a newspaper.

Gary's train arrived, twenty minutes late. Not like those Swiss trains, Bernie thought, always on time. He walked through the double doors into the lobby and she welcomed him into her waiting arms. She didn't want to let go.

"Hey! Happy to see you, too, baby," he said into her ear.

She inched back to look at his face. "I missed you. I hate being apart," she stated. He took her hand and started toward the exit to the street, but Bernie planted her feet and didn't move. Gary stopped and turned, eyebrows raised.

"I hate being apart," she repeated, and pulled him back to her. He dropped his weekend bag to the floor.

"So let's not be apart then," he said, looking into her eyes. "We're not kids, Bernie. Let's be together."

"Logistically..."

"Logistically," he grinned, "we'll make it work. Do you want me to move here?"

Bernie couldn't believe what she was hearing. Gary was willing to move to Rhode Island to be with her. He would leave his teaching job at NYU for her?

She shook her head. "No, I want to come to you. All I'd have to do is get my credentials to practice in New York. I just don't want us to be apart from each other anymore."

"Okay," he said. "Let's figure it out this weekend." He picked up his bag. "I'm starving. You gonna feed me or what?" He held out his hand.

Karl Berset telephoned Henri Rutz from his office.

"*Salut*, Karl! How are you?"

"How am I? I'm still reeling. Why didn't you let me know you'd found her?"

"What are you talking about?"

Karl stood in his office, looking out the window at the steel-gray sky. Darker clouds hung over the lake. "What?"

Henri repeated the question. "What are you talking about, Karl? I haven't found anyone yet."

Karl dropped into his chair and pressed the telephone tight against his ear. "What do you mean? She just showed up here. Simone. Simone Marceau. My daughter. Bernadette's daughter." He was sweating again. It dampened his armpits, trickled down his back. He felt that thing clutch his heart again, crushing it in its grip.

"Karl, I don't know who came to see you, but I'm still tracing leads. Bernadette Maguire gave birth to a son, not a daughter, but beyond that I haven't been able to confirm anything yet. Who is this Simone Marceau?"

Karl tried to speak, but the words wouldn't come. The air was being pulled from him. He'd just handed over twenty thousand Swiss francs to – to who? Who was that girl? He winced from the pain in his chest and he bent forward from the waist, his head almost between his knees.

"Karl, are you there?"

"Oh God," he cried, and fell to the floor, bringing the telephone down on top of him.

Over dinner at the Flying Horse, Bernie and Gary talked about their future.

"It's not like I'm trying to rush things between us, Gary. I just don't want to waste any more time without you. Life is better with you." She felt no anxiety or trepidation stating what she knew to be true.

"Bernie, I feel the same way. When my marriage ended, I figured that was it for me. Friends tried to fix me up, but I just couldn't see myself with any of those women. They were either bitter over their own failed marriages, or carried so much baggage with them…"

"I have baggage, too," Bernie said, averting her eyes.

He gripped her hand, forcing her to look up. "I know your baggage," he said softly.

"Not all of it, Gary." She bit the inside of her cheek, something she hadn't done for a while. Her dentist had admonished her about it.

"I know you, Bernadette. And I choose to be with you, baggage and all." He smiled. "And you choose to be with me, warts and flaws and baggage."

She waited until their plates were cleared before telling him about the letter from Michael.

"He sent a photograph," she said, pulling it out of her bag. She handed it to Gary, who smiled when he looked at it. "Your son has your good looks," Gary said, glancing up at her. "Beautiful family." He handed the photo back to her. "So he knows everything?"

"He knows that I gave birth to him, and he understands why I couldn't raise him. I didn't tell about Karl Berset, but if he asked me, I would. He even thanked me for doing what I did. I don't think he'll ever think of me as his mother, Gary. The Eichers are his parents, plain and simple. But he invited me to Fribourg anytime, said I would be his guest at the hotel." She looked at him hopefully. "Maybe we could go back together?"

Gary laughed and stirred his coffee.

"What's funny?" She smiled with him, not understanding.

He shrugged. "I thought we might return to Switzerland if we got married." He shifted in his chair and scratched his neck.

Bernie's lower lip dropped. "Oh. Wow. I wasn't thinking about marriage. Were you?"

"Someday. Not tomorrow. But someday, yes."

Wow. Marriage. Bernie thought her chances were over, and she'd accepted it. Being single wasn't the worst thing in the world, and it was better to be lonely and single than lonely and married, she reasoned. She'd handled enough divorces in her practice to see how painful divorce could be, for everyone. Gary knew that pain. But he wasn't talking about the immediate future, just the general, vaguer future, and that was okay.

"Someday is good."

"Let's go home," he said.

CHAPTER TWENTY-SIX

Fritz Gruber worked in the office next to Karl. A quiet, nervous man, he'd been with the bank since he was eighteen years old, and looked forward to retirement in six months. He heard a loud thud and jumped from his chair. Ever since the terrorist attacks in New York the previous year, he was on edge. Even in Switzerland, where no one thought anything could happen. Fritz looked out the window of his office but saw nothing different, just gray and brown office buildings, clouds heavy with snow, a traffic light changing on time. He stepped outside his office and saw the faces of the people who sat at their desks, all turned to him. Six faces, all with the same look of concern. All eyes on Karl Berset's closed office door.

"Did you hear that?" he asked, wringing his hands. "What was that noise?"

One of the young women stood up and pointed. "It came from inside his office," she said. "Sometimes Monsieur Berset gets angry on the telephone and once he threw a paperweight against the wall. But this sounded different." The others nodded.

Fritz knew of Karl's temper, too, and kept his distance. He knocked lightly on Karl's door. When there was no answer, he glanced back at the workers who were staring at him, then put his hand on the doorknob. He twisted it and pushed the door open as the bank employees all craned their necks to see.

"Karl?" The man poked his head in, and saw nothing. He ventured into the office and suddenly cried out, "Call an ambulance! Hurry!"

Someone picked up a phone and started dialing. "What is it? What happened?"

Fritz turned. "Get the emergency kit, please," he instructed the young woman, who ran to find the box of supplies kept in the office. He looked down at Karl, unmoving on the gray carpet, the telephone on top of his body. Karl's face was colorless and Fritz was quite certain he must be dead.

Within minutes, two emergency workers entered the office building and ran to the back. Fritz pressed himself against a far wall and stared out the window. The medics administered CPR to Karl Berset and hoisted his body onto a stretcher. His face was covered with an oxygen mask as they carried him out to the waiting ambulance, and with the siren roaring, the ambulance disappeared.

Fritz Gruber picked up the telephone unit and replaced the receiver, and as soon as he did, it rang. He looked at the phone, then lifted the receiver to his ear. He turned his back and spoke in a low voice, and after he replaced the receiver, he circled around the door of Karl's office.

When he exited Karl's office, the young woman was staring at him. "Monsieur Gruber, will Monsieur Berset be okay?" Her eyes were huge.

"I think so," Fritz replied. "Apparently he was talking on the telephone with a friend, and he may have received some bad news. That was his friend, calling back. I told him that they had taken Karl to hospital."

The office was subdued; people returned to their work, but quietly. Fritz Gruber sat at his desk and wished his retirement day was tomorrow.

Nani set the date: May 17, 2003 would be the day she married Alain Bouchard. Alain said he could take care of all the paperwork. He found an apartment for them near the university, "with two bedrooms," he'd said, stroking her hair.

"A guest room," she murmured.

"I was thinking a nursery," he replied into her neck. Nani knew well how to prevent a pregnancy. She would not be pregnant until she wanted to be pregnant.

"Of course, sweetheart," she said.

She wrote a long letter to her parents. In it, she told them all about Alain, his fine family, his good job, and his financial situation. And she knew it wouldn't make any difference. They would never leave their little village to come to Switzerland for the wedding. They had never even been to Athens, never been on an airplane. Alain said they could have another wedding in Greece, for her parents, but if they couldn't make the effort to see her here, then she didn't want to see them.

She set up a bank account at the SwissBank, in her own name, and deposited twelve thousand francs into it. The rest of the money went into her account at the Helvetia Bank, the one Alain knew about. It would help pay for her wedding dress and accessories. And this way, she also could tell Alain that she had some money in the bank when they combined their accounts. He didn't have to know about the SwissBank account. Not now, anyway.

Monsieur Rosolen, the owner of the Hotel de la Rose, offered the restaurant for the couple's reception, although he said he couldn't close it off completely on a Saturday evening, but they could use half of the room for their wedding dinner with guests. Nani thought it might be nice to have a wedding dinner away from her place of employment, but Alain liked the idea, so she relented. They would be married in a civil ceremony at the Registry Office on Friday afternoon and have a reception at the hotel on Saturday evening. She was going to take two weeks of vacation! Alain suggested Italy for their honeymoon, and since Nani had never been there, she was excited and happy. He showed her brochures of the Amalfi coast, and it reminded her of Greece. Naturally, he'd asked her if she wanted to spend their honeymoon in Greece, but she shook her head. No, if her parents were going to be thick-headed about this, then she could be stubborn as well. They would not get a visit from their daughter. They hadn't even sent any money for the wedding. Not that they had much, but for all the money Nani had sent to them since she started working at the hotel, she thought they should provide something of value for their daughter's wedding.

Lying next to a sleeping Alain later that night, Nani wondered if she could go through with it. Alain snored, and she thought about spending the next fifty years next to this giant man.

She turned her back to him and stared at the wall. Her financial burdens would be lifted by marrying Alain; she wouldn't always be counting centimes, stealing food from the restaurant, adding water to the shampoo bottle. Alain was an only child and stood to inherit a sizable estate when his mother died. The old bat just kept living, though. Nani thought seventy-two was long enough. Time to go, old lady. Make room for us. Madame Bouchard owned a chalet in Gstaad, an apartment in Zug, and the house she lived in just outside of Fribourg. And she hadn't offered any of them to Alain as a wedding gift!

Alain turned and flung his arm over her. He whispered into her neck, "Nani, love, turn over." She rolled her eyes in the dark and flipped onto her back.

Bernie turned onto her back and waited for her pulse to slow down. Gary lay next to her, still breathing hard.

"Wow," he said. He turned his head toward her and repeated, "Wow."

Bernie grinned. Physical and emotional intimacy, a winning combination. She'd had plenty of awesome sex, but with the wrong guys. She'd had mediocre sex with one very nice guy, she recalled. But with Gary, she had everything.

She raised herself up on one elbow and pulled the sheet over her chest. "Will your kids be okay with this? If I move in with you?"

He clasped his hands behind his head and she noticed a few gray hairs in his armpits. "Well, they like you. They told me so last weekend after you got on the bus. I didn't even have to ask them. Justin said you were cool. I asked Nicole if she thought so, too, and she agreed."

"Really? Oh, I'm glad. Because this is a lot for them. Their mother is getting married next month. It's a lot to get used to."

"They'll be alright. I think sometimes they feel bad for me, being alone."

"You're not alone anymore," Bernie said softly.

"When do you think you'll be ready to move?"

Bernie fell back on the bed and looked at the ceiling. "Well, I'd have to apply to sit for the bar in New York, or apply for a waiver. New York may grant it based on my years of practice here in Rhode Island. I have a few open cases, nothing much. My lease here is up at the end of May." She looked at Gary. "So maybe we're talking about early June?"

"Actually, that might work fine. Classes at the university end in early May, the kids are done in June. We should really find a bigger apartment, though. Two full bedrooms, don't you think?"

"Yes, or three. Are they terribly expensive in Chelsea?"

"They are! Everything is, Bernie. But we don't have to live in Manhattan, you know."

"But you're close to school. Neither of us owns a car, and I don't really want to. No, we'll look for something in your neighborhood. I like it there."

"Next month we'll look. Valentine's Day weekend. The kids will be at the wedding. I'll set up a few views ahead of time."

It was moving fast, Bernie thought, but life moved fast. Sometimes she couldn't believe she was forty-four years old; it felt like yesterday she was twenty-six. Law school, the bar exam, working long hours, running at full speed. Going back to Switzerland to look for Michael. All the drinking, all the sadness. Until now. She'd seen her son, and now he knows who she is. She found love with her old friend Gary, and she was going to move to New York to live with him. She wanted to return to Switzerland, to see Michael, to meet his parents, his wife, his new baby.

"What's wrong, love? You're frowning," Gary said.

"Nothing. I'm just thinking." She rubbed at her forehead to smooth it out. "Let's plan a trip back. In May. Can we go in May?"

"To Switzerland? This May?" Gary let out a breath. "Bernie, I want to go, too, but there's so much happening in May."

She sat up and pulled an old t-shirt over her head. "I know, but this is the time to go, Gary. We'll have the new apartment by then, your classes will be ended. We'll be back before the end of school for the kids. Michael invited me, Gary. I want to be there, with you. For his birthday."

He smiled at her. "Look at you. You're all fired up."

"Back in October, I went to spend time with Joan. I never expected to find Michael. It was something of a miracle, really. And I believe in miracles, Gary. I found my son, only I didn't tell him, because I didn't want to upset him, or his family. But now he knows I'm his birth mother. And he seems to be at peace with it. Please, let's go. He's offered us a room at the hotel! Gary, life is too damn short. We may never have the chance to go again."

He pulled her down on top of him, his hands running across the worn cotton of the shirt until he reached skin. Gently, he lifted the old t-shirt. "Yes, Bernadette, let's go. Let's go back to Fribourg," he said, as she lowered her mouth to his.

Michel was speaking to a hotel guest when Nani arrived for work. He glanced up to see her walking through the lobby toward him, but focused his attention on the man standing in front of him, and barely nodded at her when she called "*salut*" to him. When he finished with the guest, he listened to her making noise in the back room, hanging up her coat, pouring a cup of coffee, her clackety heels on the floor behind him.

I know now that she was the one, he thought. No one else but Nani. Lucia had helped convince him when he related the story to her.

"She did it, Michel. That girl has always had a thing for you, and this is probably her sick way of trying to get closer to you." Lucia crossed her arms over her chest and paced the small kitchen. The baby was sleeping, so she kept her voice low.

"I just can't believe she would do something like that. Lulu, how would she know who my natural father is?"

Lucia huffed. "Maybe she doesn't know who he is. Maybe it's all a lie, a ruse to get you interested. I mean, how could she know?"

He shook his head. "That's my point, how could she know?" He paced around her, following the little circle she made on the kitchen floor.

Lucia uncrossed her arms and put her hands on her husband's shoulders. She began to massage gently, working on the knotted-up muscles, working her way behind him to knead his back. "My love, you are so tense. Does it matter who this man is? I still don't believe she knows, but what does it matter, when Bruno has been such a good father to you? Besides, I'm sure if you asked Bernadette directly, she would tell you. Don't play Nani's game."

Lucia always made sense. He felt himself relax under her touch. Turning to face her, he opened his arms. "I don't want to wake the baby, but Lulu, I need you." His eyes searched his wife's face. "You are more beautiful to me now than ever."

She tilted her head back and held out her hand. "Come then, and show me how much you've missed me." It was all he needed to hear.

Michel smiled at the memory of their lovemaking the previous night as he absentmindedly tapped his fingers on the counter.

"Well, something is making you happy," chirped Nani from his side. He cut his eyes to her and his smile faded.

"Actually, I was thinking about my wife and baby. That always makes me smile," he said with a hard look.

Nani lowered her eyes, then raised her chin. "Well, Alain and I have set our wedding date," she stated. When he did not respond, she said, "We will be married at the registry on May 16, and have a dinner reception here in the restaurant the following day, Saturday the seventeenth. I hope you and your wife will be able to attend." She reached her hand out to rest on his arm, but thought better of it and tucked it in her pocket.

Michel gave her a withering look. "You're having a dinner here? At the hotel?"

Nani tossed her hair back. "Monsieur Rosolen offered half of the restaurant to us for the reception. Alain liked the idea. I'm going to have one of those chocolate fountains. They're very classy." She raised her eyebrows to him, as if seeking his approval of her plans, but Michel kept his face expressionless as he stared at the computer monitor.

"Well, May is still over three months away, Nani. A lot can happen in that time." He hit the keys hard to log off and picked up his messenger bag. "I must go. Have a good night." He disappeared in the back to get his coat and scarf.

When he reappeared, he walked right past her, calling "Good night!" as he sailed out the door.

Henri Rutz entered the University Hospital of Lausanne and asked for Karl Berset's room, then ran down the long corridor until he reached the last room on the right. He saw a pretty nurse in the room, taking Karl's blood pressure, so he ducked back outside until she left, then entered to see his old friend.

"*Salut*, Henri," Karl said. "How are you?"

"Me?" Henri shook his head. "Forget me, Karl. You scared the shit out of me."

"Sorry about that," Karl said with a tight smile. "Sit, please." He closed his eyes for a moment.

Henri pulled a chair close to the bed. He rested his forearms on his knees. "So, tell me. Do you remember what happened yesterday?"

"Doctor says I had a mild heart attack. Could have been much worse." Karl grimaced at the memory and looked around the hospital room with disdain.

"We're too young for this stuff, Karl. You quit smoking, right?"

Karl nodded. "Two years ago. There's just been a lot on my mind lately."

"Well, sure." Henri sat back and crossed one long leg over the other. "That was a strange conversation we were having yesterday. About a girl named Simone."

Karl winced and Henri shot to his feet.

"Should I get the nurse?"

Karl raised his hand and motioned for his friend to sit. "No, I'm fine," he said. "Henri, a girl came to see me. Just showed up at the office yesterday, unannounced. I figured she had to be my daughter, that you'd found her and somehow forgot to tell me, I don't know. Anyway, she mentioned Bernadette, and said some things that just convinced me she was the child. My child. She told me her name was Simone Marceau."

Henri poured water from a plastic pitcher and handed a cup to Karl, who took small sips. Henri pulled a little notebook from his shirt pocket and began scribbling.

"Simone Marceau?"

Karl nodded. "I thought she was the girl. Henri, I gave her money."

Henri stopped writing and stared at his friend. "How much money?"

"Twenty-thousand Swiss francs," Karl whispered.

Henri stood up so fast he almost knocked over the table holding the water pitcher. "What? Are you kidding me? Where did you get that kind of cash?"

Karl held a finger to his lips. "Keep your voice down, will you? I had it in a locked drawer in my desk. I keep cash there."

"You're a banker! Why do you keep all that money in a drawer?" Henri set his notebook and pen on the bedside table. "I can't believe you had twenty thousand francs in your desk drawer."

"Actually, I had thirty thousand. Since Ella threw me out, I've been withdrawing money every day and stashing it in the drawer. I think she's going to divorce me, and I wanted to have some money readily available. But when the girl showed up, I don't know, I panicked. I wanted to keep things quiet, and I was positive she had come looking for money."

Henri clapped one of his palms to his forehead and he slumped in the chair with his mouth open.

Karl started to laugh. "It's absurd, isn't it?"

Henri shut his eyes. "Yeah, absurd. Well, you had your reasons, I suppose." He opened his eyes and poured some water for himself. After downing the contents of the plastic cup in one gulp, he picked up his notebook and pen again. "What did this girl look like, can you remember?"

"Sure. She was short, thin. Dressed in black. Long dark hair in a ponytail. Dark eyes. Pretty eyes." He looked at Henri. "Does that help?"

"That describes half the girls in this country. What else?" His pen hovered over the paper.

"Wait. She carried a bag, black. Big, a shoulder bag. It had three pink flowers on it."

Henri nodded as he wrote. "Who else did she speak to yesterday?"

"Probably Carmen at the reception desk. Yes, Carmen was the one who called to tell me she was waiting."

"Okay, let me see what I can do. I'll talk to Carmen. Maybe she remembers something. Listen, you rest and get better. That's the most important thing right now." Henri stood up and turned to leave, but stopped at the door. "Karl, does Ella know you're here? The kids? Do you want me to call her?"

Karl grimaced again and shook his head. "No, don't call her. I don't want her to know," he said. She'd probably dance a jig, he thought, and closed his eyes.

CHAPTER TWENTY-SEVEN

Bernie knew Gary had something planned for Valentine's Day because he asked her three times to remind him what time her train would arrive. She took a later train on Thursday afternoon, one that would get into Penn Station by eight. That way she'd have an extra night with him. Friday was Valentine's Day, a day Bernie had always considered a waste. Of course she felt that way; husbands usually remembered their wives on Valentine's Day, not their mistresses. How many years she'd spent the day alone. No calls, no cards, and certainly no red roses. This year was different, though. Gary's ex-wife was getting married. And Gary had set up five apartment viewings for Saturday.

That morning, she'd shopped for new underwear, and couldn't help but think about the day she and Lisa skipped class in Fribourg to go to Placette, the only department store in town. Bernie had selected a purple matching set for her deflowering at the hands of Karl Berset. As she sat on the train and watched the lights along the Connecticut shoreline twinkle like a never-ending necklace of diamonds, she remembered how naïve she'd been. And how the whole experience had hardened her. How she never trusted men completely again after that, how she convinced herself that sex was enough, that love didn't matter. When all she was trying to do was cope with life. With Gary now, she understood. Finally.

She crossed her legs and pulled a book from her bag. It's February 13, and in three months, we'll be in Switzerland, she reminded herself. Gary couldn't get two full weeks off, so they planned an eight-day trip. Fly out of New York on the twelfth, a Monday, fly back home the following Monday. They would still be able to go back to Schwarzsee, and hopefully celebrate Michael's twenty-fourth birthday. She couldn't wait to see the baby, Jean-Bernard, who would be nearly five months old. Still, Bernie would not think of herself as a grandmother. She smiled and opened her book.

Nani read that in America, couples usually celebrated Valentine's Day with little gifts or a romantic dinner in a restaurant. She dropped hints all week to Alain.

On Thursday, she showed up for work and received the same short greeting from Michel. For weeks now, he had been polite but aloof. They did not kiss hello or goodbye anymore, and it seemed to Nani that he couldn't wait to leave the minute she arrived, as if she were contagious. Something was definitely wrong between them, but Nani couldn't bring herself to broach the subject with Michel. She couldn't bear to hear him tell her what she already knew.

When Alain stopped in to visit at midnight, she did not mention any of this to him. She thought it best to keep as much distance between Alain and Michel as possible. They would never be friends, and Nani didn't want to be friends with Lucia, anyway. Perhaps she could convince Alain to move away from Fribourg, start a new life, but she knew they'd be stuck here as long as his mother was alive.

Alain bent low to kiss her. She knew they made a strange-looking couple when they walked together. He was so much taller, and even when Nani wore high heels, she reached only to his chest level. He mentioned the height difference early on in their relationship, and she told him it didn't matter when they were horizontal. He laughed at that, and repeated it at least once a week now, usually when they were in bed. It got to where she wanted to scream at him to just shut up about the stupid height difference.

"Nani my love," Alain said, "my mother has invited us to her house tomorrow for lunch. We can take the bus to Plaffeien."

Nani's face fell. Valentine's Day with his mother?

"Oh, Alain, baby. I was hoping to spend the entire day with just you." She kissed him lightly, pulling on his lower lip with her little teeth.

He drew back, and touched a finger to his lip. "Well, I think she has something to tell us. She sounded very excited on the telephone."

Perhaps she is giving us a big wedding gift, Nani thought. The chalet in Gstaad would be nice.

"Okay, we'll go tomorrow. But don't you have to work tomorrow night as well?" She gave him a little pout, like a five-year-old would do if she were denied a second cookie.

"Yes, and you work on Saturday night. But we will have our Sunday," he said, smoothing her hair back from her face. She reached up and took his hand, drawing it away from her head.

Nani gave him a small smile. Yes, Alain, we will have our Sunday, she said to herself. And with any luck, we will have a new house, thanks to mama Bouchard.

Henri Rutz showed up at the Banque Cantonale Vaudoise right after the doors opened. He saw a middle-aged woman at the front desk and approached, stopping just in front of the desk.

"*Bonjour*," he said, looking down. The woman glanced up and broke into a smile at the sight of such a handsome man.

"*Bonjour, monsieur*," she responded, taking in his clean looks and muscular body. He wore well-fitting dark trousers, a chocolate-brown sweater, likely cashmere, and a tan leather jacket. Very sharp, Carmen thought.

"Are you Carmen?" He smiled again, showing dimples in his cheeks.

"Yes," she breathed as the color rose in her cheeks. She knew her lipstick was probably chewed off by now, but she gave him her best smile anyway. "How may I help you?"

He put out his hand. "I'm Henri Rutz, a friend of Karl Berset. I was wondering if I could ask you just a few questions."

She fluttered her eyelashes without realizing it. A friend of Monsieur Berset! Carmen patted her hair, wishing she'd had her roots touched up. "Of course. We are all very concerned for Monsieur Berset."

Henri grabbed a chair from the little waiting area and pulled it next to Carmen's desk. His thighs were muscular under the trouser fabric, she noted, and his dark hair was just receding from his brow. He was very dashing, like James Bond, she thought, momentarily distracted.

Henri leaned forward and took a small notebook from his pocket. "Carmen," he said, and Carmen smelled his minty breath. "Do you remember the young woman who came to visit Karl, er, Monsieur Berset, yesterday morning? Without an appointment?"

"Of course I do," said Carmen, happy to help. He had gorgeous gray-green eyes. And no ring on any of his fingers, either. "I remember her well. A small girl, dressed in black."

"Yes!" Henri sat back and smiled. "I'm hoping you'll tell me everything you remember about her."

Carmen gazed at Henri. I wonder why he wants to know, she thought. It didn't matter. If she could help him out, he would be pleased. The telephone rang at her desk. She looked at it with alarm, then looked at Henri. He sat there, waiting, smiling at her with those dimples.

She swiveled around in her chair and faced the woman whose desk was behind her. "Sara? Would you take the calls until I'm finished here?" Sara nodded and picked up the telephone. Carmen swiveled back to Henri, her hands flying to her hair again. Oh dear, a hot flash. She braced herself for the surge of warmth, feeling the heat on her face, on her neck.

"Carmen?" Henri leaned forward again. "Are you not well?"

She slid her hand across the surface of her desk and switched on the small fan. A cool breeze provided some relief. Having this handsome man so close to her certainly didn't help matters.

"Yes," she sighed. "Just a little warm, that's all. The air in this office doesn't circulate." She peeked at him and he shifted in his seat. Carmen averted her gaze from where she really wanted to look and tried to focus.

"Whatever you can recall, Carmen," Henri prompted.

"Yes, let me think," she said, as her body temperature returned to normal. "Small girl, dressed in black. Long dark hair in a ponytail. Attractive." She glanced up at Henri, who was writing in his notebook. "Um, she carried a large shoulder bag. Also black. It had some pink flowers on it." Henri nodded and kept writing.

Carmen shut her eyes. She tried to picture the girl who walked in and asked to see Monsieur Berset. "Oh!" She cried and Henri looked up. Carmen pointed to the small waiting area opposite her desk. "She sat over there to wait, and she picked up a magazine. And then she took eyeglasses from her bag, bright red eyeglasses. Not something I would have chosen," she added in a conspiratorial whisper. Henri looked at her and grinned.

"I think your eyeglasses suit you perfectly," he said, glancing at the plain wire-rimmed spectacles on Carmen's desk. Carmen blushed again and rubbed her nose. "Is there anything else you can remember, Carmen?"

Carmen. I love the way he says my name, she thought. Anything else. Carmen thought hard. "She had an accent, but I couldn't place it. She didn't say much, you know? Oh, wait, she had a pin on her bag, one of those canton flag pins."

"A flag pin? What did it look like?"

"Well, I know my cantonal flags. It was Fribourg, black and white." She clasped her hands in front of her and, seeing her ragged fingernails, resolved to get a manicure that afternoon.

Henri snapped his notebook shut. He put a hand on her arm and Carmen buckled slightly. "Thank you, Carmen. You have helped tremendously." He stood up and Carmen found herself staring directly at his zipper. "I hope to see you again."

Carmen reluctantly drew her gaze upward, just as Henri Rutz turned and exited the bank building. The telephone rang and she heard Sara say, "I'm going on my coffee break."

CHAPTER TWENTY-EIGHT

Michel was arranging magazines in the hotel lobby when the mail arrived. He greeted the mailman and accepted the stack of envelopes, then returned to his desk as a couple approached him with questions about day trips from Fribourg. After providing them with brochures and suggestions, he turned back to the mail. As he leafed through the pile, his eyes rested on one letter. Addressed to him at the hotel, from Bernadette Maguire in Rhode Island, America. He glanced around the lobby, and, seeing no one, tore open the white envelope and pulled out a card, with a photograph of the ocean on it. He opened the card.

Dear Michael,

Thank you so very much for your letter and photograph. What a lovely family! I look forward to meeting your parents, your wife, and beautiful little Jean-Bernard.

Michael, your letter meant everything to me. Please know that I did not want to upset you while my aunt and I were staying in your hotel. It was truly a coincidence that I saw you that day, but when I saw your face, I knew you were the boy I'd given birth to in 1979. I just knew. Dr. Schmidt confirmed it for me, but I didn't want to confront you with the news, especially as I wasn't sure how much you knew about your adoption. My friend Gary and I are planning a visit in May. Yes, I know I was just in Switzerland not long ago, but I would very much like to meet all of you. As long as your parents are in accord with this, we will come. Please let me know if it is okay, and I will purchase tickets. We look to arrive on 13 May and depart on 19 May. I know

it is not a long visit, but my friend does not have much vacation right now. My e-mail address is at the bottom – please use that for speed.
All the best to you and your family, Michael.
Bernadette

First he entered the dates into his phone. Then he blocked off the dates for her arrival on the hotel's computer. Michel glanced at her letter again. She is bringing a friend, not her aunt. Maybe a boyfriend? Should her room have one bed or two? Could he ask her in an email?

He typed in her email address and began the message:

Dear Bernadette – We are so happy to welcome you and your friend to Fribourg and the Hotel de la Rose, arriving Tuesday 13 May 2003 and departing Monday 19 May 2003. Please advise if you would like two single beds or one double bed.

And I hope you both will join us for dinner at our house while you are here. Very much looking forward to seeing you again, I am

Yours,
Jean-Michel

Michel reread his message, checked for errors, and hit 'send.' He would tell Lucia that evening and together they would inform his parents. There was no reason for Klara to be upset about this, he hoped. She would be in Fribourg for his birthday. Was she aware of that? Of course she would know, he thought. Perhaps that was why she chose the dates. Michel smiled. As long as his parents were happy about it, he and Lucia would welcome Bernadette and her friend to his birthday celebration.

Gary had planned a special weekend with Bernadette, and most of it turned out the way he'd hoped. He met her at the train station and took her to a Japanese restaurant, which they both loved. They kissed like teenagers in the taxi back to Chelsea, and spent most of the next day in bed. He left the apartment early in the morning, saying he wanted to get coffee and croissants, and returned with a bouquet of red roses and a box of chocolates. They toured the Metropolitan Museum of Art and ate at home, after Bernie insisted that going out to dinner on Valentine's Day, especially on a Friday, would be maddening. They picked up lobster and crab pot pies, salad, and a pint of coffee ice cream. Gary had a bottle of Pinot Grigio chilling in the fridge, and it was the best Valentine's Day Bernie had ever known.

On Saturday they toured apartments, both deciding on one in the meatpacking district on West 13th Street. It had two big bedrooms, and Gary said that it would work, especially if Justin ended up at NYU the following year. The extra bedroom would be for Nicole, and Bernie wanted to let her decorate it. She thought about Roxana's wedding, which had taken place the previous evening. Gary hadn't mentioned it, although she was sure one of the kids had texted him after dinner. He didn't say, so she didn't ask.

On Sunday morning, while they were reading the Times and drinking coffee, Gary's phone rang.

"Hey Jus," Gary said, setting down the paper. He held the phone to his ear and Bernie saw him pale.

"Shit, when? Where?" Bernie sat forward, watching him. He ran a hand through his hair and listened.

"We're on our way." He snapped the phone shut and took a deep breath.

"Honey, what is it?" Bernie rose to her feet as Gary did.

"Nicole's in the hospital. Justin said something about dehydration." She looked in his eyes and saw fear, the same kind of look Joanie had that time, when the twins were babies, and Mandy spiked a fever. It turned out fine, but Bernie always remembered that look, and Gary had it.

"Go get dressed, we can leave in three minutes," she said. They left everything and hurried to get out the door. The wait at the train station was ridiculous; everyone seemed to be going to Greenwich. Roxana and her new husband were already in Cancun, having flown out on Saturday.

"Didn't you say Roxana's sister was staying with the kids?"

"Yeah, Justin didn't mention her, but she'll probably be at the hospital," Gary muttered.

"What else did Justin say?" They stood on the platform, waiting for the train. Gary shifted from one foot to the other; he couldn't stay still.

"He said she fainted about an hour ago, after she got out of bed. He said her skin was white and pasty, and she was incoherent, so he called the rescue." Gary removed his glasses and wiped at his eyes. "Nicole doesn't eat enough, I keep telling her that."

The train arrived and they boarded in silence. Bernie knew it was true; Nicole had an eating disorder. She wasn't getting the nutrition she needed. It was another forty minutes to Greenwich.

"Justin's meeting us at the station. He's got Roxana's car," Gary said. "I'll find out where the hell Stephanie is. Damn, I should have a car," he added with exasperation. Bernie linked her arm through his and pulled him close.

"All teenage girls worry about their weight, honey. Nicole's petite anyway, but it's best to have her checked out by a doctor." Bernie was more worried than she let on, as she recalled watching Nicole shift food around her plate, but she didn't want to draw conclusions without knowing the facts. She wasn't with the girl often, so she really didn't know.

"Roxana is oblivious, Bernie. I tried talking to her about it a few months ago, but she was more concerned with planning her wedding. I've noticed it, too, believe me. The girl doesn't eat. Roxana told me I was being silly. But I think she needs help. There've been a lot of changes in her life lately." He gazed out the window.

Bernie squeezed Gary's arm. "Whatever I can do to help, you know I will."

He squeezed back. "I know, babe."

The special lunch at Alain's mother's house in Plaffeien turned out to be anything but special, in Nani's opinion. She'd worn Alain's favorite pale blue sweater and a longer black skirt, not one of the shorter ones she favored. Her black boots gave her a little height, and she was careful about her makeup as well, sticking with soft pink lipstick and just a little eyeliner and mascara. She'd met Madame Bouchard only once, and remembered the hard lines in her face when she'd looked Nani up and down.

Lunch consisted of beef liver in a casserole. Nani managed to choke down small bites with gulps of red wine. She saw Madame Bouchard eye her wineglass as Alain refilled it, twice. Nani didn't care. She hated beef liver. What a stupid thing to serve for lunch, anyway, she thought. Roasted chicken would have been a better choice. Everybody likes chicken.

"My Alain tells me you have set a date for May 16 to wed," Madame said as they sipped coffee from small delicate cups. Nani had just put a sizeable forkful of almond cake in her mouth and could only nod. The cake was dry and crumbly. Nani drank the rest of her coffee and swallowed.

"We marry on the Friday, and have the supper celebration at the hotel on Saturday, mama," he said, smiling at Nani. She noticed that he extended his pinky finger as he drank. Oh, for crying out loud, she thought, my fiancé looks like a prig.

"At the hotel where you work," murmured Madame, fixing her eyes on Nani. "And Nani, will you continue to work after the wedding?" She held the fine porcelain cup in her wrinkled old hand. She also stuck her little finger out, and Nani imagined Madame had instructed Alain to do the same when he was a small boy. "Or perhaps there will be babies soon." She raised an eyebrow at her son, whose face reddened. He looked down at his coffee.

"No, I plan to continue working," Nani said brightly, ignoring Madame's stern look. "After the honeymoon, of course."

"Yes, well, of course you are welcome to use the chalet in Gstaad for your honeymoon if you wish," she sniffed. "And I'm very hopeful that the two of you will live here with me as a married couple. There is so much room in this house, and we could be a family, together again, Alain."

Nani almost dropped the empty china cup. Live with her? Was she crazy? She looked to Alain, who seemed at a loss for words. She kicked him under the table. Alain jumped in his chair and cleared his throat.

"Mama, such a generous offer. Nani would like to see some of Italy, so we will spend our honeymoon in Amalfi." His voice wavered as he caught his mother's eye. "But we will consider your offer to live here, of course. I found an apartment near the university, but of course we could save money by living in this house, isn't that right, sweetheart?" He laid his enormous hand over hers.

Nani couldn't believe what she was hearing. She knew Alain was a mama's boy, but there was no way they would live in this house with that witch. Oh, they were going to have a big fight tonight, she knew that for certain.

CHAPTER TWENTY-NINE

As winter turned to spring, Henri Rutz continued the painstaking work of trying to find out who had scammed his old friend Karl Berset. He still had not been able to get to the adoption records, so all he knew was that Bernadette Maguire had given birth to a male child on May 18, 1979. The attending obstetrician was a Dr. Hanna Schmidt. He wondered if he might be able to get something from her. Nearly twenty-four years later, she would be in her fifties by now. He could turn on the charm, see if it might work the way it had on old Carmen at the bank.

Meanwhile, he called one of his old buddies in the Fribourg police department. Lukas Bachmann had been there for over twenty years; he might remember something. The guy had a mind like a steel trap.

"Lukas! It's Henri."

"Henri, old friend, how are you? How is the private eye business?

"Busy, busy. When are you going to retire, Lukas?"

"Ah, never. The wife won't let me. She likes shopping too much. What can I do for you, Henri?"

"I'm doing a little investigating for an old friend. Does the name Simone Marceau mean anything to you?"

There was a beat of silence before Lukas spoke.

"Simone Marceau. No, doesn't ring a bell. But I can do a computer search, see if anything comes up."

"Great. Hey, who works the streets at night these days?"

"Oh, you'd want Alain Bouchard. Remember him? Big, quiet guy, enjoys the late shift. Is this Simone girl a prostitute?"

"Don't know. Might not even be her real name. Alain Bouchard, you say? The tall, dark guy? I think I remember him; he's been with the department what, about ten years? Maybe he'd recognize her from a description."

"Yeah, he's been with us about ten years now. Been on night shift for the past three. Let me give you his cell number."

"Thanks, Lukas, and let me know if you learn anything."

"Will do, Henri."

By April, Bernie was readying for the move. Her sister Joanie had a hard time accepting her decision, and told her so.

"Bernie, you don't even really know him. I mean, I know you were friends in college and everything, but people are different twenty years later. What if you get down there and move in and it doesn't work out?" Her frown lines had settled into her face, Bernie noticed. Joanie frowned a lot more than she smiled. But when Bernie looked at her sister, she still saw the blonde cheerleader from their teenage years, the party girl voted Homecoming Queen and Most Popular in high school.

"What if it *does* work out, Joanie?"

Joanie pursed her lips. "I'm just saying that you've been at loose ends for years. Different men. Oh, don't roll your eyes at me, Bernie. I probably only know a fraction of it. And I don't care; it was your choice. But now this one guy is really nice to you and you're ready to pack everything in and move to New York City, of all places."

Bernie smiled. "Kind of like when you were, what, twenty-three and got your first apartment, and Lou moved in? Like that?"

"Lou and I got married. We're still married." Joanie crossed her arms over her chest.

"Well, I'm nearly forty-five years old, Joanie, I think I know what I'm doing."

"Hope so," she said in a barely audible voice and turned her back to her sister.

Bernie wiped her hands on a towel in the kitchen. "Where's Lou, anyway?"

"He drove over to the house to pick up Joan," Joanie said, putting the ham in the oven.

"And the girls?"

"Probably upstairs." She pulled her phone from her skirt pocket.

"What are you doing?" Bernie stared at her sister as she tapped buttons on her phone.

"I'm texting them." She snapped her phone shut and looked very pleased with herself.

"Are you kidding me?? Bernie shook her head. "Why didn't you just call upstairs?"

"They wouldn't hear me. They've always got those earplugs in, but if I send them a text, believe me, they'll get that."

Joanie emptied a bag of frozen corn into a heavy pot, added water from the faucet, and set the burner to low. She took an oblong pan from the refrigerator, removed the plastic wrap and covered it with foil, then placed it in the second oven above the stove. When Joanie and Lou remodeled their kitchen four years ago, Bernie thought it was crazy to have two ovens. Now she understood. Joanie emptied a large plastic bag full of baby carrots into one more pot, added water, and set it on another burner. She turned that burner on low and covered the pot. Corn, green bean casserole, baby carrots. Joanie was all about balancing the colors of her vegetables. Ham and another casserole of potatoes au gratin were in the oven. Yellow, green, orange, pink. Joan had made a tiramisu, and Bernie, of course, brought wine. And chocolate bunnies for the girls, who probably wouldn't touch them. Too fattening. She thought about Nicole, who'd been improving, thanks to therapy with a psychologist, a nutritionist, and the support from her parents. Early treatment had proved essential to Nicole's recovery, and two of her friends had stepped forward to seek help, too. The three girls got together as a kind of teenage support group. Well, as long as it worked, Bernie thought.

"I'm not moving across the country, you know," Bernie said, helping Joanie to set the table. "Joanie, look at me." Her sister set down a fork and looked up. She wasn't smiling.

"I really care about Gary, I always have. My life, it's been a mess, you know that. Mom dying last year, making peace with Timmy Lyon, then going to Switzerland and seeing my son." Bernie looked at the ceiling and blinked hard. "Joanie, Gary settles me. I'm happy with him, and I'm a better person when I'm with him."

Joanie stepped around the long table and held her arms out to her sister. "Okay," she nodded as they hugged. "Okay, Bernie, go and be happy. You deserve that." Bernie held her older sister and couldn't recall the last time they'd felt so close.

That evening, once she was back home in her apartment, Bernie pulled out her phone and called Timmy Lyon.

"Hey, Bernie! How are you?"

"Fine, Timmy, I'm fine. Happy Easter. Listen, I just wanted to thank you."

He laughed, that big, hearty laugh and Bernie smiled at the sound. "Uh-oh, what did I do?"

"You reconnected me to Gary Baptista. After my mother died. He contacted me, and we're together now, Tim. And, and we're happy."

She heard Timmy exhale on the other end. "Wow, I'm really glad to hear that. Gary's a good guy. That's really great news."

"Yeah, we think so, too. The timing was right. Actually, I'm moving to New York next month. Right after we return from Switzerland."

"No kidding! You and Gary are going to Fribourg? You sure you don't want me along?" He laughed loudly again, and Bernie heard him call out, "It's my old friend from college, honey."

"We're staying in Fribourg. You probably didn't know, Timmy, but my aunt Joan, you remember her from the wake? We traveled to Switzerland together back in October, after the funeral. And...I met my son there. It was totally a coincidence, well, maybe it was, or maybe it was meant to be, but I met Michael. My boy." She listened to the words catch in her throat. "It's a very long and complicated story, but the bottom line is, he's a wonderful young man, and everything has worked out for the best. Everything turned out okay, Timmy."

There was a moment of silence. Bernie imagined Timmy might be reliving those last few weeks in Fribourg, when he discovered Bernie's pregnancy and assumed it was his child, and the way their friendship shattered when he learned it wasn't his. Perhaps she had said too much. It wasn't necessary, she reasoned, but after all, they did have that history.

"Good, Bernie," he said, and she could have sworn she heard his voice break. "Happy for you."

Bernie swallowed. "I have to go, Tim. You take good care."

"You, too Bernie." He clicked off.

Bernie wiped her eyes. So much history. And an uncertain but promising future.

She opened her laptop and typed a quick message to Hanna Schmidt, letting her know they were coming next month. Hanna would know everything now, anyway, from Klara and Lucia.

Last, she picked up the phone and called Gary.

"Did you call to read me a story before I go to sleep?" His voice was like cream.

"I called to say good night and to tell you to get up here soon," she said with a laugh. Gary had rented a U-Haul truck and was driving up to Providence to pack up her belongings. They decided to take the larger apartment in Chelsea at the end of April; this way, it would be set up when they returned from Switzerland.

"I'll see you tomorrow afternoon, honey. Sweet dreams."

CHAPTER THIRTY

Alain stood at the far corner of the office he shared with another detective and tossed his sandwich wrapper into the wastebasket across the room. It hit the rim and fell on the floor. With a curse, he strode to the basket, picked up the wrapper, and tossed it in. The red light blinked on his telephone, and he picked up the receiver. Pressing a button, he listened to a voice message. Alain remembered Henri Rutz, who had retired a few years ago. Henri asked Alain to send a text to his cell phone to let him know when it would be convenient to talk. He concluded by stating that he might have some good information on a case. Alain replaced the receiver and rubbed his fingers over his chin and cheeks. He opened his phone and typed a message to Henri: could they meet for coffee tomorrow at three?

At three o'clock in the afternoon the next day, Alain shook hands with Henri at the Tilleul tea-room on the rue de Lausanne.

"Good to see you again, Alain, and thanks for meeting me," said Henri.

"I remember you from years ago," Alain said. "I was a rookie with a lot to learn." He thought Henri looked good for a man his age; trim and fit, well-dressed. Alain sucked his stomach in and thought he should exercise more, especially with his wedding in just three weeks.

"Time goes by quickly, no doubt about it," Henri remarked. "Lukas said you're the man who knows the streets around here."

"Hope I can help," Alain replied, taking a seat. They ordered coffee and Henri asked for a slice of butter cake.

"One for you, too, monsieur?" The young woman smiled and tilted her pretty head at him.

Alain shook his head. "Not today."

"So, Henri, what's the news?" Alain poured sugar and cream into his coffee and stirred.

"I'm working on a case for an old friend. There's a woman involved," Henri began.

"Isn't there always a woman involved?" Alain said and both men laughed.

Henri waited until the girl had placed the cake in front of him and wiggled away before speaking again.

"I believe she might be from Fribourg, and if so, you may have had dealings with her, since you work nights."

"Is she a prostitute?"

"She could be. But we know she's a con artist, and she scammed my client out of a lot of money. She gave a name that could be fake, but have you ever heard of a Simone Marceau?"

Alain sipped his coffee. "No," he said, shaking his head, "that name is not familiar to me at all. Did Lukas run her through the computer?"

Henri nodded. "Yes, and nothing came up. I'm pretty sure it's a fake name."

"Can you describe her?"

"Here's what I've got," said Henri, pushing aside the plate and pulling his notepad from his shirt pocket. "Short. Long dark hair. Dressed all in black. Carried a large shoulder bag with some pink flowers on it, and one of those little pins of the Fribourg flag." He squinted at his handwriting. "That's why we think she's from here." He glanced up briefly. "Oh yes, and she wears bright red eyeglasses." He tucked the notepad back in his pocket and looked at Alain. "Sound familiar at all?"

Alain would not meet Henri's eyes. He made a point of scratching his head and looking down at something on the floor. He covered his eyes by rubbing his forehead and said, "Hmm." He pressed his lips together so hard his teeth hurt.

"Nope. Can't place anyone with that description," he said finally, looking at the half-eaten piece of butter cake. When he met Henri's gaze, he kept his face expressionless. "Sorry, Henri. Wish I could have been more help." He drank the rest of his coffee and set down his cup. Reaching in his back pocket, he pulled a ten-franc note from his wallet and laid it on the table. "I need to go. Sorry I can't stay and chat."

"Hey, I've got this," Henri said, pushing the bill back to Alain.

Alain stood and clapped Henri on the shoulder. "Good luck finding her," he said and left the café. Halfway up the cobblestone street, Alain ducked into an alley and fell to his knees. He couldn't breathe. He pressed his forehead against the cold stone side of the building.

That evening, at midnight, Alain entered the hotel, as he always did. Nani buzzed him in and kissed him with passion. When they sat down for coffee, she remarked, "Aren't you the quiet one tonight? What are you thinking about, my love?"

Alain ran a hand from Nani's shoulder, down along the length of her arm. Her dark red sweater was soft and warm, even though it reminded him of blood. She warned, "Don't start anything here. You know we can't."

"Nani, tomorrow the weather will be almost like summer. I want us to have a picnic at the lake. We'll take the bus. Just you and me, baby." His fingers continued their up and down route, from her shoulder to her wrist.

Nani saw that his eyes were shiny, and she knew she was lucky to have someone so in love with her. "Okay, Alain, we'll have a picnic by the lake. I'll pack a basket in the morning."

He touched his lips to her warm cheek and she turned her face to meet his lips. Before she could kiss his mouth, he rose and said, "I must get back to work. See you tomorrow morning, my Nani." And with that, he was gone. Nani stared after him as he walked out the door. She stood up and locked the entrance door behind him. Something special for us tomorrow, she thought.

The next morning, Nani received a text message that read, "Will be at your apt at 11." So he wasn't picking her up from work this morning, she mused. Strange, Nani thought, and snapped her phone shut. Michel breezed into the hotel just then, his jacket slung over his shoulder.

"It's already warm," he said by way of greeting. Nani knew their relationship had changed over the past few months, but she tried to concentrate on her new life with Alain. After their one big fight on Valentine's Day about his mother's offer to have them live with her, Alain had visited his mother and told her they would prefer to have their own apartment. Madame Bouchard was not happy, and reminded him that he had never been so bold since he met that girl. But he did stand his ground, for her, and she appreciated that. Pulling him away from his mother would prove to be a challenge, but Nani was ready. A man must leave his mother when he marries. His wife must be number one in his mind. She knew Michel felt that way about Lucia. He treated her like a goddess. And, she realized, Alain treated her that way, too.

"Yes, Alain and I are having a picnic at the lake today," she called to Michel.

"Nice weather for that," he said from the back room, where she heard him banging around.

"I'm off then, Michel. Have a good day."

"Same to you, Nani," he called from the kitchen.

Alain was prompt. He rang her bell just as Nani was folding napkins to place on the bottom of the picnic basket. She'd stopped at the market on the way home and purchased bread, cheese, salami, grapes, and a bottle of wine. She'd rolled a knife and a corkscrew into a linen towel and laid them in the bottom of the basket, then filled it with food. She found a bar of milk chocolate in the cupboard and added that, too. Sweet for her sweetie, she thought with a smile.

She descended the stairs to let him in, and walked back up ahead of him. Usually when they climbed the stairs, he made a complimentary remark about her behind, but this morning he said nothing after giving her a quick kiss on the cheek. She trudged up the stairs ahead of him in heavy silence.

She finished packing the basket and pulled a thin jacket from the hook behind her bedroom door. Still he said little, and Nani wondered if perhaps he'd had another quarrel with his mother. She held the picnic basket out to him and he took it with a smile, then held his free hand out to her. Together they took the stairs to the pavement and walked the short distance to the bus stop.

She couldn't stand it any longer. She turned to Alain and raised her face to see him.

"Are you alright, my love? You're so quiet today." She felt him grip her hand a little more tightly.

He looked down at her with his big blue eyes, his droopy eyelids, and he looked so sad, she thought. Alain smiled. "Everything will be fine, Nani."

The bus ride was quiet; Nani looked out the window and tried to quell the uneasiness she felt inside. Her skin felt prickly and she couldn't wait to get off the bus. Alain was always so attentive, so loving. He touched her often, sometimes to the point where she wanted to swat him away, as if he was simply an annoying insect hovering around her face. But not today. Today he sat on the bus with his hands in his lap, turned slightly toward the center aisle so his knees had room. The few times Nani glanced at him, he seemed to be somewhere very distant, and it unnerved her.

Twenty-five minutes later, they arrived at the lake. Nani saw that other people had the same idea, and Alain suggested they climb a small hill to be by themselves. This made her feel better; he wants us to be alone, she thought. Wanting more privacy was a good sign. Alain set the basket on the ground and spread out a thick woven blanket he'd brought with him. They sat cross-legged next to each other and took in the magnificent view. Nani edged closer to Alain so that their thighs were touching.

"Are you hungry, love? We could eat now, maybe nap later," Nani said, opening the basket.

"Yes, let's eat," Alain replied simply.

They ate all of the food; well, Alain ate most of it. Nani could see that he was hungry. She picked at the salami, taking small bites and chewing for longer than necessary. She tried to feed him a few grapes but his cup of wine was always to his lips. In fact, Nani had very little wine and Alain drank most of the bottle. She noticed that he didn't offer to fill her cup, but she didn't point it out, the way she usually would. He's just relaxing, she thought. He can nap here all afternoon, with his head in my lap. I'll stroke his hair and soothe his worries, whatever they are. And in time, he'll tell me what is bothering him. That's what married couples do, they communicate.

But Alain didn't nap. He didn't even stretch out. After the linens and utensils were packed away in the basket, he stared out over the lake, and the mountains that lined the horizon. In a quiet voice, he said, "I don't want us to have any secrets, Nani."

Nani brushed away an ant that was crawling up her leg. "Of course not, sweetheart. I will always be true to you." She felt it crawling again, but when she looked, there was no ant. Does he have a terminal disease, she wondered? Has he been unfaithful to me? She turned to look at him.

"Do you know a man named Henri Rutz?" He spoke in a low voice, even though they were alone on the hill. He continued to stare straight ahead.

Nani felt the sun on her head, hot, and she wished she'd brought a hat. "No, I've never heard this name. Why, Alain?"

"Did you go to the Banque Cantonale Vaudoise in Lausanne recently?"

The lake began to rotate in front of her, as if it was on an axis. She shut her eyes to stop the spinning. "Why are you asking me this question, Alain?"

"I need to know, Nani. Did you go to see a man named Karl?"

She opened her eyes and now the mountains started to spin. Nani bent her knees and rested her forehead as nausea broke within her. She knew she was going to be sick.

"Nani?" His hand on the back of her neck caused her to gasp. "Who is Karl, Nani?"

"He is the birth father of Michel Eicher." She would not look at Alain, but heard his sharp intake of breath. She raised her head, looking straight ahead, willing the mountains to stay still, and spoke.

"I wanted to tell him to stay away from Michel, to not upset things."

"How do you know about him?" Alain's voice was so calm, Nani thought. As if he was in a trance. As if he could hypnotize her with her voice, and she started to feel better.

"Um, Bernadette Maguire told me. She was the American woman who came to stay at the hotel last fall. She is Michel's natural mother, and she told me. I don't know why she did."

"And why is Michel's parentage any of your business?" His voice sounded different, sharper now, as if it could slice her in two.

Nani felt a shiver go through her body, in spite of the hot sun on her head. How much does Alain know, she wondered. Why has he not asked me about the money?

"Well, you know, we're friends at work and all." She turned her face to Alain. "It was a stupid thing to do."

Alain's hand gripped her tiny wrist, and she flinched under his viselike grasp. "You sent the anonymous letter to him, saying you knew who his father was? You took the stamp, but you used it on that letter, didn't you, Nani?"

She had no words. Her lower lip dropped, but there was nothing. The well of lies and excuses had dried up.

He released his grip on her and turned back to stare at the lake.

"Alain..."

"Henri Rutz told me that a con artist visited Karl Berset. I don't know the details of his investigation, Nani, but I'm guessing you tried to extort money from him."

"No!" she cried in protest, but he raised his massive palm to quiet her.

"I think it would be best for us to not be married." Each word was a stone, pelted from a distance, hitting its target. "I cannot marry you if I cannot trust you, Nani. And I don't think I can ever trust you now."

There was stillness on the hilltop. The earth paused, waiting for an eruption.

To her own surprise, Nani didn't cry. Or carry on. She knew he was right. She twisted the ring off her finger and laid it on the blanket next to Alain's foot. He didn't move to pick it up and it lay there, sparkling in the midday sun.

She rose to her feet and picked up the picnic basket. "I will go now, Alain. I am so very sorry."

He looked up at her from where he sat. Nani could see his cheeks were streaked with tears. "I know you are," he said, swiping at his cheeks. He cries, yet I cannot, she thought. What kind of heartless monster must I be?

She walked to the bus stop and rode back to Fribourg by herself. That evening, she telephoned Monsieur Rosolen, the owner of the hotel, and tendered her resignation, telling him that there was an emergency in her family and she had to return to Greece at once.

"Please say goodbye to everyone for me," she said.

Nani packed up the few things she owned. She looked at the simple white silk dress hanging in her closet, wrapped in clear plastic. She would leave it behind; let the landlord do what he wanted with it.

On Monday morning, she closed her account at the Helvetia Bank and tucked the bank check into her bag. Then she walked to the SwissBank and transferred nine thousand Swiss francs to the Bank of Greece, where she had always kept a small account. The remaining three thousand francs she would use to pay for a flight home.

Nani left the bank and walked two doors down to the travel agency, where she purchased a one-way ticket to Athens, business class for the first, and likely last time. In the afternoon, she boarded a train to Zurich and watched Fribourg disappear from the window. I will be a very wealthy woman in my village, she thought. Perhaps my parents will even forgive me. And surely there must be one nice young man still left in the area.

CHAPTER THIRTY_ONE

The ride to JFK Airport was comfortable, thanks to the car service Gary had reserved.

"Remember the bus from Providence to Boston? This is better," Bernie said with a laugh. Gary held her hand.

"Last time I flew from JFK was about eight years ago. I'm sure it's changed since then."

"Well, everything's changed now," Bernie replied, and they fell quiet. Gary had been deeply affected by the events of September 11, and nearly two years later, the scars were still fresh.

At the Swiss terminal, they rolled their bags behind them and headed inside.

"It's different," Gary noted. Bernie looked around at the increased security. "Has Fribourg changed that much, too?" he asked. "Please tell me it hasn't."

"Not so much, but you'll see a few updates. They have a McDonald's now; you don't have to take the train to Lausanne."

"Wonderful," he said, his voice dripping with sarcasm. "We're not going anywhere near that place."

"Deal," Bernie said with a laugh.

They checked in and stopped for a quick bite and a beer before boarding. Every seat on the airplane was sold, and poor Gary was stuffed into a middle seat. Bernie switched with him so he had the window, which wasn't much better.

"Business class would have been nice," he said.

"At ridiculous prices. Don't worry about it," she said, patting his hand. "I hope you can sleep tonight. I brought earplugs for both of us."

They arrived in Zurich and it was Tuesday morning. Gary was pleased to find the train station was attached to the airport, down two levels by escalator. Once they'd cleared customs and picked up their bags, they waited for the connecting train to Bern. With unwavering Swiss efficiency, they arrived at the Fribourg train station before one in the afternoon.

"What do you think?" Bernie turned to Gary as the train slowed to a stop.

"This part looks the same," he said. She could see him as he was, quiet and mannered, knowing he was observing the awkward dance between his friends Bernie and Timmy. He kept his feelings for me buried, she thought, and squeezed his hand.

"I love you," she whispered in his ear, and felt the pull of his grin against her lips.

They rolled their bags down from the platform to the main station.

"The inside is a little different. You'll see," she added, leading the way down the ramp. How familiar everything was now, she marveled. Just as she had with her aunt Joan seven months earlier, Bernie led Gary outside, to the covered area where the taxis waited. She half-expected to see the same driver, but it was a young man with blue hair and a tattooed neck who drove forward.

"Hotel de la Rose," Bernie said to the driver, who nodded and hit the gas pedal hard. They lurched forward and sailed through the streets. Gary fixed his gaze out the window, trying to absorb it all.

"We'll have plenty of time to explore all the places we missed when we were students," she said.

"How did the time go by so fast?" Gary shook his head and pushed his glasses up his nose.

They arrived at the hotel, and the driver pulled their bags from the trunk. Bernie handed him a ten-franc note, and he nodded again and sped away.

"You're sure they're expecting us?" Gary's eyes darted around the lobby. "I've never set foot inside this hotel, you know."

"They're expecting us," said Bernie, walking ahead of Gary to the reception desk. And just like the day that she and Joan arrived, no one was there. She waited for a minute and finally tapped the bell. Turning to Gary, she whispered, "Nothing but the best!" She nudged her shoulder against his.

And there he was. Her son. Grinning from ear to ear when he saw her. Michael stepped from behind the reception area to embrace Bernadette.

"Michael," she said. She almost added 'my son' and remembered not to do that. When they finally pulled apart, she introduced him to Gary.

"Michael, this is Gary Baptista. Gary, please meet Jean-Michel Eicher." Michael extended his hand to Gary.

"Sir, welcome to the Hotel de la Rose."

"Please call me Gary. Very nice to meet you."

"You as well." Michael stared at Gary for a long time before turning to Bernie.

"Everything okay? You were expecting us, yes?" Bernie wondered if perhaps Michael had forgotten.

Michael hurried back behind the desk, his face and neck bright red.

"Yes, well, we have the best room for you both," he stammered. "Number 400. The boss said okay when I explained who you are." He glanced up, again fixing his eyes on Gary.

"That's very kind, thank you," Bernie said, pulling out her credit card. Michael waved it away.

"No, not for the room, please. Bernadette, you and Monsieur Baptista are guests of the hotel." He lowered his voice to a whisper. "You have to pay for food and drinks, though."

Bernie laughed. "That's only fair! Thank you again." She noticed that Michael kept looking at Gary, and a thought seized her. Does Michael think Gary is his birth father? Oh no, she'd have to set him straight on that.

"You leave next Monday, correct?"

"Yes, correct. The day after your birthday." She met Michael's eyes and held them for a long time.

"Yes. My birthday is on Sunday. Will you come to our house then? You can meet my parents, and Lucia, and of course, Jean-Bernard, who is nearly five months old now. And Dr. Schmidt," he added. "We can be all together." He looked again at Gary and smiled.

"Yes, of course." Bernie turned to Gary. "Honey, would you mind if I spoke with Michael for just a moment?" She leaned in to whisper in his ear and Gary drew back, eyes wide behind his glasses.

"Um, let me just use the men's room, please," Gary said. He looked to Michael, who pointed across the lobby. Gary nodded and walked away.

Bernie stepped closer to her son. "Michael, Gary is a very special friend. He and I were students together here in Fribourg." She rested her hand on his arm. "But he is not the man who fathered you, if you were wondering."

Michael ducked his chin and nodded silently. "I thought perhaps…" his words fell away.

Bernie glanced back at the empty lobby. "Michael, I know who your father is, and I know where he lives. If you really want to know, I will give you the information. He is married, and he was married at the time." She saw him raise his head to look at her. "I didn't know that he was married at the time, and although I went willingly with him, he did deceive me. He never knew that I became pregnant, he never knew that you existed until last fall."

"You saw him?"

Bernie nodded. "I had to close that chapter in my life. If you fccl you need to open it, I'll understand. But I don't know that he would want a relationship with a son he has never known. Either way, it's your decision. We're here for a week. You can think about it and let me know, okay?"

"Okay, Bernadette," Michael said quietly. "Thank you."

Gary and Bernie spent the week walking around Fribourg, remembering old places and finding new ones. They spent a day in Schwarzsee and another in Gruyères. One night a dinner at Hanna's house and another a raclette at the Chasseur. The days flew by and it was Sunday, their last day.

"Are you ready to see everyone today, Bernie?" Gary buttoned his shirt and tucked it into dark gray trousers. He ran a comb through his hair and slipped into shoes.

Bernie pulled an emerald green dress from the hanger where it had been since they arrived. This was the dress she'd bought specifically for Michael's birthday, in a color and style well suited to a forty-four year old woman with green eyes and hair the color of carrots. She walked to the window and looked at a blue sky dotted with puffy clouds. The trees along the river were covered in that lovely light green fuzz that signaled summer's imminent arrival, and she saw row after row of red and yellow tulips standing straight and tall along the riverbank.

She stepped into shoes and sprayed her hair, hoping to keep it from spiraling out of control.

"Shall we?" Gary held out his arm.

They arrived at the house where Klara and Bruno Eicher had raised a little boy into a grown man, where that grown man now lived with his beautiful wife and their new baby. Bernie and Gary were welcomed with hospitality and warmth to the Eicher family. Michael and Lucia, Klara and Bruno, Bernie and Gary, and Hanna Schmidt ate and drank and talked and laughed. Little Jean-Bernard slept in the next room, oblivious to the noise surrounding him.

After dinner, Michael asked Bernie to take a walk outside. He offered his hand to Bernie as they walked the lane that wound around the farmhouses and passed tidy garden plots of new growth. The ground was pungent with the smell of spring, and everywhere around them there was new life bursting forth. He led her to a small bench, where they sat and turned to each other.

"This day has been perfect, you know," he started. "I am grateful to know you, Bernadette."

Bernie smiled and swallowed down a lump. She vowed not to cry, not on his birthday.

"Michael, you are an exceptional young man. It fills my heart to see you with your family, and...to know I did the right thing twenty-four years ago." Bernie blinked hard against tears that had a will of their own.

"You are my family also." He squeezed her hand.

Bernie looked off into the distance, at the expanse of green, at the rolling hills that led to higher peaks. She took a breath. "And what about our conversation earlier this week, Michael? About the man who fathered you?" She met his eyes, the soft brown eyes that were the same as Karl Berset's but so very, very different.

He shook his head with determination. "No. I do not need to know him."

"He knows that you exist. Well, he knows I had a child; I didn't give him much more information. But he may try to find you; there's always that possibility, you know."

"And if he does, fine," Michael replied evenly. "I want nothing from him, and I offer nothing to him."

Bernie pressed a tissue to her eyes. "Come on, let's rejoin everyone. They'll be sending a search party." They stood together. "Will we have a birthday cake?" She smiled brightly at him.

"No, not a cake," Michael replied. He turned to Bernie and grinned. "Lucia will wait for you before she prepares our special dessert."

When they stepped into the kitchen, Bernie heard laughter and cooing from the living room and knew that the baby must be awake. Michael again took her hand and led her to meet Jean-Bernard, the most beautiful baby she'd ever seen, and she wasn't just saying that.

"Bernadette, will you come with me to the kitchen, please?" Lucia handed her son to Klara, who was only too happy to oblige. Bernie followed Lucia into the kitchen.

"Today, instead of a birthday cake, Michel asked for a chocolate fondue." As she prepared it, she continued. "He said what makes this fondue special is that you need to mix two different chocolates together to make the best fondue." Lucia turned her pretty face to Bernie. "You know that the best cheese fondue is, how we say, '*moitié-moitié*,' half

Emmanthaler and half Gruyère cheese? Well, the best chocolate fondue is made with the Toblerone…" Lucia took a bar of Toblerone chocolate and broke it into the small ceramic pot, "…and the Tobler bittersweet chocolate." She opened a different bar and broke it into the pot, then added cream. She handed a long wooden spoon to Bernie.

"You stir it together over the fire."

Bernie began stirring and watched the chocolate and cream mix together. Lucia reached up and pulled a bottle from the top shelf. She held it up in front of Bernie.

"Kirsch, just a little." She splashed the clear cherry brandy into the chocolate and Bernie breathed in deeply.

"You keep stirring and I will do the rest." Lucia set plates with fresh strawberries, cubes of butter cake, small slices of Mandarin orange, and slices of banana. She brought the base of the fondue pot to the table and lit the flame. Bernie carried the pot by its long handle and set it over the flame, and everyone was called to the table. At each place was a long, thin fork.

When everyone was seated, and baby Jean-Bernard settled into his crib, Michael cleared his throat and rose to his feet.

"This is the best birthday celebration I could have. And I am a very lucky man. My bella Lucia is my best friend, and the mother of our precious son." He bent to kiss his wife and turned to look at Klara and Bruno.

"My parents raised me to be the man I am today. Thank you for giving me everything I ever needed." Klara touched her cotton handkerchief to her watery eyes and smiled back at her son. Bruno nodded and reached for his wife's handkerchief.

"Dr. Schmidt, Hanna, you helped to bring me into this world, and you did the same for our little boy. And you connected me with my parents. *Merci*." He laid his hand over his heart and nodded to Hanna.

"And to Bernadette and Gary, our guests. Gary, I see the love you have for Bernadette and it makes me happy." He turned his face to Bernie on his left. "And you, Bernadette," he said, his voice cracking, "you chose to keep me. And then, selflessly, you chose to give me an opportunity. I cannot thank you enough for that." He swallowed hard and kissed Bernie on the cheek.

"And now," Michael said, "let us all share my birthday fondue!" He sat and raised his dessert fork. Everyone else followed his lead, spearing a piece of cake or fruit from the plates in front of them and together, seven forks were dipped into the chocolate fondue.

THE END

ABOUT THE AUTHOR

Martha Reynolds ended an accomplished career as a fraud investigator and began writing full time in 2011. Her debut novel, CHOCOLATE FOR BREAKFAST, was named 2012 Book of the Year (Women's Fiction) by Turning the Pages Books. CHOCOLATE FONDUE continues the story of Bernadette Maguire.
She and her husband live in Rhode Island, never far from the ocean.
Her Facebook author page is Martha Reynolds Writer
Follow her on Twitter @TheOtherMartha1
Read her blogs at http://MarthaReynoldsWrites.com

32468297R00165

Made in the USA
Charleston, SC
19 August 2014